The Angeluscustos And The Wonderful Waterfall

ELIZABETH ANDERSON

ISBN:1508781966
ISBN-13:9781508781967

DEDICATION

To all of my grandchildren, especially the real Hannah, Brennan, Julia, and Emma.

CONTENTS

ACKNOWLEDGMENTS

Cover Photography by K. D. Witmer

List of characters and Definitions

In Indiana:
   The Angeluscustos-

   Emma West

   Julia West

   Brennan West

   Hannah West

   Kyle and Debby West, their parents

In Pennsylvania:

   Robert Waest, union soldier and ancestor of the Wests

In the mountains of Serenia and at Glacère:
   Mr. Higgley - a rabbit

   The Gwencalon ("Shining Heart") - the holy man of Serenia

   Ugo – leader of the Barbegazi of Glacère

   Amea – Ugo's wife

   Sachi – a Barbegazi of Glacère

   Fiscus – a Barbegazi boy

At Charlesville and Chavornay Castle in Serenia:
   Sergai – butcher in Charlesville

   Marthe – cook at the castle

   Duffy – her son, spy for Lord Bernald

   Bruno – a footman at the castle

   Arabella – the former queen's horse

   Rascal, Rouget, Blaze, Minuit – horses from the castle stables

   Mouser – the castle cat

Hobo – the former king's dog

Duke Topo – leader of the dungeon rats

King Charles – late king, killed ten years ago

Queen Marianne – late queen, died ten years ago

Prince David – future king of Serenia

Rudolf Alexandre Frederic Georges Henri
Chavornay II - King of Serenia in 1478

Duke Ferigard – brother to Queen Marianne,
Prince David's uncle and regent

Frederick, Lord Gabin – Duke Ferigard's son,
Prince David's cousin

Berkel – Captain of the duke's guard

At Ravenswood-
Henri, Lord Bernald – Baron of Ravenswood
and godfather to Prince David

André, Olivier, Jérome, Lieutenant Cerles –
Lord Bernald's men

Others:
Hans, Greta, and Pietre of Longmeadow

Prince Lethin of Kummer

Lords Schuman and Rheiner of Oberwald

Lords Altvater and Einstadler of Unterwald

Lord Perrault of Meerwald

Lords Killian and Witmer of Nidwald

Lord Spielburg of Mittewald

Definition of names and terms

Angeluscustos – guardian angels

Barbegazi – miniature people of the mountain heights, covered in white fur and with huge feet that allow them to ski through the snow on the mountain slopes. They whistle to warn valley residents of avalanches.

Charlesville – capital city of Serenia, located in Mittewald

Dragons de Neige – snow dragons, domesticated white dragons who prefer to live on the snow capped mountains and provide quick transportation for the Barbegazi into the valleys when needed

Einsiedler – broad chested, strong legged horses, bred for use in mountainous areas

Filleul – godson

Glacère – Barbegazi village where the Gwencalon sought refuge

The Holy One – Serenian term for God

Kummer – a neighboring country to Serenia

Landesgemeinde – an open air meeting where adult men in Serenia vote by a show of hands for the next king

Parrain – godfather, a close friend of a child's parents who becomes a second father to the child

Regent – one who rules on behalf of another who is too young to rule

Schulmappe – a leather bag with a long strap and a flap closing, usually worn across the body to carry personal belongings, especially when traveling

Serenia – the land of the five Cantons, a world somewhere beyond our own

1 AN UNUSUAL SUSPECT

The letter came on a Thursday. Brennan had gone to the mailbox, hoping that perhaps today at last the new LEGO catalog had arrived, but it had not. Instead, nestled between the phone bill and an ad for hearing aids was a plain, white paper, folded in thirds like some kind of flyer and smudged with dirt in a pattern that looked remarkably like paw prints. Scrawled across the front, and none too neatly, were the words:

"Hanna Brenan Julia Ema West,

#5 Turtle Lane, Springwold, Ind."

The back was sealed with a blob of red wax with some kind of crest on it.

"Hmph!" he said a he slid a finger under the flap to open it. "Atrocious spelling!" Brennan had just learned the word "atrocious" in English class and he was rather pleased to have the chance to use it, even if no one was about to hear him. Before he could finish opening the letter, he heard a shout from the side yard. The older of his two younger sisters, Julia, was running towards him, her long legs quickly covering the ground, her shoulder length light brown hair flying behind her.

"What did you get?" she panted, hazel eyes sparkling with interest. "Did the catalog come? Did I get anything?"

"The catalog didn't come, but we all got a letter." He showed her the letter. "It's addressed to all of us."

"Wow, not very well, though." Julia was 12 and very proud of her spelling.

"Yeah," Brennan responded, "I think it must be from one of Emma's friends. Only one of them might spell this badly."

"I don't think even they are that bad," Julia objected. "Most of them can at least spell our names. Let's open it!"

"I was going to," Brennan responded, "but I think we should get Hannah and Emma and open it together."

"Just open it now. They won't mind."

"Yes they will," Brennan objected. "I'm waiting 'til we get in the house."

Julia made a grab for the letter, but Brennan, having anticipated his impatient sister's move, had shoved it back into the stack of mail and started towards the house. Scarcely daunted, Julia raced past him, leaped onto the wooden porch, and flung herself into the house.

Brennan, who believed his fourteen years removed him from the impetuosity of Julia's youth, followed at a more sedate pace. His hair, a little darker than hers, was neatly combed as usual across his wide forehead, his somewhat round face fixed in a pensive pose. He imagined himself to be the scholarly one of his four siblings. Were he to categorize each of them, he would call Emma, his 9 year old sister, the cheerful one; Julia, the impatient one; his oldest sister, Hannah, the bossy one, and himself, the scholarly one. He was really, really good with numbers especially. To be honest, he mused, Hannah wasn't really bossy. He supposed she just seemed bossy because she was so much older than the rest of them. Honestly, she was actually pretty nice. . . most of the time.

When Brennan got inside, Julia had already found Hannah in the family room and was calling Emma from her bedroom.

"Hurry up, Brennan," Julia urged. "I want to see what's in it."

"Yeah, Brennan," Hannah added. "This better be good! I was reading my new library book when Julia interrupted me."

"What's going on?" Emma asked, puzzled.

"We got a letter from one of your idiot friends," Brennan answered, waving the envelope.

"Not one of her friends. I told you they can write better than that," Julia corrected him.

"Just open it," Hannah directed, with the slightly bored affectation of an eighteen year old.

And so, open it Brennan did. The inside of the paper was remarkably clean and smooth, but the writing was clearly that of the one who had addressed the outside. The words, however, were perplexing. In large print, someone had written:

Kum now. The Prince needs your help.

Go thru waterfall on

Little Bear River. You will be mett.

"Ooh!" Julia sighed. "A mystery! Let's go!"

" How do you go through a waterfall?" Emma asked.

"It doesn't mean through," Brennan explained patiently. "It means 'to.' This kid can't spell, remember."

"To, through. Who cares! This is like a scavenger hunt! Let's go!"

"No, Julia," Hannah intervened. "We aren't going anywhere. Mom and Dad are in town and would be worried if they came back and we were gone."

"We could leave them a note," offered Julia.

"No," Hannah said firmly. "We don't know who wrote this. It could be a joke."

"Yeah," Brennan agreed. "Some kids could be down there at the falls waiting for us to come so they can laugh at us."

Julia pouted, "Spoilsports!"

"Or," Emma added, "it could be a kidnapper waiting to grab us and hold us for ransom!"

"Or a serial killer," contributed Brennan.

"Or a robber waiting until we leave to break into the house!" added Julia.

"Or," Emma said thoughtfully, "It could be real."

Hannah shook her head. "Yeah, it could be any of those, but it's probably just a joke. Let's just hang onto it for a while and see if anything else happens. Agreed?"

"Yeah."

"Sure."

"I guess so. But what if someone is really in trouble?"

"If someone is really in trouble," Brennan answered, "they should call the police or talk to their parents."

"But what if they can't?"

"Enough, Emma," Hannah intervened. "Brennan is right. If someone is really in trouble, I doubt we could do anything to help him. It's a joke, okay. Now, forget it. We better finish our chores before Mom and Dad get home, or we won't be going to the movies tonight!" She reached over and plucked the letter out of Brennan's hands.

"Hey!" he objected. "I was the one who got it out of the mailbox. How come you get to hold it?"

"I'm the oldest and Mom left me in charge."

Since both of those statements were obviously true, no one challenged her further. Reluctantly, they wandered off to finish any unfinished chores.

Hannah folded the letter again as she headed for her bedroom. Turning the letter over, she noticed what she had not seen before. The stamp in the corner was strange. Rather than the normal postage stamp that you stuck on an envelope, it appeared to be an ink image that had been stamped directly on the letter. It seemed to be a coat of arms held by two lions standing on their hind legs. The coat of arms itself had a wide, white diagonal stripe running from the upper left to the lower right corners. Above the stripe was what looked like the French fleur-de-lis and below it were five stars. Below the shield was an elaborately unfurled banner on which the words "Crois qu'il soit" were written.

Going to the computer on her desk, Hannah googled coats of arms and searched diligently for the distinctive shield. Nothing. She tried fleur-de-lis and fleur-de-lis + stars, but still she found nothing. Then she tried the motto. It translated as "Believe it will be." "Hmm," she murmured. "That is a kinda positive idea. I wonder where on earth this stamp is supposed to be from?"

Finally she logged off the Internet and sat back in her chair. If this was a joke, it was certainly an elaborate one. The stamp did not look homemade. It looked real, just not real American. Puzzled, she slid the letter into her center desk drawer. Better wait and see if anything else happened. She sure wasn't going to the falls with her younger brother and sisters based on this letter, at least not today.

Putting it out of her mind, she went back to the family room where she retrieved her half finished book and curled up on the couch. Joining Emma, Julia, and Brennan, she set herself back to work. Still, her mind kept returning to the letter. What if it was real somehow? No, it had to be a joke. This was America. There were no princes in America to need their help. Resolutely she forced the letter out of her mind, turning her thoughts to the book that somehow seemed suddenly so very mundane.

ELIZABETH ANDERSON

2 A DREAM BRINGS A SHOCKING REVELATION

The wind blew softly through the branches of the tree that stretched above her head, shielding her from the warm sun, and lifting the short strands of her dark hair. She sat on a large rock, its surface cooled by the shade of the tree, looking out over the valley spread before her.

Here and there patchwork fields nestled against each other, separated at times by clumps of woods or the roofs and walls of farmhouses and barns. In the center of the valley wound a rushing stream of nearly white water. Foam, she thought, churned up by its swift passage over a rocky bed, or perhaps sediment from the rocks themselves. To her left the woods seemed more solid, stretching most of the way across the flat land and up the lower slopes of a mountain that protected the far reaches of the valley.

Behind it were even more mountains, studded with dark green trees on their lower reaches and gradually changing to bare rock that became snow covered near the mountain peaks.

Just above the tree line on the closest mountainside her gaze was caught by the tall towers of a castle, glowing white in the rays of the sun. Had the sun not shone directly on its turrets, she might never have seen it, she realized, as it seemed to fade into the background of a stretch of snow or glacier that reached its fingers down the length of a valley behind the castle. From her vantage point, the castle seemed innocuous enough, almost fairytale-like, reminding her of Cinderella's castle at King's Island, the amusement park her family had visited frequently over the years. Still, she felt a quiver of nervousness in her stomach, a feeling of unease, almost as if someone in the castle were watching her across the valley, watching her with anger and suspicion. Although she imagined that to be silly --- after all, she was too far away for anyone to see her on this mountainside, much less be able to tell who she was --- still she found herself getting up from the rock and moving back into the shelter of the tree's trunk.

Suddenly a mist began to settle into the valley, obscuring first the tops of the mountains, then gradually the forests, and finally the floor of the valley. Surrounded by the greyish white cloud, Hannah crouched, feeling cautiously for the rock on which she had been sitting. She didn't dare move far for fear of tumbling down the slope into the valley. Her fingers touched the rock's face, and gingerly she slid to her knees on the now dampening grass. She would sit with her back against the rock and wait for the mist to clear, she decided.

How long she sat there, Hannah had no way of knowing. But when at last the mist began to lift, she sensed a difference, darkness. The sun no longer shone down on her and as she reached down to the grass to get to her feet, she realized that it wasn't grass at all, but stone that she sat on. Bewildered, she reached back to the rock behind her back, comforted as she felt its rough surface. But then the mist disappeared and she realized that she no longer sat on the mountainside, but on the stone floor of a long, shadowy corridor. She scrambled to her feet, frightened and confused. What she had mistaken for the boulder on the mountainside was actually the rough-hewn stone of the corridor wall. Where on earth was she? And how had she gotten here? And even more importantly, how did she get out of wherever here was?

She looked around her more carefully. By the flickering light of a torch on the wall across from her, she could see that the hallway stretched maybe fifteen feet in each direction before ending in what appeared to be a solid wall. Well, that couldn't be. A hallway must go somewhere! No one built a hallway and then walled up the ends of it. But which way should she go, to the right or to the left? A rasp of sound from her left, followed by a hollow cough made up her mind, and she crept cautiously toward the noises. Someone was there. Maybe she could find out what was going on.

As Hannah reached what had seemed to be the end of corridor, she realized that the hall actually turned sharply to the left and that the noise had come from around the corner. A few feet beyond the corner, another flickering torch cast weird, moving shadows on the walls. Someone coughed again, and Hannah moved quietly around the corner and down the hallway, feeling her way with a hand against the wall. When she felt metal instead of stone, she stopped. The torchlight barely reached where she stood, but in the edges of its intermittent light she realized that she had reached a barred cell. A dungeon!

She had somehow ended up in the castle dungeon! In the cell before her, a shadow in the corner coughed again, stood slowly and looked directly at her. She shrank back, but apparently he couldn't see her because he turned and moved to a thin slit of window high in the wall, looking up at the narrow sliver of night sky that was his only glimpse of life beyond the cell. As he tilted his head up, the moon must have emerged from behind a cloud because suddenly it lit his face as if a spotlight had been turned on and Hannah stifled a gasp. She could only see his profile, but it was that of a young, man, perhaps in his late teens or early twenties, with a straight nose, a firm jaw line, and thick, black hair. A shadow along his jaw might have been the start of a beard, or perhaps it was only a shadow. As she watched, he began to speak, his voice hoarse and strained.

"God, please send them quickly. I don't know how much time I have left. I don't ask for myself, you know. If I die in the fight, so be it. But fight we must. We cannot lose this land to Evil. Please let them come."

Hannah opened her mouth to speak to him, reaching out to grasp the bars as she did so, but her fingers closed over air as the moonlight disappeared and the torch suddenly went dark. Disoriented, she stood her ground, reaching out first on one side of her and then on another, trying without success to find something solid to hold to. The stonewalls and the cell seemed to have disappeared with the light, leaving her alone in a vast, black nothingness.

"God, help me," she cried, and at that moment she felt herself falling. She hit the floor with a jolt, banging her elbow hard against something as she fell. As she rubbed her elbow, she realized that the darkness was no longer complete. Instead, grey light slipped from between curtains, her curtains. She was back in her bedroom. She had fallen out of bed, whacking her elbow on the nightstand. Had it all been a dream?

She had read the letter. She had hunted for the coat of arms that she saw on the strange stamp. Had her subconscious created a dream based on the letter? A handsome prince in trouble? And where else would you find a prince but in a castle? And yet. . .it had all seemed so real. She crawled back into bed, pulling the tangled covers back up over her shoulders, but try as she might, she couldn't go back to sleep. The mountain valley, the stamp with the distinctive coat of arms, the dungeon, and the young man in the cell kept chasing one another through her mind. Finally, the brighter slant of sunlight through the gap in her curtains teased her eyes open, and she saw by the clock that it was just after 7:00. Her dad, a minister, would have gotten up early for personal devotions and by now would surely be making breakfast. Soon her brother and sisters and mother would rise as well.

Grabbing her robe from the foot of her bed, Hannah padded barefoot down the hall, through the family and living rooms, and into the kitchen. Her dad, hearing her mumbled "Morning," turned from the stove where he was frying bacon and smiled.

"Morning, Sunshine. Have a bad night? You look a little the worse for wear."

"Thanks, dad!" she answered sarcastically, rubbing the back of her head. "But you're right. I had. . . I had a weird dream and then I fell out of bed."

"Fell out of bed, huh? One of those dreams where you dream you are falling and then you do?"

"At the end, yeah, but before that it was so strange."

Her dad dished some bacon onto a plate and scooped some scrambled eggs from an iron skillet that had been in the oven keeping warm.

"Okay, Hannah. Dig in and tell me about the dream while you do. I've already prayed for the food."

As Hannah scooped up the eggs and bacon, she described her dream, which remained surprisingly fresh in her mind. She was puzzled to see her dad's brow wrinkle in concentration as she talked. Finally she ended, "But there was that letter that we got yesterday, so I thought I wondered if there was some connection."

"Letter? What letter? Where is it?" her dad demanded.

"It's in my desk drawer. I suppose we should have told you and Mom about it, but I just thought it was some kind of a kids' joke, although the stamp looked funny."

"Hannah, go get it for me, please."

Hannah took a good look at her dad's suddenly serious face and got up to hurry to her bedroom for the letter. When she returned and handed it to her, he glanced at the stamp and at the broken wax seal, then opened the letter and quietly read it.

"Hannah," he said finally. "Get your brother and sisters for me. I have something to show all four of you."

Hannah, Brennan, Julia, and Emma, all barefoot and pajama-clad were perched on stools at the kitchen island when their dad came back, followed closely by their mom. He carried an ornately carved wooden box that none of the children had seen before, setting it carefully on the counter before them. Their mom smiled encouragingly as she also perched on a stool.

Their dad, however, remained standing. He slipped a key from his pocket, inserted it into a brass lock in the box, and withdrew a parchment scroll that he carefully unrolled and turned so that they could read it. At the top of the parchment was the duplicate of the image stamped on the letter the kids had gotten.

Here, however, the lions holding the crest were a bright gold as were the stars at the bottom of the crest. The fleur-de-lis was the deep, sky blue of a cloudless day. The letters of the motto, "Crois qu'il soit." were also picked out in gold, shining in the early morning sunlight.

The paper itself read in somewhat faded and yellowed ink:

"Let it be known that by this order, signed

by my very hand, I, Rudolf Alexandre

Frederic Georges Henri Chavornay II,

King of the Five Cantons of Serenia,

hereby declare Robert Bruce Waest and

all of his descendants to be Nobles of

Serenia. They shall bear the title of Lord

and Lady hence-forth in Serenia as

hereditary Angeluscustos, sent by the

Holy One when they are needed to defend

the honor and the law of the King."

Signed this 2nd day of Januarie

in the year of Our Holy One

1478.

There followed the scrawl of a name that must have been that of Alexandre Frederic Georges Henri Chavornay II of Serenia, but was so filled with loops and swirls that it was impossible to read.

"Who is Lord Robert Bruce Waest?" demanded Julia.

"Yeah, and where is Serenia?" asked Brennan.

"That's the same seal as on the letter!" exclaimed Hannah in wonderment.

"What's an angel- us- cus, whatever?" piped in Emma.

"Hush, kids, and wait a minute," their mother laughed. "Give your dad a chance to explain. It's kind of complicated."

"It's okay, Debby," their dad assured her, "They're just excited. He turned back to the kids. "I'll answer all your questions," he smiled, "but let me start at the beginning. In 1778, your great, great, great grandfather was a soldier in the Continental Army."

"Wait," interrupted Brennan. "You said you were starting at the beginning. According to that paper, the beginning must have been in 1478, not 1778."

"I'll explain that in a minute, Brennan," his dad responded. "Anyway, it was 1778, your ancestor, whose name was Robert Bruce Waest, was a soldier fighting the British."

"Oh, yeah," said Brennan again. "1778 would have been the American Revolution."

"That's right. Your, well, just let me call him Robert for simplicity's sake, had been separated from his regiment of the Pennsylvania Regulars during the Wyoming Valley Massacre. The patriots had been tricked by the British and between the British soldiers and their Indian allies, nearly 300 Pennsylvania volunteers were massacred. The rest ran for their lives into the Endless Mountains.

"The Endless Mountains?" interrupted Julia. "I've never heard of them."

"They are a part of the Pocono Mountain range in eastern Pennsylvania," Debby contributed. "Remember we talked about the Poconos when we studied geography last year."

"I remember," Emma chirped in. "They aren't very tall mountains, though, are they?"

"Tall enough," Debby answered. "Kyle, you'd better continue your story."

"Yes. It's just getting to the interesting part," Kyle agreed. "Anyway,

Robert was trying to get away from the British soldiers and join up with some of the other survivors. By now it was just before nightfall and the British had chased him into the mountains. He managed to slip away from them by crawling into a crevasse between two big rocks, working his way in as deeply as he could. He found to his surprise that it wasn't just a crack between the rocks, but a passageway that opened into a beautiful valley with snow capped mountains." He paused at a gasp from Hannah. "Yes, Hannah. I imagine it was the valley you recently saw."

"What's he talking about, Hannah?" asked Julia. "What valley?"

"I'll tell you later," Hannah said. "Let Dad finish."

"Robert started down the mountainside, thinking he would reconnoiter and try to figure out where he was and where his regiment was. He walked for quite a while through a really thick forest until finally the ground leveled out and he came upon a well-worn road. He figured he had reached the valley floor and that if he followed the road he would find someone to tell him where he was.

He wasn't in a uniform . . . like most soldiers he couldn't really afford one, but he did have his rifle with him, loaded and primed, and he was a good shot. About the time he had walked along the road for a few minutes, he heard horses coming at a gallop. He didn't want to encounter any more Redcoats or Indians, so he hid behind a tree.

What he saw was a young man on a white horse being chased by three other men who were shooting at him with bows and arrows. Just then, one of the arrows hit the man on the white horse, knocking him to the ground. As the others reached him, the young man struggled to rise and one of his pursuers aimed at him again. Robert raised his rifle and shot the man before he could release the arrow. The other two men looked around fearfully, and then, grabbing the reins of their wounded friend, turned their horses and raced off the way they had come, the injured man slumped over his horse's neck."

"Wow," Brennan interrupted. "Were these more British soldiers? I thought most of them fought on foot."

"They weren't the British," his dad answered, "and Robert wasn't in

14

Pennsylvania anymore."

"Then where was he?" asked Emma?

"He was in Serenia."

"Serenia?" Julia repeated. "But you haven't told us where Serenia is yet?"

"Give me time, Julia. Be patient," her father admonished. "Now, where was I?"

"Robert had just driven off the attackers," Hannah contributed.

"Right," her dad said. "So, seeing that the attackers were gone, he called out to the injured man that he was a friend, and moved slowly back to the road. The wounded man was weak from the blood that was pouring from his shoulder, so Robert helped him into some cover in the woods in case the men came back. He used his knife to dig out the arrow. Then he tore off part of his shirt to use as a bandage to stop the bleeding . . ."

"Euh," Julia interrupted. "Wasn't it all sweaty?"

"Better than nothing," Brennan said wisely.

"Yes, better than nothing," their dad concurred. "Anyway, then he prayed that God would help the man's arm to heal quickly. The man thanked him for saving his life. Then he asked who he was and where he had come from and that is where things got interesting. It turns out the man had never heard of Pennsylvania, or the United States, or the British.

The story goes that he was really suspicious of Robert, then, and just told him his name was Rudolf. Rudolf's horse hadn't gone far when he had fallen off, so Robert was able to get it and help Rudolf mount. Then he somehow got on behind him to hold him on, and following Rudolf's directions, guided the horse along the road until they were met by another group of men. This time they were friends of Rudolf's so everything was okay." He paused and poured himself a cup of coffee from the coffeemaker.

"The really interesting part was that when Rudolf's doctor took off the

15

bandage Robert had put on to clean the wound, there was no longer a wound there!"

"So he really hadn't been shot at all," Brennan concluded.

"Oh, he had been shot all right," Kyle answered him. "Remember that Robert had to dig out the arrow."

"But then he prayed for him," Hannah concluded.

"And God had healed him, just like that?" asked Emma, astonished.

"According to the family legend, yes, He had."

"Wow!" said Brennan.

"Humph!" Julia retorted. "Just family stories like dad said!"

Hannah had a question. "But we still don't know where Serenia is and how he got there. I mean, all he did was go through a crevasse in the mountains, so he should still have been in Pennsylvania or at least close to it. Was this some weird group of people living in an isolated valley?"

"Well, yes and no. Serenia is a country in another world, one that is sort of parallel to ours. Sometimes, when serious trouble threatens Serenia, a portal opens between the worlds and people are able to pass through from one to the other for a brief time. That crevasse in the mountains was a portal. It had been opened by the Gwencalon, the wise man of the Serenians --maybe we would call him a prophet, like in the Old Testament -- in the hopes that The Holy One, their name for God, would lead the right person through the portal to save the king."

"The king?" repeated Brennan.

Julia was more skeptical. "You are just making up a story, aren't you, Dad? There really is no Serenia, no portal to another world."

"Portals," chirped Emma, "make me think of Harry Potter and port keys!" Everyone laughed.

Kyle sipped his coffee. "No, Julia. I wish it were just a story, but it is real."

Debby thought it was time she contributed to the discussion. "Your dad is making a long story out of this, and I suppose that's okay. It is his family that is involved, after all, but let me condense it for you. Because Robert appeared just when the King of Serenia needed help and saved him from sure death, the King rewarded him by making him a nobleman of Serenia. . ."

"Which is why he was called Lord Robert Bruce Waest," Kyle inserted.

"And also why he was made Hereditary Angeluscustos of Serenia," Debby concluded.

"But what's that angelus thing?" Emma asked again.

"An angeluscustos is like a guardian angel," Debby explained.

"In this case," Kyle continued, "your ancestor and all of his descendants became the Angeluscustos of Serenia. Whenever the King of Serenia needs help, one of his descendants goes to the King's aid."

"Hey, did you ever have to go?" Brennan asked his dad.

"No," his dad answered regretfully. "Most of my lifetime things have been pretty calm in Serenia. I understand there was a war with a neighboring country, but your Uncle Russ went to see about that since he wasn't married at the time. Saved the Queen and the Prince, but couldn't save the King. He was killed in an ambush."

He cleared his throat. "Time in Serenia is different than here," he explained. "That's why when it was 1778 in Robert's time, it was only 1478 in Serenian time."

"Wow, so now it is about 1714 there, right?" calculated Brennan.

"I'm not really sure, because time there doesn't move quite like time here."

Hannah was puzzled. "I don't get why our family is involved."

"Yeah," Brennan added. "What makes us so special? I mean, how could we help the King more than his own people? Doesn't he have soldiers and armies?"

"Your dad hasn't given you the most important information yet," Debby said. "Hadn't you better, Kyle? Especially in light of the letter and Hannah's dream?"

"Yes, I know." He took a deep breath. "Okay, kids, here's the deal. You know that Robert Waest and his descendants became Angeluscustos for the royal family of Serenia. The Gwencalon, or "Shining Heart" who is a holy man in Serenia, contacts us and directs us to the portal, the doorway into their world, when we are needed. Once we cross through the portal, we are granted special powers --- whatever is needed by the King --- and we do what needs to be done and then we come home. Our powers only work in Serenia, so when we are here, we are back to being normal people."

Emma's forehead was furrowed in puzzlement. "Dad, do you mean that we are angels?"

"Well, in a way, I guess, but only when we are in Serenia."

"But we don't have any wings!" she argued.

"No, but not all angels have wings all the time. We work only with Serenia and only when they need us. The rest of the time we are just regular people."

"Why didn't you ever tell us this," asked Hannah, a little offended. "This makes us special, supernatural!"

"That is exactly why, Hannah. We are not special and it is important that you don't think we are. Nor are we supernatural! When was the last time you flew or walked through a wall? Only when we are on a mission in Serenia do we have any special powers."

"Ah, what kind of powers?" Brennan asked, visions of Spider Man flying through his mind.

"I can't answer that," Kyle explained. "Whatever is needed."

"But why us kids and not you and Mom," asked Julia. "We're just kids! What can we do?"

"Speak for yourself!" Hannah objected, feeling every inch the adult after her 18th birthday.

"Yeah, Julia," seconded Brennan.

"It is not our choice," Debby reminded them. "The request always comes from Serenia and it is always specific. If the Gwencalon wants the four of you to go, there must be something only the four of you can do."

"You mean you think we should actually go?" Hannah asked.

"I don't see that you have a choice," her dad said softly. "You've been asked to come and you saw why."

"The dream."

"Yes, Hannah, the dream."

"What dream," asked Emma.

And so Hannah related her dream once more. When she had finished, her brother and sister were beside themselves with excitement and could scarcely be persuaded to eat the cereal that their mom set in front of them. The bacon that Kyle had cooked was still crispy and warm, so they eventually gobbled that down too, washed down with milk. But the eggs their dad had scrambled for them, though warm, had dried out in the oven while they talked.

After breakfast they conducted a heated discussion over what to take along. Over his mother's objections, Brennan stuck his Swiss army knife and his cell phone in his pocket.

"You won't have cell towers, you dope," Julia argued.

But Brennan was adamant. "I have apps I might be able to use," he retorted, "a compass, a calculator. . . lots of things."

"Humph!" Julia snorted in distain. "I'm going to pack a change of clothes in my backpack along with a pen and paper in case we need to make notes."

"Matches," Emma contributed, "in case we need to build a fire."

Remembering the locked bars in her dream, Hannah asked her dad for a collection of old keys he had long been collecting, and Emma stuck in a set of lock picks from her Sherlock Holmes Detective Kit. Debby made them pack a change of clothes and toothbrushes and toothpaste.

"Just because you'll be in another world is no excuse for bad hygiene!" She admonished. But then she also made sure they had bottles of water and granola bars and the kids each stuck in their favorite cookies or candy bars.

Soon they all had bulging backpacks and were ready to set off on foot for their great adventure. In the end, their parents had insisted on going with them at least part of the way, and the group moved quietly through the woods behind the house and down to the riverbank. Leaves drifted slowly from the trees as they passed them, flashing gold and red in the beams of sunlight that filtered through the overhanging branches. Under foot, twigs and drying leaves crunched noisily, the only sounds beyond the occasional scurry of a rabbit or squirrel hurrying out of their way.

As for the Wests, not one of them spoke. Kyle brushed branches aside, holding them for the others to pass safely by. Debby watched for Emma lest she, as the smallest of the four, might stumble over a root and fall. Emma, of course, had no need of such care. She had wandered these woods hundreds of times and the way to the river bank was as well known to her as her own bedroom.

Each of them was lost in thought. Kyle, somewhat disappointed that he himself had not been included in the request, wondered why all four of his children had been called for. Was that the prince that Hannah had seen in her dream, and if so, who had imprisoned him?

He had talked at length with his brother, Russ, when he had returned from Serenia and knew that the prince, only nine at the time, had been safely left in the care and guardianship of his maternal uncle. The rule of the country itself had been invested in a council of elders, which included the uncle, and other luminaries of the country. Things should have been stable, and in fact, had been stable for some ten years. What now could have put the prince in jeopardy?

Debby, who had herself learned of Serenia and the entire hereditary Angeluscustos affair only after she and Kyle had married, was more than a little concerned about what her children were going to encounter. She had tried to broach the subject with Kyle while the kids packed, but he had assured her that they would be okay, that they would be protected. She didn't like to doubt, but she just couldn't feel comfortable letting them go off on their own like this. They were all so young! Hannah, of course, was nearly an adult, but even her life had been pretty sheltered. What did any of them know about a world like Serenia? What did she know, for that matter?

Hannah, remembering her dream and the lonely figure in the cell, wondered how on earth the four of them could do anything to save him. They were nothing special, just kids with no particular talents beyond music. Maybe she should have brought along her guitar. She imagined herself playing a song and singing with Emma to distract the guards while Brennan and Julia slipped behind them to release the prisoner by . . . what?

That was a stupid idea. What on earth were they going to do? Still, she supposed they would have to think of something. Was he handsome, she wondered, this mysterious prince? Would he have dark hair, with a lock that drooped lazily over his forehead and that he kept ineffectually pushing back? Would his equally dark eyes glitter with unshed tears as he thanked them for saving him, gazing deeply into Hannah's eyes? She shook her head to clear it of that compelling image. They would have to do something to help, but she had no idea what it could be, what they could possibly do.

Brennan's thoughts were a bit more positive as he focused on the idea of helping free the prince. He saw himself, like Frodo Baggins the Hobbit, fighting his way up a mountain to throw a magic ring into a volcano thereby saving the kingdom of Serenia from utter destruction. Nothing would stop him, he vowed. He would face any struggle with determination. After all, the prince was counting on them. Perhaps there would be sword fights. He would be empowered with excellent swordsmanship, he imagined. And he settled into pleasant images of himself gallantly fighting off a dozen warriors single handedly.

Julia wanted to talk. She wanted to ask her dad more about the special powers they would have in Serenia. She imagined herself soaring above the ground while frustrated Serenians ran below her, shaking their fists and shouting as she flew away. Or perhaps she would have special healing powers. The prince would be wounded, in the shoulder like the king in the story her dad had told, and she would gently heal the wound. He would fall in love with her, naturally, and she would accept his offer of marriage and become, one day, the Queen of Serenia. Well, maybe she shouldn't share that dream with anyone just yet, she considered, and so remained silent as she followed along, dreaming of handsome princes, crowns, and beautiful dresses.

Emma of all of them was the most pragmatic. Although both excited and a little frightened, she accepted without question that whatever Power had sent for them had a certain purpose for them to accomplish. Likewise, she had no doubt that they would accomplish that purpose. Why else would they have been summoned? So she marched along, wondering if there was anything else she should have packed to bring.

When they reached the riverbank, Kyle stopped them and gathered them around him.

"You should go on by yourselves from here," he said. "The falls are only about a mile down the river. Just follow the directions in the letter and you will be fine. Good luck! We'll see you when you return."

"Hannah and Brennan," added Debby fiercely. "You watch out for your sisters! I want to see all of you back here unharmed, understand?"

"Deb," Kyle soothed. "They'll be fine."

And, after a flurry of hugs and kisses, the four began to pick their way through the weeds that grew along the river's bank. Just as they reached a bend in the river that would hide them from the sight of their watching parents, Emma alone turned with a cheery smile and a farewell wave.

"Kyle. . . ."

"They'll be fine, Deb." Kyle hugged her to him. "Let's go home."

3 THE MEETING

As they neared the falls on the Little Bear River, Brennan began to notice the absence of noise in the woods around them. No more sounds of animals skittering away, no more calls from birds in the trees above, only the sound of the water rushing more and more rapidly to their right. The tumbling river was not very deep, only a couple of feet, but the current caused by the cascading falls and the presence of tumbled boulders in the river bed had always made the river off limits to the kids before. Brennan wondered that their parents had let them come this way alone. Still, they weren't going to play in the water, just meet whomever had been sent for them. They shouldn't have to get their feet wet at all, he mused.

Louder and louder grew the sound of the water until at last they turned a final bend and could see the falls itself in all its magnificence. As waterfalls go, it was probably not so significant, not a Rhine Falls or a Niagara Falls. But to the kids, who had never seen either of those, Little Bear Falls seemed gigantic. In misty splendor its waters crashed over the rocks at the top of the falls, tumbling some twenty feet to the pool below where they foamed and roiled around granite impediments, before surging down the riverbed to the west.

Hannah, who had unconsciously been leading the group, halted and looked about her. She could hear nothing above the roaring of the waters and she could see nothing but trees and bushes and weeds on either bank. No one waited impatiently for them.

"No one is here," Julia said, echoing Hannah's thoughts. "I thought someone was supposed to meet us."

"Yes, they were," Hannah answered, searching between the trees for some suggestion of movement. "Someone has to take us to the portal."

"Maybe they got tired of waiting," Brennan contributed. "I would have. After all, the letter came yesterday. They probably thought we would come right away."

"What are we going to do?"

"I don't know, Julia." Hannah's voice was edgy with uncertainty. "Let's walk a few feet into the woods in case someone is there. Brennan, you take Julia and Emma, you come with me." She turned to catch her sister's eye, but Emma was no longer there.

"Emma? Emma! Where are you?"

But no Emma answered her call. Emma, remembering the wording of the letter "Come through the falls . . . ." had quickly spotted a line of flat-topped boulders rising above the foam of the turbulent waters and leading straight to the waterfall. . And there, in the midst of the falls, she had also spied the long ears and grey whiskered face of a rabbit, leaning out from the curtain of water and beckoning to her. So she had gone, stepping carefully on the damp stones to take the soft paw of the rabbit and step through the curtain of water. On the other side, she was surprised to find herself dry as she released the paw and faced the rabbit.

"Hello," she said.

"Hello," he answered, wiggling his whiskers. "You must be Lady Emma. I am Mr. Higgley." He tilted his head to the side to study her from head to foot. "You are smaller than the rest." He looked back at the screen of water, which fell more quietly on this side. "Where are they? Didn't they come through? Tsk, tsk. Now I shall have to go back after them."

"Wait," she said, reaching out a hand to stop him. He paused and looked at her questioningly. "You can talk!"

"Well, of course I can talk. So can you! Where's the surprise in that?"

"But rabbits where I live don't talk!" Emma insisted.

"Of course they do," Mr. Higgley contradicted. "It's just that you can't understand them there. Here, you can understand all of us, just like the Gwencalon, because you are an Angeluscrustos."

Emma could think of nothing more to say than, "Oh."

"Stay here," he ordered. "Sit behind that rock over there," he pointed to a large, nearby outcropping of rock just to the left of the falls, "and don't move! T'would be bad if anyone saw you just yet."

And with that, he disappeared back into the screen of water.

"Emma. Emma, answer us. Where are you?"

Brennan, Julia, and Hannah continued to call their sister to no avail. "She can't have fallen into the water," Brennan mused, "or we would have heard her yell for help."

Julia and Hannah turned as one to look at the swirling, angry waters.

"Look," Julia said, pointing. "Isn't that a rabbit sitting on that rock in the middle of the river?"

"What?" Brennan said. "Rabbits don't like water, do they?"

Hannah saw that indeed a rabbit did sit on a flat-topped rock, seemingly oblivious to the water that swirled around him, as he gazed at the three kids, his nose twitching.

"Poor thing. Maybe he washed up there and got stuck," Julia suggested. "We should rescue him." And with that, she started onto the row of stones that seemed to lead straight to the falls.

"No, Julia, wait!" Brennan called, but it was too late. Julia had already stepped onto first one and then a second rock. The rabbit, with the typical contrariness of any animal that a human is intent upon saving, turned and scampered from stone to stone away from her and straight to the falling sheet of water.

"Of course!" Hannah suddenly exclaimed. "The letter said through the falls, not to the falls. Come on Brennan. I think that rabbit is our guide." She grabbed his arm and started after Julia.

"But what about Emma?" Brennan objected.

"I think she has already gone through!" Hannah answered. "Come on!"

"Don't pull, Hannah! You'll make me lose my balance," he complained.

Mr. Higgley, for of course it was he, stopped on a narrow ledge onto which the water cascaded, turned toward Julia, sat back on his haunches, and extended his right paw to her with a courtly bow. Surprised and enchanted, she none-the-less took his paw, just as Hannah, towing a still protesting Brennan behind her, reached Julia and clasped her arm. And just like that, the three followed Mr. Higgley through the falls.

As she stepped out of the water and onto the hillside, Hannah immediately recognized the valley of her dream, spread out before her. Dumbfounded, she found herself unable to move or speak. Julia, however, had spied Emma, asleep by a rock a few feet away, and with a cry of delight, she ran over to shake her awake, Brennan at her heels.

"Oh, hi," Emma said sleepily. "It took you guys long enough!"

"Long enough!" Brennan sputtered, indignant. "You only disappeared five minutes ago. I looked at my watch!"

"It was forever," Emma said. "I got tired of waiting and fell asleep."

"The Gwencalon says that time moves a little differently in your world than here,"

Mr. Higgley explained. "He says time here is vertical and time in your world is horizontal.

"Why, you are talking!" Brennan exclaimed. "Hannah, the rabbit talks!"

28

Hannah pulled herself out of her reverie and joined her brother and sisters gathered around the rabbit.

"Oh, sorry," Emma said. "This is Mr. Higgley. I think he came to get us."

Mr. Higgley bowed, low. "Charmed, Lord and Ladies."

"Nice to meet you, Mr. Higgley, " Hannah replied.

The others murmured their hellos as well, gazing open mouthed at the rabbit.

"Wait," Brennan interrupted. "You said time here is vertical. How can time move vertically? That doesn't make any sense."

"Only know what I'm told, only know what I'm told," Mr. Higgley answered.

Brennan continued. "So a whole decade, a whole millennium could pass here in a minute in our time?"

"Oh, not so much, no, not so much," Mr. Higgley responded. "But that is the way it goes, yes."

"Oh, Mr. Higgley," Emma hastened to say. "I'm glad you had me sit behind the rock because some men came by just below me on that path." She pointed down the hillside. They wore some kind of black uniform and carried guns. I'm sure they didn't see me."

"Oh my, oh my," Mr. Higgley worried. "How long ago, Lady Emma?"

"Oh quite some time before I fell asleep. I watched for awhile, you know, to be sure they didn't come back."

Mr. Higgley looked around him and motioned the others closer. "We must move quickly before another patrol comes along. They are looking for the Gwencalon, you see, but they will never expect him to be with the Barbegazi, no, but with the Barbegazi he is. Come!" And he waved his paw to urge them on.

"Come on, guys," Hannah seconded. "Let's go with Mr. Higgley."

"Yes, come, come," Mr. Higgley urged hopping off on some mysterious trail only he could see. Julia and Emma fell in on either side of him with Hannah and Brennan following closely.

For some time they seemed to follow the curve of the mountain, bearing ever so slightly up at the same time. The ground was still covered in short grass and liberally sprinkled with bright flowers, some clustered among the huge rocks that pushed up here and there. Julia suddenly stopped and pointed to some star-shaped white flowers with yellow centers. "Hannah, look! Aren't those Edelweiss?"

"Yes, they are, I think! Aren't they pretty?"

"Can we pick some flowers? Those pink ones over there are really nice, too," Julia motioned to a clump of feathery flowers waving gently at the ends of long stems that pushed out of a crevice in a rock. Emma was already reaching for the flowers with a cry of delight.

"No, no, no!" scolded Mr. Higgley. "We must hurry on. Another patrol will come by soon and we must be well ahead of them through the pass. Besides," he added, "It gets dark quickly in the mountains. We must reach the caves of the Barbegazi before nightfall. Pick flowers some other time."

Reluctantly Emma and Julia left the flowers and hurried after the hopping Mr. Higgley. Hannah heard Brennan's mumbled complaint of "Girls!" and shushed him. A brother-sister squabble was the last thing they needed. Though she had not noticed it before, shadows had begun to lengthen on the valley floor as the sun dipped closer to the mountains to their left. She hurried her pace, forcing Brennan to step up his as well. She had no desire to be stuck on an open mountainside for the night.

Soon they reached a wide dirt road that wound steeply upward toward an obvious gap between the mountains. Mr. Higgley lifted a paw to halt them.

"Be very still," he cautioned. As they stood silently, he hopped onto the road, perked up his long, pink ears, and listened intently in both directions.

"Come, come," he urged. "We are well ahead of them, I think, but we must still hurry." And with that, he started up the road with the four Wests following after him.

Though the road was steeper, Hannah found the footing much easier. The grass had been slippery and her tennis shoes had not provided much traction. Still, as they moved higher, the air became thinner, and she could hear all of them gasping for breath.

"Can we rest a minute?" Julia asked, panting.

"Please, Mr. Higgley?" Emma begged.

Mr. Higgley turned to the four who had been lagging farther and farther behind him. "Oh, my, oh my," he worried. "For just a moment. We really must hurry. If the patrol passes us, we will have to spend the night on the mountain. We must go on in just a moment. Rest, rest!" he urged, and Julia and Emma collapsed to the road. Hannah leaned against a rock, hands on her knees as she fought to get her breath. Brennan, however, scrambled onto the top of some rocks and pulled binoculars from his pack. Training them down the mountain, he began to slowly sweep them from right to left, struggling to catch any glimpse of movement between the trees and rocks below them.

Suddenly, he called urgently, "Mr. Higgley. I think I see them coming. Some movement a ways below us."

"Oh, dear, oh dear," Mr. Higgley said, wringing his paws. "Quiet then, and let me listen." And again he stretched his long ears, and listened intently. "Yes, yes, they are coming. Up, up," he motioned to Emma and Julia. "We must hurry now. They are closer than I had hoped, but we should still beat them." And, spurred on by the sense of urgency, the girls struggled to their feet and the small group hurried along the road.

In only a few minutes they had reached a relatively level patch of road that plunged quickly into a narrow rock passage. The sun was well behind the mountains now, and Mr. Higgley grabbed Emma's hand to guide her through the pass.

31

"Hold hands," he urged. "It is dark here, but we are almost there." Emma reached for Julia, who in turn took Hannah's hand and she Brennan's. Brennan had decided that as the only male in the group (he found it difficult to count Mr. Higgley), he needed to bring up the rear. If the patrol caught up to them, he thought, he would try to hold them off while the girls escaped. He had spied a fallen branch as he had clambered down from the rocks at their rest stop and as they had hurried on, he had been methodically stripping it of branches. It wasn't much as a weapon, he admitted, but swung at the legs of unsuspecting men it might buy them a moment or two to get away.

Mr. Higgley pulled them quickly along the passage and out into the sudden light of a rising moon. Spread before them was another valley, narrow and deep, twinkling with the lights of farmhouses on the mountain slopes and clumps of lights along the lower slopes and on the valley floor. Those must be towns, Hannah thought, wondering to which of the towns they would be going. But Mr. Higgley had left the road now, and, having dropped Emma's hand, was hopping from rock to rock up the mountain.

Luckily the moonlight clearly illuminated the rocks that he climbed, and with little difficulty the four were able to scramble after him. Brennan was forced to drop his tree branch and use both hands to steady himself as he climbed, but still he kept looking down behind, worrying that at any moment the patrol would burst out of the passage behind them. In the bright light of the moon, a casual look up the mountain by one of the men would immediately reveal their presence. Suddenly, however, he realized Emma and Julia, had disappeared from sight.

"Hannah," he whispered loudly. "Where did they go?"

"Here, Brennan," she answered, grabbing his arm and pulling him into a shadow between rocks where the moonlight didn't reach. Mr. Higgley stopped them with a soft paw, explaining, "This is where I leave you. The Barbegazi are inside and will take you from here."

"What about the soldiers?" Brennan asked worriedly.

"I'm a rabbit," Mr. Higgley smiled. "I'll just hide until they pass and then head home to my family. They won't be looking for me, you see.

Not for me!"

"Will we see you again," Hannah asked.

"Who can say? Who can say?" Mr. Higgley replied. "Hurry now. They are waiting. "

And so Hannah and Brennan continued into the shadow, slipping and sliding on the dark rocks that sloped gently downward, and gradually realizing that the shadow was actually an opening into a cave. And soon, the darkness began to brighten and they could see the flicker of torchlight as the cave opened into a large cavern. In the torchlight Brennan could see a group of four figures waiting for them, among whom he picked out Emma and Julia. The other two barely reached the level of Emma's shoulders, and as he and Hannah approached them, he realized that they were short, bearded men with huge feet and covered in white hair all over their bodies. Unlike dwarves whose bodies were shortened but whose hands were often normal sized, these two men were perfectly proportioned small adults except for their huge feet.

Brennan thought they looked a little like tiny Yetis, those mythical snow monsters of the Himalayan Mountains. But these little men were dressed in white shirts and bright yellow pants, held up by black suspenders decorated with white flowers. They looked amazingly like pictures of German lederhosen that Brennan remembered seeing in his geography book.

One of the small men waved them closer. "Lady Julia tells us you are the Angeluscustos the Gwencalon sent for. We are Ugo," he thumped his chest, "and Sachi. We are the Barbegazi with whom the Gwencalon has been sheltering."

Sachi bowed low to Hannah and Brennan and murmured "Pleased to meet you."

Julia, who had readily taken the lead in this encounter, introduced her brother and sister to the Barbegazi. Sachi eyed them carefully and then shook his head. "The Gwencalon has been waiting for you, though I can't imagine why. I would have thought he would call in tall, strong men, not mere children."

Brennan, offended at this comment, drew himself up to his full five feet 10 inches and looked down on the Barbegazi. "We seem to be taller than you, at any rate," he intoned.

Ugo laughed and slapped Sachi on the back as Sachi scowled. "Right you are, Lord Brennan. Sachi is just disgruntled because the snows haven't fallen yet. We move around much easier in the winter, because we can ski down the mountains. Much faster than walking, you know. But never mind. We will do what we can to help you, right Sachi?"

"Humph," Sachi snorted. "We'd better get you to the Gwencalon. And I suppose you haven't eaten either, so we'd better get some food for you."

With that, he and Ugo took the torches from the holders along the walls. Sachi handed one to Hannah and one to Brennan before taking the final one himself and starting deeper into the cave. Hannah, Brennan, Julia, and Emma followed with Ugo bringing up the rear.

4 THE GWENCALON

The Barbegazi led them through a series of caves and tunnels, many of which had clear marks where iron tools had chipped away at the walls. As they reached another cavern, so large that the light of their torches did not reach the ceiling, they suddenly heard voices and the scuffle of feet from behind them.

"The patrol?" Brennan asked Ugo.

"Shush, yes. But speak softly! If we can hear them, they can hear us." He whispered to Brennan. "Did they follow you here?"

"No, I don't think so," he answered. "I climbed a rock when we rested for a moment and I could see them coming, but I only caught a glimpse of them through the trees. I'm sure they were too far behind to see where we went." He paused and then continued. "Could they have found my staff?"

"Your staff?" Sachi asked, his brow wrinkling in annoyance.

"Yes. I found a strong branch to use as a weapon in case we needed it," Brennan explained, "but I had to drop it when we started to climb the rocks. I had stripped off the smaller branches so they will know someone has used it."

"What a dunderheaded thing to do!" observed Sachi.

"Never mind," Ugo said. "Everyone knows about these old mines. They may just be searching them to be sure the Gwencalon is not hiding in here. I will lead them astray. Follow Sachi."

So Sachi, shaking his head and muttering under his breath turned to lead them on while Ugo disappeared in another direction. Emma moved back to Brennan's side and whispered. "I think that was a very smart and brave thing to do, Brennan, making a weapon!"

"Yeah, I thought so to, but it hasn't turned out so well!" he answered.

"Don't worry." She patted his arm. "It will be okay!"

The light from their four torches lit a rough circle about them beyond which stretched a blackness that seemed impenetrable. Yet Sachi walked unerringly across the floor, his large feet flapping against the dirt and rock. The sounds of voices behind them soon faded into silence as they reached opposite wall of the cavern.

Sachi lifted his torch and seemed to search for something. Julia, who was just behind him, caught sight of a red smear on the rock just to the edge of the torchlight. Sachi grunted in satisfaction when he saw it, turned to his right, and moved quickly along the wall until he came to its end at the opening of another tunnel. He motioned them all inside, and when they had obeyed him, he pressed against the wall near the opening and with a grinding sound the wall closed behind them.

"What about Ugo?" asked Hannah.

"He will join us soon enough," Sachi answered. "From now on we must go without the torches." He took their torches and rolled them on the dirt floor to extinguish them. "Take each others' hands," he instructed, waiting to see that they were holding on to one another before taking Emma's hand and putting out his own torch, leaving all three of them on the ground.

His voice was a sibilant whisper as he instructed, "We will soon come to a tunnel that connects to the one where Ugo is leaving a false trail. Until he has joined us and we can close off that tunnel, we must be very quiet and move in darkness."

Then, with eveyone firmly connected, Sachi began to move forward, feeling his way along the wall with his free hand. Julia felt Emma's hand tighten in hers, a suggestion of the fear she felt in the utter darkness. Julia squeezed back and then firmed her grip on Hannah. Once again, Brennan had opted to bring up the rear. None of them had ever experienced darkness like this. Here, below the earth, no stars, no moonlight, no light from house windows could reach them. It was as if each of them had suddenly become totally blind.

After what seemed like a long time of shuffling in the dense darkness, Sachi felt the rough-hewn edge of the tunnel opening and stopped the group. In the distance they could suddenly hear voices again.

"This way," someone cried. "There are fresh soot marks on the ceiling from a torch. Someone has just gone down this tunnel!"

"Do you think it is the Gwencalon?" asked a second voice.

" I don't know," the first responded, his voice growing slightly louder. "But if it is and we catch him, we will be well rewarded this night! Now, no more talking. We don't want to warn him that we are coming!"

The voices were silent, but now the shuffle of boots on the floor echoed through the tunnel as the soldiers hurried past the opening at the other end. As even those sounds died out, they heard a soft, "Now!" and again the grating of stone against stone as the opening to the tunnel closed.

Sachi spoke again. "Ugo will lead us on, now. But still, hold hands. We must go farther before chancing light!"

They shuffled on in the vast dark for several minutes until finally the Barbegazi came to a stop. "Why are we stopping?" Julia whispered to Hannah.

"Shush, I don't know!" Hannah whispered back.

"Okay to talk now," Sachi said as with a scrape of rock on rock and a spark of fire he lit the torch that Ugo was suddenly holding. Ugo passed the torch to Sachi, lit another from it which he handed to Brennan, and then, lighting a third, motioned Brennan to the front.

"Lord Brennan, you are tallest, so now you must lead with Sachi," he instructed. "Again I will follow." In the torchlight, the kids could see a flight of stone steps disappearing up into the darkness, made easier to climb by a thick rope fastened to metal rings fastened to the rock wall every couple of feet. Following Sachi, Brennan began to climb, the others following close behind. The steps seemed to go on forever, and soon Hannah found herself pulling herself up with one hand on the thick rope and urging Emma up the steps with her other.

Finally, however, a subtle change in the air and the whisper of wind against her face caused her to lift her eyes from the steps to look up the stairs. A slight lightening of the darkness and a sudden rush of cold air heralded the end of the stairs and an opening out of the cavern. With Julia and Emma, she emerged into the cold night to a moon washed, snow covered landscape that stretched before them in gentle undulations. In the distance, tucked into a slight depression, too shallow to be called a valley, lay a cluster of stone cottages.

"Welcome to Glacere," Ugo said with a smile, waving his arm at the village before them. "Isn't our village a pretty one?"

"Yes, yes," grumbled Sachi. "Time for sightseeing later!"

Ugo rolled his eyes, but followed along as Sachi led them quickly towards the village. In the distance slightly darker shapes moved about on the snow, herded toward a barn-like structure by another Barbegazi, and Hannah guessed they might be cattle, though why anyone would have cattle this high on the mountain she could not guess. Surely little grass could be found beneath this snow. From what she remembered of pictures her grandparents had shown her of a trip to the Alps in Switzerland, mountain areas like this were usually rocky, rather barren landscapes without much vegetation.

She reached a hand to brace Emma who had lost her balance in the deep snow. Her own tennis shoes were soaked and snow dampened her jeans to mid calf. Emma, the shortest of the four, was wading nearly knee deep in the chilling snow. Hannah glanced with envy at the Barbegazi. Using their large feet like snowshoes, they skimmed across the snow, only stopping from time to time to wait for the ungainly four who struggled valiently through the drifts.

"We usually bring guests in by air," Ugo explained apologetically, "but with the extra patrols that the duke has ordered, we could not have collected you by the waterfall without unwanted notice. This was the safest way."

Sachi pointed to a taller building, set apart somewhat from the others in the village which they were slowly approaching. "We are almost there. See, smoke rises from the chimney. There will be a nice fire going."

"Good," Julia complained, rubbing her arms as she struggled to wade through the snow, "I'm wet and freezing!"

"You will be warm inside," Ugo assured her. The cottage, although somewhat larger than the rest in the village, appeared, like the others, to be made of stone with a steeply pitched slate roof and wooden shutters on the windows.

As they reached the building, Ugo pulled open a heavy wooden door and urged, "Go in, all of you. The Gwencalon is inside."

The small room into which they stepped indeed wrapped them in warmth, aided by the blankets that were handed to them by a smiling Barbegazi woman. She hurried from one to another, giving them the warm, wool blankets, and then guiding them to seats near the fire that roared in the fireplace that dominated the room.

"This is my wife, Amea," explained Ugo, proudly. "She will see that you are comfortable and warm. Amea, these are the Angeluscustos."

"Welcome to our home," she smiled. "Sachi, Ugo, help me with the drinks, please," she ordered, sweeping her long blue dress out of her way as she moved to the fire to ladle steaming cider from a pot that was warming there into thick pottery glasses that she passed to the others to distribute.

In the flurry of being settled with blankets and the hot cider, Hannah at first did not notice the man who sat quietly in the corner of the room, but his amusing exchange with Emma caught her attention. Exhausted from the long walk, Emma had gone immediately to plop down in a wooden chair in the far corner of the lamp-lit room while the others had milled uncertainly just instead the door. She slid out of her backpack and set it down next to her chair. Next to her sat a rather plump man with long white hair and a beard that covered most of his chest. Instead of the pants and shirt worn by the Barbegazi, he wore a long blue robe that reached to his ankles and was tied at his waist with a braided sash of crimson. His rosy cheeks and kind blue eyes made her feel comfortable at once and reminded her strongly of someone.

"Ah, Mr. Higgley saw you safely to the Barbegazi before going home, I see," he commented.

Never the shy child, Emma smiled and said, "Yes, he took good care of us. He is ever so nice." She paused and then asked him, "Are you Santa Claus?"

"No, child," he chuckled, "I am not. I am the Gwencalon. And you must be Lady Emma, the youngest of our four intrepids."

"Oh, no," Emma replied. "I am Emma, the youngest of the four Wests!"

At that, Hannah, feeling the responsibility of her advanced years, approached the corner and asked, "If you are the Gwencalon, you're the one that we have come so far to see. Can you tell us what you need us to do?"

"Yes, yes, my child. But first, sit down and drink your cider while Amea brings you some stew. You must be very hungry and tired by now, for you have indeed come a long way."

"Yes, we have," agreed Brennan, sitting on the floor in front of the fire. "And we weren't really dressed for the last part of it."

"No," the Gwencalon agreed. "But no clothing that you have would really work here. Tomorrow we will give you clothing that will help you fit in" he smiled at Brennan, "and keep you warm. Now, let's eat. We have waited supper for you and I fear we are all very hungry."

The woman called Amea bustled about, filling bowls with fragrant stew, which Sachi and Ugo helped her distribute. Julia lifted her bowl to her nose and sniffed before asking, "What kind of stew is this?"

"Beef," Amea answered, smiling. "We don't have it often, because mostly we keep milk cows, but tonight is special."

Emma tasted carefully and then smiled at Amea. "This is very good!"

Amea nodded her thanks as she handed the Gwencalon a bowl. For some time, the only sounds in the room were the crackle of the fire and the clatter of spoons as they dipped again and again into the bowls. Finally, the Gwencalon laid aside his bowl and began to speak.

"Serenia, where you are now, is a country divided into five cantons, four of which are mountain valleys, and the fifth of which, Meerwald, lies between the mountains and the Great Sea. On this side of the Great Sea, for many, many miles in both directions, the mountains reach down to the very edge of the water with only rocks and cliffs at the shore. Only in our canton of Meerwald do you find safe harbors, sandy beaches and flat, verdant fields.

This has been very useful to Serenia and has made us rich over the centuries through the tariffs that others must pay to ship goods from our harbors. Think of Serenia as a capital T. The top of the T is the canton of Meerwald, butted up against the sea. The other cantons form the leg of the T, stretching back in a series of valleys formed by the great river Chavornay, from which the royal family takes its name. Just south of Meerwald lies Nidwald, then Mittewald, where the capital and the royal castle are located. Then south of Mittewald are first Oberwald and finally Unterwald.

Just over the mountains to the east lies the country of Kummer, with whom we have always had friendly relations. But about fifteen years ago, the King of Kummer died, and his cousin became the ruler. He grew tired of paying the tariffs and suggested that we divide Meerwald with him so that he could have direct access to the Great Sea. Our king, of course, would not agree and so ten years ago the Kummerian armies attacked over the mountains. King Charles quickly raised an army against him, and in the great battle that followed, the Kummerians were defeated and retreated back to their own country.

Unfortunately, King Charles was wounded in an ambush on the way home and died before I could get to him, leaving only his son, the young prince to rule. Queen Marianne convinced the Council of Elders to choose her brother, the Duke Ferigard from Meerwald, to be the young king's guardian until he came of age. I warned against that choice, for the Duke is an ambitious man, but in her grief, the queen looked to her close kin for support. Alas, the queen herself died only a month later, when a sickness spread through the cantons, taking many lives."

"I have a question," Brennan interrupted. "Who are the Council of Elders?"

The Gwencalon paused a moment before answering. "The Council of Elders are a group of ten representatives of the people who serve as a group of advisors to the king. They serve alone except in times of war when they are joined by the Council of Lords, the ten Lords of Serenia. Traditionally, the king has appointed two elders from each of the five cantons, but no law says that he must. In fact, he may choose whomever he wishes as long as they are not members of a lord's family."

He sighed. "In these last ten years many things have happened. The duke gradually replaced the elders, one by one, forcing them to retire and replacing them with men who were loyal only to him. A few months ago, a series of mysterious accidents began to happen to me: a hunting accident, a loose stone that fell from the castle wall, a run-away horse. Finally, I had a yearning one morning for some cod for breakfast, so I went out in a dingy to fish. My boat began to sink and I was too far from shore to swim, but Sachi here saw my distress from the mountain top and whistled up some help for me."

Sachi interrupted here to explain. "From the mountains, we Barbegazi can see avalanches and other dangers that those below us can not see, and we whistle to warn them of danger."

"Yes," the Gwencalon continued, "he whistled loud and long and some fishermen who were mending nets looked out to sea and saw me. By the time they reached me, I was treading water and the boat was already gone. That was one attempt too many on my life, so I decided it was time to disappear. The fishermen took me to shore far from the village and told no one that they had seen me. And I came here with the Barbegazi to hide from the enemy."

"Who is the enemy?" asked Brennan. "Do you know who wants to kill you?"

"I would guess it is Duke Ferigard," the Gwencalon answered, "but alas, I have no proof. "

"Why would he want to kill you?" asked Julia. "Did you do something to him?"

"No," the Gwencalon shook his head. "But I had begun to suspect that he wishes to become King of Serenia, not just Regent for prince David. I have even wondered if he had something to do with the old king's death. Those who shot him were never caught, and it was only assumed that they were a remnant of Kummerian soldiers. I am afraid I began to question the replacement of all of the Elders on the Council, especially when two of them died suddenly. Even the soldiers at the castle all come from Meerwald now, all from the duke's own lands." He shook his head. "I must have seemed too suspicious."

"So he tried to have you killed," concluded Brennan.

"Yes, I think so. With me missing and presumed dead," he continued, "the duke has already appointed another Gwencalon. The Gwencalon," he explained modestly, "serves as the spiritual leader of Serenia and also a close advisor to the king.

"I suppose he picked another of his henchmen?" questioned Hannah.

"A henchman indeed," replied the Gwencalon. "He has appointed his younger brother."

"Wow!" Brennan exclaimed.

"But what about the prince?" asked Julia.

"The prince has a godfather, the Lord Bernald, who was very close friends with the late king. But more and more the duke has discouraged Lord Bernald from seeing the prince. The prince is at lessons or he is out hunting in the mountains with the royal huntsman or he is off visiting his relatives in Meerwald. Lord Bernald, like me, had become suspicious. . . suspicious and angry. Now it seems no one has seen the prince in several weeks and the duke has put about the word that he is very ill. The new Gwencalon says he has been to see him and fears for his very life. The entire country is to pray for his recovery, but I am afraid he will not be allowed to recover."

"But, he didn't look ill when I saw him," Hannah objected. "only lonely and despairing."

"When you saw him?" the Gwencalon questioned sharply. "When and where did you see him?"

Embarrassed, Hannah, explained. "I didn't see him in person. It was a dream. I dreamed that I was in a castle dungeon and he was there, locked in a cell."

"So that is where they have put him, the rogues!" muttered the Gwencalon. "We must get him out! That is why I called for you, you see. On Wednesday the prince will turn eighteen. He will be of age and can be chosen to rule on his own. I don't believe his uncle the duke intends for him to live that long."

Emma gasped.

"Then we must save him," Hannah cried anxiously.

"Yes, we must," the Gwencalon, concurred. "But first we must have a plan and I must explain to you just what you can do that most of us cannot. You have certain special powers here, you know."

"Powers?" repeated Julia. "Can we fly?"

"No," the Gwencalon responded with a chuckle. "No flying. But as you already know, you can speak to animals and understand when they speak back to you. You have already talked with Mr. Higgley, of course."

The kids all nodded.

"Beyond that," the Gwencalon continued, "I don't know what you might be able to do. Other powers you will need to discover for yourselves. What you must remember, however, is that your powers have been given to you to help others. Do not misuse them! They will only appear when you truly need them, and they will only work in this world."

"So the powers cannot just be turned on and off?" asked Hannah.

"Not exactly, no. Once they are on, as you put it, they stay on, ready for you to use as you need them."

"Do we have to say some special words, like a spell or something?" queried Brennan.

"No," the Gwencalon answered. "Your powers are not magic. You will have no magic wand to wave, no incantations to repeat."

Emma wanted to know what an incantation was and that interrupted the discussion for a moment while Julia explained to her. Then the Gwencalon continued.

"You have been called here as soldiers of The Holy One. You call Him God, I believe. He has all power and when you need extra help to complete the mission He has sent you on, He will supply that power."

"But how? I mean, how do we let Him know we need help?" Julia asked.

"How do you do it in your world?"

Emma answered that one. "We just ask, and then we have faith."

"Right answer, Lady Emma. That's what you will do here also," the Gwencalon concluded. "Now, however, we must formulate a plan."

5 A PLAN IS MADE AND ACTION BEGINS

The Gwencalon's plan contained none of the intrigue and pitched battles that Brennan had expected. In fact, he found it disappointingly dull, not at all the type of thing an Angeluscustos should be involved in. It did not occur to him that since he had only found out that day that he even was an Angeluscustos, he was hardly in a position to decide what was or was not appropriate for one.

In disgust at the simplicity of the plan, he considered complaining, but the girls were listening so intently and nodding so approvingly that he knew no one would listen to him anyway. So he bided his time. Things had a habit, after all, of seldom working out the way they were planned. They might be in a fight yet, so he'd better find another hefty pole to use as a staff . . . like Little John in Robin Hood, he thought. In the meantime, he listened.

The Gwencalon explained that although many in the King's castle had been replaced with Duke Feragard's men, the kitchen staff and scullery maids, and maids of all work had not. The cook's young son passed messages to a loyal man from the village at the foot of the mountain that provided meat for the duke's table. Under the guise of delivering meat or of collecting scraps to feed his pigs, the man was able to keep up on all the information that the maids and kitchen workers were able to glean.

The duke, like many aristocrats, viewed servants as nearly invisible, and so they were often able to overhear news of interest. They had not found out, however, that the prince had been imprisoned. They still thought he was confined to his bed, gravely ill and that news they had reported to the Gwencalon through the twisted network that began with the cook's son and ended with the Barbegazi. Hannah's dream had provided vital information, for the Gwencalon knew it was not a dream, but rather a vision from the Holy One.

The conspirators would need to go to the castle, find their way to the dungeon, free the prince, and take him safely to the Barbegazi, whose knowledge of the mountains and their mysterious caves and mines could keep him safe from any pursuers. The Gwencalon paused a moment before going into more detail and Hannah wanted to know what would happen then.

"Will the people be loyal to the young prince," asked Hannah, "or will they follow the Duke and his men?"

The Gwencalon nodded, pleased at her question. "Oh, yes. They are loyal to the royal family. Only those who are of the Duke's lands are loyal to him. That is why he must be rid of the prince. With no one from the immediate royal family left and a Gwencalon and Council of Elders who support him, he can insure that he will be chosen king. After all, he has been the de facto ruler for the last ten years so people will easily accept him if the prince has died."

"Then what will we do once we have brought the prince to the Barbegazi?"

"Once we have rescued him, the duke will not be able to continue with his plan, because we will produce the prince to the people at the Landsgemeinde."

"What's that?" Julia questioned.

"The Landsgemeinde? It is an open air meeting where the Council of Elders and the Lords of the cantons will present the candidate to become king and the people will vote by raising their hands," the Gwencalon explained. "But the Landsgemeinde will not happen until the young prince's birthday which is still a few days away." He smiled. "We will have quite a surprise for the duke that day!"

"How will we get into the castle and down to the dungeon? Will we have to overpower the guards?" Brennan asked, hopefully.

"That shouldn't be necessary," the Gwencalon answered, frowning. "The Duke and his men are not as familiar with the castle as they believe themselves to be. The servants who have worked there all of their lives know secret ways in and passages from room to room that are no longer used."

"Cool!" Emma interjected. "Secret passages! This is going to be fun!"

"This is not a game, Lady Emma," the Gwencalon cautioned. "But yes, secret passages and castles and dungeons are things you have probably not seen before. We will put them to good use. In the morning, we will go down to the valley below where one of the noblemen I can trust will meet us to take you to the village below the castle. There, you will meet up with the butcher who will take you on to the castle as he goes to make a delivery.

You will be hidden in his wagon so no one sees you, of course. Because he makes the trip to the castle each day, he knows the guards and they will let him pass without much of a search. Once at the castle kitchen, you will sneak into the building and someone will be able to help you find the dungeon." He frowned and shook his head.

"If we had only known that the prince had been locked in the dungeon, we could have found a way to get a copy of the dungeon keys. But alas, that we did not know and so," he gazed intently at each West in turn, "getting the prince out of his cell will be your problem to solve once you are in the castle. Mayhap the servants will be able to help, but you must find a way. You will have all day to figure out a plan because you cannot leave the castle until after dark. Then you will be led out of the castle through a secret entrance and back to Lord Bernald." He cleared his throat.

"What if something goes wrong?" Brennan asked. "Shouldn't we take some weapons along with us?"

"What weapons do you know how to use, Lord Brennan, a bow, a flintlock?" the Gwencalon asked quietly.

"Uh, none, I guess," Brennan admitted, blushing. "But shouldn't we be trained? Shouldn't we be taught how to use a sword or a knife or something?"

"You are here to rescue," the Gwencalon admonished sternly, "not to go about slaying people!"

Brennan subsided into a glum silence as the Gwencalon continued.

"Lord Bernald will supply you with everything you need, but remember, you have special powers from the Holy One that will appear just when you need them."

Emma and Julia nodded in understanding, but both Hannah and Brennan seemed somewhat dubious. Brennan thought surely he could talk Lord Bernald into supplying some weapons. His Swiss army knife was useful for lots of jobs, but it was hardly a weapon to protect his sisters against armed soldiers. And no self-respecting ruler would imprison an important hostage and just leave him unguarded. How would they overcome the dungeon guards without weapons?

Hannah's concern dealt not with weapons, but with the lack of specificity in the plan. She wanted to know exactly what would happen and when it would happen and she thought that the plan became way too vague after they reached the castle. Still, she supposed that since no one had known that the duke had locked the prince in the dungeon until she had told the Gwencalon, that part of the plan couldn't have already been worked out. They would have to figure that out after they got there and that made her very nervous. It wasn't that she didn't trust God, because she did. And it wasn't that she expected Him to tell her every step of His plans for her and the others, but a little more information would have been reassuring. She sighed. The Gwencalon was speaking again, so again she listened.

"Tomorrow, your task will be to rescue the prince from his uncle," the Gwencalon continued, "but now, I think we all need a good night's sleep." He motioned to Amea, who scooped up a pile of covers and bustled forward. Apologizing that the house had neither enough beds nor beds that were long enough for the Wests, she began laying layers of thick covers on the wooden floor before the fire. Sachi mumbled a good night to them, talked quietly with the Gwencalon for a moment, and then slipped out the door, letting in a cold blast of air. Soon, with everyone, even the Gwencalon, snuggled tightly in blankets before the fire, Amea and Ugo put out the lamps and disappeared into another room. Quiet settled over the little house as one by one its occupants slept.

But Emma couldn't sleep. First she worried about Mr. Higley. Had he gotten home safely or had some soldier seen him and decided to have rabbit stew for supper? Emma quickly said a prayer for his well-being. Surely he was okay. The Gwencalon would not have sent him to meet them if he was likely to die doing it, she thought. And then her mind turned to the next day. Once they were in the castle, would she be able to pick the dungeon lock with her lock pick set, she wondered? If not, how would they steal the keys from the guards? One of them would have to get the guard's attention, she supposed, but what if that person was then caught? Then they would be back where they started with someone else to rescue. And what about these special gifts? What on earth could they be? Well, she decided. Those were God's problems, not hers, so she might as well get to sleep and let Him worry about them. And with that, she turned over and went to sleep.

Hannah and Julia had nodded off quickly, Hannah drowsily wondering what her parents were doing back home, and Julia dreaming of castles and princes. But Brennan, still miffed over what he saw as a majorly deficient plan, tossed and turned on his pallet. Where could he get a knife, he wondered? Surely he should have some weapon hidden on him so he could protect his sisters. They were his responsibility. Even though Hannah was older, she was still a girl. Girls were supposed to be taken care of by guys, he mused, totally ignoring the fact that his sisters were certainly as capable as taking care of themselves as he was. And how on earth could he be guardian and potential rescuer, he fumed, with only a Swiss army knife as a weapon. It was utterly unthinkable! He would just have to keep on the lookout for any weapon that someone might have left carelessly lying around, he mused. After all, surely God would expect him to arm himself for battle!

Hannah became aware of subtle movement and quiet noises in the small house and rolled over, opening her eyes. Amea, Ugo, Sachi and the Gwencalon were gathered around a wooden table, sipping what smelled to her like hot chocolate. A lamp was lit, and no light seemed to be coming through the window, so you assumed the sun must not yet have risen. As she sat up, stretching, she saw that Brennan and Julia were also waking. Emma, already up, perched on a stool beside the fire, munching on a slice of bread.

"Ah, you are awake," Amea greeted them. "Have some breakfast. There is bread and honey and hot chocolate."

"Yes," the Gwencalon added. "Do come and eat. We need to get moving before the sun rises."

Julia got slowly to her feet, yawning. "You mean it is still night?"

"Not night exactly," the Gwencalon smiled. "But not really morning either. I'd like us to get down the mountain before the farmers get out in the fields. While you eat, Amea will get you warmer clothes to change into. It will be warmer once we reach the valley, but you will stand out less if you are dressed like us."

Breakfast was a quiet affair as the kids hurried through their food. Then, Amea swept the girls into her bedroom where they donned long brown leather pants with warm, long sleeved white shirts topped with forest green buttoned jackets made of thick wool. There were also soft black socks and black leather boots.

"Sachi guessed pretty well at your sizes, I think," Amea commented in a satisfied tone. "We knew you were coming, of course, so we had gathered some clothing and boots in several sizes, but Sachi, who has several friends in the valley who have children about your ages, thought he could come close to the sizes you would wear. I think he did well!"

And in fact, he had. Julia's trousers were perhaps a bit large, but not much. Even the boots fit pretty well. Amea also handed each of them a leather bag to wear over their chests for the belongings from their backpacks.

"These are called Schulmappes," she explained. "Everyone uses them and they won't call attention to you." She looked askance at Emma's Disney Princess backpack. "The ones you brought would mark you immediately as strangers."

Hannah agreed, and the girls hastily emptied their backpacks into the Schulmappes and hung them across their bodies.

When they exited the bedroom, they saw Brennan had also been outfitted. Instead of jeans and a sweatshirt, he also wore long leather trousers, black boots, and a dark woolen jacket over a white shirt. And he, too, had been supplied with a Schulmappe. Amea and Ugo handed each of them a thick, hooded cloak like the ones the Gwencalon and Ugo now wore.

"Sachi has our mounts ready," Ugo explained. "They are well-trained Dragons de Neige and will take us quickly down to the valley. Once there we will pick up horses."

"We get to ride horses?" Emma asked. "Cool!"

"What are Dragons de Neige?" Brennan asked.

"Come outside and see," the Gwencalon said, smiling. And so out they all went.

The early morning mist was heavy on the mountain, hiding from view all but the closest houses. Rocks and walls seemed to suddenly appear from the damp clouds as the Gwencalon led them unerringly through the village and onto an open area where low vegetation grew among the scattered rocks on the gently sloping ground that had been swept virtually free of snow by the fierce mountain winds.

As they stepped carefully over a narrow stream, Brennan began to see dark, humped shapes emerging from the fog. And suddenly, they found themselves among their mounts. The long snouted, ridged back animals placidly grazed on the thin grass, flicking their heavy tails from time to time. The white of their thick hides would make them almost invisible against the snow covering the mountains, Hannah thought, eyeing them warily. Brennan, too, was hesitant.

Hurrying to the Gwencalon's side, he asked. "Are those dragons?"

"Dragons? Yes, Dragons de neige, Snow Dragons." The Gwencalon chuckled. "I forgot you don't know about them. They will carry us down to the valley very quickly and safely."

"Do they breathe fire?" Julia asked in awe.

"Only when they have eaten something they shouldn't have," laughed Ugo. "Here, let me help you on."

Each of the animals wore a leather saddle with a high front and back settled snuggly across their shoulders. Behind the saddles, wings quivered, opening slightly and closing again as if the dragons realized they were soon to be flying.

Ugo helped Julia climb into a saddle, adjusting the stirrups to fit her long legs, as Sachi helped first Hannah and then Emma onto similar dragons. The Gwencalon hoisted himself effortlessly onto his dragon, gathering the reins into his hands confidently, as Ugo and Sachi mounted their own dragons. But Brennan stood beside the remaining beast, hesitating. The ridged tail flashed from side to side and the wings flexed repeatedly as he watched. Suddenly the dragon's head swiveled on its long neck and the bright, yellow eyes twinkled at Brennan.

"So get on, young human," the dragon prompted. "I won't eat you!"

Blushing furiously, Brennan stammered, "I was just wondering if I needed to adjust the stirrups," and everyone laughed as Brennan climbed on. Then one by one the dragons unfurled their wings, and beating them majestically, rose into the clouds. After a moment or two, Brennan found himself wishing that the weather had been clear so that he could have enjoyed what must have been a marvelous view. Instead, the misty, greyish-white clouds drifted by him as they circled and then descended into the valley.

In just a few minutes the Snow dragons dropped out of the mists and settled with ease onto a meadow far greener than the one they had just left. Sachi and Ugo helped everyone dismount and then Sachi headed toward a thick stand of trees just to the north of them.

"Wow," Julia commented. "That was fun!"

"Kind of scary, though," added Emma, "since all you could see were clouds."

"Yeah," Brennan broke in. "The view would have been really great without the fog."

"Early morning in the mountains is often like this," the Gwencalon explained. "Before long, though, the sun will burn away the mist and bring us a clear day."

"Is the castle far from here?" asked Hannah, straining to see any glimpse of it through the still persistent mist.

"In the next valley," the Gwencalon answered. "It's safer to land here and go on with horses. Ah, here they are now."

Sachi and a taller figure were leading a group of sturdy mountain horses toward them. The stranger wore a long, deep blue cloak which he had thrown back over his shoulders as he walked. His thick brown hair hung nearly to his shoulders and dark eyes appraised them from his clean-shaven face.

"These are Einsiedler," the Gwencalon told them, pointing at the horses. "They are good for these mountains. . . strong legs, deep chests, sure-footed. They are good riding horses. And this," he clasped the taller man on his arm, "is Lord Bernald. He has brought us the horses and will guide you from here on. I must return with the Barbegazi for now since I would immediately be recognized. The duke must continue to think I am dead until we are ready to confront him. Henri, these are. . . ."

"Yes, " the man nodded, "the Angeluscustos." He bowed deeply to the four Wests. "You are most welcome and most needed. Let us mount our horses and ride for Mittewald and Charlesville, our capital city. Shepherds will be moving their herds to the pastures now and we do not wish to meet too many of them this morning. Please put your hoods up so you are not seen to be strangers."

"This is the Meadow of the Larks," the Gwencalon told them, in the canton of Nidwald. Remember that in case any of you should be separated from the rest. An eagle that lives above this meadow watches it closely for me. If you come here, I will know and someone will come to get you."

"Thank you," Hannah said. "We will do the best we can."

"Your best will be all that is needed, child," the Gwencalon responded. Hannah turned and hurried after the others who had already picked out mounts from among the Einsiedler.

The horses were not excessively tall, only about 15 hands high, and everyone except Emma was able to scramble into their saddles without help. Lord Bernald tossed her into her saddle easily and handed her the reins with a smile, adjusting the stirrups to fit her shorter legs. Soon they had left the Gwencalon and the Barbegazi standing with the Dragons de Neige and were trotting along the valley, keeping to the foot of the mountains and away from the houses that clustered into villages here and there.

In the distance smoke rose lazily from cottages and farmhouses as housewives began stirring up fires that had been banked for the night. They passed a lone shepherd with a small brown dog, herding a group of shaggy, white and black sheep. The shepherd raised a hand in greeting as they trotted past, and Hannah instinctively lowered her head, avoiding his eyes as if he would not see her if she did not look directly at him. Soon they had left the shepherd and the wide valley far behind and were moving along a steep road that snaked its way up a mountainside. As Hannah looked down to her left, she realized that she could no longer see the valley in which the Dragons de Neige had deposited them.

The road which they climbed had worked its away around to the far side of the mountain and now she could only see trees below her and the lower slope of another mountain beyond through the clearing mist. Evergreens grew on each side of the road, both above and below them, thickening into a forest as they climbed. Soon the terrain flattened out somewhat into a higher mountain valley with buildings lining the road on both sides and reaching up the mountainside. As in the valley, these houses differed from those of the Barbegazi. Constructed on wide planks of dark wood rather than stone, they stretched to three or four levels, on the valley side.

On the back side, most of them butted against the mountainside so that often the second or third floor opened onto the grassy slope. The roofs were steep pitched and crowned by stone chimneys from which here too, smoke rose to the sky. The village seemed much larger than that of the Barbegazi, and judging from the sounds she began to hear, the townspeople were beginning to stir. Here and there the wooden shutters had already been thrown open, and a few houses down the street, an industrious housewife had already hung a comforter over a balcony railing to air. Beyond the village, she could just glimpse the road which continued to wind back and forth upon itself as it led farther up the mountain to the stone walls of the castle from her dream.

Lord Bernald suddenly guided his horse off the main road and into an alley that led behind the first buildings. Here at the outskirts of the village, Hannah saw that the buildings were only a single row deep, backed against the alley rather than the mountainside. As they passed behind the first houses, he stopped to dismount, gathering the reins of Emma's horse as the Wests slid off their mounts. Hannah saw a fenced hillside to the left that already held several horses and in front of it, the open door of a stable. A young boy, maybe Julia's age ran out to take the reins of their horses, leading them back into the dark recesses of the stable without a word.

"This way. Stay close now," Lord Bernald cautioned, as he led them farther along the alleyway. Soon he turned down some stone steps between two buildings and paused on a landing to knock quietly on a wooden door. Seemingly of its own accord, the door swung open, and Lord Bernald quickly ushered the kids inside.

As the door shut behind them, they stood for a moment as their eyes adjusted to the sudden darkness of the room. A thick cloying smell permeated the building and Hannah shivered as she realized where they were. This must be the butcher's shop, she thought.

"I had almost given up on you," a voice murmured, as a man hurried farther into the dim room. "No problems, I hope?" A thick set man, he had a ruddy complexion and greying hair still streaked here and there with the carroty red color of his youth.

"No problems," Lord Bernald answered. "Are you loaded and ready to go?"

"Yes, of course. We only need to load the children into the wagon." The butcher, for that is what he was, now turned to the Angeluscustos with a bow.

"I am Sergai. I have a special compartment in my wagon in which you will hide as we go into the castle. Duffy, the cook's son, will help you out while I go about my business. It will be a tight fit, but the journey is a short one. Come now."

He began to lead them through a forest of hanging carcasses and between blocks of ice. "This is how I know the Barbegazi so well," he explained. "They bring me blocks of ice from the glacier to keep my meat cold. I furnish the entire valley as well as the castle with meat," he remarked proudly. "Watch your heads, now."

They quickly arrived at another room, separated from the first by a heavy wooden door. This second room was somewhat brighter, lit by a lantern that had been placed near a wagon. Hitched to the wagon, a brown horse with a long shaggy mane and tail, turned to look at them before returning complacently to his breakfast of oats that had been placed in a wooden bucket before him. Sergei teased a rope out of a crack in the wooden back of the wagon and pulled. A wide section board dropped open to reveal a compartment scarcely large enough for two adults. Luckily, the Wests were not yet adult sized in width though the three oldest were certainly tall enough.

"In you go," Lord Bernald urged. "Lady Emma, you first. Lie crosswise at the front end and then your brother and sisters will fit better lengthwise."

Emma did as instructed, scrambling into the opening and squirming her way to the front of the cavity, where she arranged herself on her side, back against the wood.

"No, feet first," Sergei instructed. "We'll help." With that, he and Lord Bernald lifted each of the others in turn, sliding them on their stomachs, feet first into the compartment. Emma wisely crossed her arms in front of her face warning, "Don't kick me!"

Soon the four were settled and the door shut, leaving them in darkness. Sergei poked the rope into the crack in the wood again.

"You can push the door open from the inside if you need to," he explained, "but only in an emergency. Otherwise, wait until Duffy opens it for you."

"Sergei is going to start off with you now," Lord Bernald cautioned, "so you must be very quiet. I will be waiting at the opening to the castle tunnel tonight to meet you when you come out with the prince. He, he is not only my prince, but also my filleul, my godson. I am very concerned for his safety. Good luck to you and may the Holy One keep you safe!"

Then they heard only a quiet murmur of voices, footsteps, and the creak of the barn doors as Sergei thrust them open. The wagon jerked into motion and just as quickly to a stop as Sergei led the horse out of the doors and then paused the close them again. Then with a heave and rocking of the wagon, he hauled himself aboard and clucked to his horse.

"Well, off we go then, Dobbin." And the next leg of their journey had begun.

6 THINGS GO AWRY

The trip up to the castle lasted only about ten minutes, but to the four packed into the wagon, it seemed like an eternity. The wagon creaked and groaned and bumped its way along the road, winding ever higher. Finally, it shuddered to a stop and then swayed violently as Sergei climbed down. The kids could hear voices and laughter from outside.

Footsteps walked along the side of the wagon and then, with a slap against the side that startled them all, a voice said loudly, "Okay, Sergei. Move on. The Duke will be wanting his meat for today. I heard he hoped for fresh venison, but the hunting yesterday was poor, so he'll have to make do with your offerings."

"And be content with it," Sergei chuckled, climbing ponderously back onto his seat. "'Tis the best meat in the valley, as well he knows. Get on then, Dobbin," he said, slapping the reins against the back of his longsuffering horse. The ride was even rougher now, bouncing them so much that Julia thought sure she would have bruises all over, and Emma became increasingly aware of the fact that she desperately needed a bathroom. At last they lurched to a stop and once again Sergei climbed down from the wagon seat.

"Eh, Duffy!" he called out. "Get out here and help get this wagon unloaded!"

They could hear the clatter of running footsteps and then moving away from the wagon, the sound of Sergei's voice as he greeted someone else.

"Robert! Upon my word! They've got you doing guard duty today and at the kitchen door of all things?" He laughed. "Has someone been stealing cook's pies?"

"Nah, the Duke has just tightened security since it is coming close to the prince's birthday and the Landsgemeinde. Who knows what strange sorts might come to see that."

"Oh, well," Sergei said, putting his arm around Robert's shoulders, "no strange sorts in my wagon unless you count the partridges I brought specially for you!" He walked back to the wagon and plucked something out of it, letting Robert get a good look at the wagon that Duffy was carefully unloading. "Cook will surely let you put these in the ice house until you are off duty. Then your lovely wife can cook them up for you for supper! Come on, let's take them to cook now."

With that, the Wests could hear both men move away from the wagon and suddenly the back panel dropped open and a gamin face with a shock of unruly red hair looked in at them.

"All right then, out you come," he said. "I'm Duffy. I've been expecting you. We got to hurry before the guard comes back."

Brennan braced his hands against the roof above the open panel and pulled himself out of the wagon. Then he helped Duffy who had grabbed Julia's arms and was pulling her along swiftly. In only a couple of seconds she was out, followed quickly by Hannah. Emma had already scooted much of the way herself and slipped out on her own after Hannah. Duffy quickly pushed the panel shut and tucked the rope pull back out of sight. He then grabbed the last hunk of meat, a ham, Brennan thought, and looked swiftly around.

"This way," he said, leading them to a low doorway and disappearing into a vaulted corridor with the Wests hurriedly following him. He stopped at a wooden door that was slightly ajar and listened intently. They could see Sergei and the guard near the kitchen door and hear a woman's voice saying, "Now get along with you. Duffy will finish unloading the wagon and then fill it with scraps for the swine while you enjoy that cold cider, Sergei. And you, Robert, had better get back to your post before someone comes looking for you."

"Or comes by and steals my wagon!" Sergei added, laughing. He slapped the other man on the shoulder. "Let's go, my friend, before we get chased out with a meat cleaver!"

The two men left, Robert grumbling that going into the kitchen hadn't been his idea in the first place. Sergei just laughed and reminded him of the two partridges that waited for him to take to his wife that evening. Duffy watched them out the door and then motioned the others to follow him into the kitchen.

"Here they are," he said quietly to the woman who was shutting the door behind the men. And to the kids he said, "This is my mum. She'll take care of you. I have work to do." With that, he dropped the ham onto a scarred wooden table and hurried out the way they had come in. The woman, with a final look at the door behind her, extended her arms wide and swept them before her like a hen with her chicks, through an archway, past a group of curious young girls who were stirring pots and chopping vegetables, and into another, smaller room, nearly filled with an oblong table and a dozen chairs. "This is the servants dining room," she explained as she stopped to examine them intently.

"Hmm," she said finally. "You are not what I expected when the Gwencalon said he had sent for the Angeluscustos, but then he and the Holy One know what they are doing." She blushed. "Oh, what am I thinking? I'm Marthe, the castle's cook. Duffy is my boy." She indicated the chairs.

Hannah and the others introduced themselves.

"I'm so glad to see you," Marthe responded. "Sit, sit! Have you eaten?"

"Yes," Hannah answered, "before we left the Barbegazi."

"But I could really use a bathroom," Emma said hurriedly.

"Um, so could I," Brennan added.

"Bathroom?" Marthe questioned, puzzled. "You want to take a bath? At this hour of the day?"

"No," Hannah explained. "They want a restroom."

"A toilet," interjected Julia.

"A loo, a water closet, a . . ." began Brennan, using every term for a toilet he could remember hearing.

"Oh," Marthe's face broke into a smile. "You mean the necessary. For the men, it is on the right of the hall beyond that door," she waved at a wooden door across the small room, "and for the women it is just across on the left. Go if you will while I set out some food for you. You have traveled far since eating and you must keep up your strength. Besides, it is nearly ten of the clock and soon will be time for the noonday mean. When you return, we will see what must be done."

The kids headed out the door and followed the hallway for quite a distance before easily finding the necessaries by their smell.

"Oh yuck!" Julia said. "I don't want to go in there!"

"Go," Hannah ordered. "You don't know how long it will be before we get out of the castle. Then we can use the woods, but for now, we better use what we have!"

The four split up, going into the respective rooms. The girls found theirs to hold a long stone bench with four wooden covers equally spaced. Emma strode purposefully to the last cover, lifted it, wrinkled her nose at the increased odor and then proceeded to sit down.

"Where's the toilet paper," she asked, as her sisters also found their places.

"I can't believe they don't have stalls!" Julia muttered.

"Don't you have some Kleenex in your backpack, I mean your Schulmappe?" Hannah asked, rummaging in hers, "Use that."

64

On the other side of the room was a trough with a pump, and the girls were able to pump water to wash their hands. They finally emerged to find Brennan standing in the hall waiting for them.

"Pretty rustic, huh?" he said, grinning.

"Don't ask," Julia said, brushing past him to head back to the waiting cook.

Marthe had laden the table with bread, honey, cheese and slices of cold meat, and filled clay beakers with cold apple cider for them and they ate ravenously. When they had finished, Hannah said, "We had better do what we came to do. The prince is not ill."

Marthe gasped, "The Holy One be praised! But the Duke said . . . ."

"Yes," Hannah interrupted. "I know what the Duke has said, but he lied. He has locked the prince up in the dungeons and we have to get him out today."

"The dungeons?" Marthe gasped again. "But why?"

"Because the Duke intends to say that the prince has died and have himself elected king in his place as his nearest relative," Brennan contributed.

Marthe clapped her hands over her mouth in horror.

"We need someone to lead us to the dungeons so we can break him out," Hannah concluded.

Marthe thought a moment, slowly dropping her hands. "Well, Bruno, he's one of the old footmen, he can take you to the dungeon. The Duke brought most of his own servants, you see, but he kept the kitchen servants, some of the maids, and a couple of footmen. How you will get the key to the cell, though, I don't know. . . ."

"Call Bruno for us. We will find a way when the time comes," Hannah assured her, praying that she was telling the truth. "When we get the prince, someone will have to take us out the secret passage after dark tonight. A friend waits there to get us to safety."

"We will do whatever we must for the prince," Marthe answered. "I will send one of the maids after Bruno."

While they waited, Brennan quietly asked Hannah if she thought she could find the prince in the dungeons, and she answered that she certainly hoped so. After all, they were talking about a castle dungeon, not a huge prison like Alcatraz that they had visited on a trip to California last summer.

Julia used the time to look around her. So this was what a castle looked like inside. She had expected something grander, but then of course these were the servants' areas, so maybe things were better for the king and his family. Stone floors, worn smooth by centuries of shoes met rough, stone, walls, bare of decorations. Two lanterns hanging from metal hooks on opposite walls provided the only illumination in the windowless room other than the light from a fireplace where a fire burned low opposite the doorway to the necessary hall. She was glad of her thick wool and leather clothing.

The creak of the opening door caught her attention away from the amenities and she gazed with interest at a dark young man, lanky and handsome in a rugged sort of way who walked in with a certain swagger to his step. He smoothed back his hair and introduced himself.

"Bruno at your service, my Ladies. . . and Lord. Marthe tells me that the prince has been moved to the dungeons. Are you quite sure? We have been taking trays up to his room, broth and oatmeal mostly, for days now. Nothing has been taken to the dungeons."

"We're sure," Julia said tartly, finding herself somehow not really liking this cocky young man.

"Well then, let me think. I know. It is nearly time for the midday meal. I will carry it to the dungeon guards to distract them and while they eat, we will go rescue the prince. I'll put some laudanum in their cider to put them to sleep, too."

"What's laudanum?" Julia whispered to Hannah.

"I think it is a drug, made from poppies. You know, like opium or cocaine, something like that."

"Is Bruno a drug dealer?" Julia asked her, scandalized.

"No," Hannah assured her. "I think before they knew how bad it was, doctors used to prescribe it as a pain killer or to help them sleep. After some wars, soldiers came back addicted to the stuff and that's when they began to learn how bad it was."

"Oh," Julia concluded. "Maybe we should warn him about it, do you think?"

"Not now, Julia. Maybe we can warn the Gwencalon or the prince later, but right now we need to concentrate on rescuing him!"

"But how will we get back past the guard with the prince?" Brennan was asking Bruno.

"We won't have to," Bruno said smugly. "I know another way out of the dungeon that will not be guarded because these men do not know about it. We can't go in that way, because it opens out onto the mountain in full sight of the castle walls. You can hide just inside the opening until night and then slip out when no one can see you. Now, wait here. I will be back soon with food for the guards and then I will take you to the dungeons." And with that, he left.

"I don't like him," Julia said to Hannah.

"What?" Hannah asked, distracted by her own thoughts. "You what?"

"I don't like Bruno and I don't think we should trust him," Julia insisted.

"I agree with Julia," Brennan contributed. "There is just something about that guy that doesn't seem right."

"Emma?" Hannah asked.

"I don't know. We should be careful."

"Okay," Brennan said. "Let's assume we can't trust him. There are four of us and Hannah has seen the prince. If anything happens, we make sure she gets away to rescue him. Right, guys?"

"Right," Julia and Emma agreed.

"No, wait," Hannah protested. "We need to stay together."

"No," Brennan disagreed. "We need to rescue the prince and get him to the Gwencalon. That is our mission, isn't it?"

"Yeah," Hannah sighed. "You're right."

"And God will watch out for us," Emma finished. And somehow, that ended the discussion.

Soon Bruno was back, his arms loaded down with a tray of food and drink. He instructed them to follow him and set off down the hall and past the necessaries. He made several other turns before finally opening a heavy door and starting down a long stone staircase. Halfway down where the stairs made a turn, he motioned them to wait and proceeded alone.

They heard him greeted with enthusiasm by at least two guards, whose voices soon faded into the distance. Then, in a moment he was back, waving them to follow him. Quickly they tiptoed down the stairs and scooted past a doorway from which the sound of voices could be heard and around a corner.

Bruno grabbed a lit torch from a wall sconce and hurried down the corridor before stopping in front of a cell where someone could be seen sleeping, wrapped in blankets. The prince! The footman pulled a key from his pocket.

"I borrowed this when they were attacking the food. By the time they wake and miss it, we will be long gone with the prince," he chortled.

"But won't they realize you must have taken it?" asked Julia suspiciously.

"It won't matter," Bruno concluded, "because I simply won't come back."

He handed the torch to Brennan, inserted the key in the lock, and turned it with a grating sound that disturbed the sleeping form on the bed. The prince got to his feet and stalked to the door.

"It is about time someone rescues me!" he exclaimed angrily. "It is vastly uncomfortable down here!"

"Your highness will be safe in only moments," Bruno assured him, pushing open the door with difficulty and ushering out the short, blond prince.

Hannah grabbed Brennan's arm, pulling him back as Julia and Emma stepped back to make way for the two young men.

"That's not the king!" she hissed in his ear.

ELIZABETH ANDERSON

7 THE ESCAPE

Brennan didn't hesitate, nor did he seem surprised at Hannah's revelation.

"Then you have to go find the real prince," he whispered back. "Take Emma with you. Julia and I will try to cover for you. And take this." He pushed his cell phone into her hand. "For a flashlight."

Bruno was plumping up the blankets on the cot, trying to make it look like someone was still there. Julia, nervous that the guards might soon be after them, stomped her foot and whispered loudly, "Come on, Bruno! Let's get the prince out of here!"

Bruno, realizing that he was trying too hard, left the cot and hurried out of the cell, pushing the door shut behind him and throwing a glare at Julia as he passed her. At least she thought it was a glare. In the dimly lit dungeon it was tough to tell.

"This way, then," Bruno said, taking the torch back from Brennan and starting off down the stone corridor. The blond young man hurried behind him and the others brought up the rear, struggling to keep close enough to the torchbearer to avoid stumbling on the uneven floor.

The fake prince said something quietly to Bruno who answered him equally quietly, and Brennan used that moment to grab Emma's arm. He put his finger to his mouth to shush her and Julia who had turned to see what was going on. "Emma," he whispered. "Stay with Hannah."

She nodded her understanding, slipping back to walk with Hannah. Julia and Brennan hurried after the footman and the pseudo prince. "Come on," Bruno urged them. "It isn't far now."

"Coming," Hannah said, but as they passed a side corridor, she grabbed Emma and pulled her into its yawning darkness. "Hurry," she urged. "Take your shoes off and let's run. I don't want them to see us if they come back to look!" She clicked on the cell phone and located the flashlight app with one hand as with the other she yanked off her boots. Emma had promptly dropped to the stone floor and pulled hers off. Holding their boots, the two pelted down the dark hallway, trying not to out run the light from the cell phone.

Suddenly Emma squealed and grabbed for Hannah. "Something just ran over my foot!" she cried in a loud whisper.

"Ooh, no!" Hannah gulped. "Just keep running. We'll put our boots back on it a minute."

Soon they reached another corner, faintly indicated by the flicker of a distant torch, and Hannah stopped Emma, gesturing to her boots.

"Thank you!" Emma responded. "Shine the light around before I sit down, okay?" Hannah's sweep of the flashlight revealed no lingering vermin, so Emma dropped to the floor to pull on her boots. Hannah held the light, passing it to Emma as she put on her own boots.

"Hannah," Emma asked. "How are we going to find the real prince?"

"I'm not sure, Emma," Hannah answered. She thought for a moment. "Let's keep going a little bit toward the torchlight. This hall wasn't lit because it is empty, so light must mean people, guards probably, and hopefully the king. Come on." She switched off the cell phone and slid it into her pack.

The girls walked more slowly now toward the distant light. Hannah figured they must be completing the third side of a large square. Perhaps when they reached the fourth side they would find the prince's cell. As they reached the end of the corridor, they heard the sounds of talking and suddenly a very loud belch, followed by laughter. Realizing that they were approaching the room where the guards were eating lunch, Hannah carefully looked around the corner, found the hallway empty of guards, and then reached back to pull Emma along with her. Lit by flickering torches, this hall was the one they had crossed before turning the corner to the fake king's cell. This must be the hallway from her dream, she thought. If so, and if she had come from the direction of the stairs, the prince would now be on her right. As the two girls crept along the stone floor, Hannah suddenly saw him, sitting with his knees drawn up on a pallet in a corner of a cell.

"Your highness," she called, remembering the title Bruno had used for the fake king.

"Who is it?" the prince asked, unfolding his length from the pallet and struggling to his feet. "Have you brought me some food?"

"No, your highness," Hannah answered. "We've come to rescue you, but we will find some food for you soon." She turned to Emma. "Emma, see if you can get this door open."

"Already working on it," Emma answered, pulling her lock picks from her backpack and inserting them into the rusty lock.

"Who are you?" the prince asked. "I don't recognize you."

"We are Angeluscustos," Emma answered as she worked.

Hannah explained. "I'm Hannah and she is Emma. The Gwencalon sent for us to help protect you until your birthday."

"The Gwencalon? But my uncle told me he had drowned!"

"Nope," Emma answered. "Still alive!"

Suddenly a voice challenged them. "Hey, get away from there! What do you think you are doing?"

All three looked to see two burly guards running down the hallway towards them.

"Hey," Hannah said, unthinkingly. "You're supposed to be asleep!" And immediately, much to everyone's surprise, both men stopped, slid quietly to the floor, and began snoring.

"Whoa!" said the prince. "I guess you are Angeluscustos!"

"How did you do that?" Emma hissed at Hannah.

"I don't know," Hannah whispered back. "I guess we just found my special power!"

"Then tell this door to open," Emma suggested. "I can't get my lock picks to work on it."

"It's probably too old," Hannah agreed. Then to the door she said, "Open up!"

Nothing happened.

"You're supposed to be open!" Hannah tried.

Nothing.

"Okay, so maybe it only works on people," she conceded to the others. "Sorry."

Emma put away her lock picks. "What about all those old keys you brought from home?

"None of them are as big as this lock," Hannah answered, gazing at the huge metal keyhole.

"Maybe the guards have keys on them. You'll have to look, Hannah."

"I think there should be a key ring somewhere," the prince contributed.

Hannah moved slowly and reluctantly towards one of the guards, who snorted and turned over as she reached him.

"I don't see anything," she reported.

"Try the other guard," Emma insisted. Mumbling "Stupid door," she grabbed at a bar on the door to yank on it just in case, and promptly fell through the door into the cell.

"Hannah!" she yelped. "I'm in the cell with the prince!"

"What?" Hannah hurried back. "How did you do that?"

"I just grabbed for it and went through it," Emma explained, reaching out toward a bar again and watching wonderingly as her hand passed through the bar.

"Wow, Emma! I think we just discovered your special power. Can you come back out and bring him with you?"

"I don't know, but I'll try. My backpack came through." She turned to the prince. "Here, your Highness, take my hand and we'll try it."

The prince took tight hold on Emma's hand and Emma walked

cautiously through the bars, pulling the prince out behind her.

"How can I ever thank you?" the prince asked. "I had begun to think my uncle was going to starve me to death in here."

"He probably was," Hannah agreed. "But don't thank us until we get you to safety. We have to get out of the castle. Do you know a way out of here that doesn't go past more guards?"

"You could just put them to sleep," Emma suggested.

"I don't want to take a chance on its not working again so soon," Hannah answered. "If another way out exists, I think we should try to use it first!"

The prince chuckled. "I played in this castle all of my life. I know lots of secret passages and tunnels."

"Then we had better move before the guards wake up," Hannah said. "Which way should we go?"

"This way." The prince started in the direction taken by Bruno and the fake prince, but the flicker of torchlight in the distance and the soft call of "Hannah, where are you?" stopped him.

"Is that Brennan?" asked Emma, who could barely hear the voice.

"I don't think so," Hannah answered. "I think it's Bruno."

"Bruno!" the prince repeated, bitterly. "We played together as children, but he is loyal to my uncle now, not to me. We'd better go another way." He started back the way Emma and Hannah had come.

Emma turned questioningly to Hannah as they followed him. "But what about Brennan and Julia?"

"The mission, remember?" Hannah answered, and at Emma's reluctant nod, she took her hand as they hurried after the young prince.

"We'll go out by the execution chamber," the prince explained as he led them past the darkened hall they had come down and quickly beyond the light of the torches. A shout of surprise from behind them caused them to stop and look back.

Bruno had obviously found the guards. He raised his torch to look their direction and the three automatically pressed themselves back against the wall, but his light did not reach to where they were. Apparently deciding that they must have gone out by the stairs, he put his torch back in a sconce and disappeared up and out of the dungeon.

"Let's hurry now," the prince urged. "My uncle may send more men to search the dungeon even if Bruno thinks we have left it. If only it weren't so dark, we could move faster, but I don't want you to fall and twist an ankle."

"Wait," Hannah said, pausing to pull the cell phone back out of her backpack. "We can use this." And she switched on the phone and tapped the flashlight app.

The prince recoiled and then leaned closer to look carefully at the light. "Is this more Angeluscustos magic?" he asked. "How does it hold the light within, it is so small. And you didn't have to light it." He waved a hand over it. "It gives light, but not heat."

Hannah tugged on his arm. "Let's go. This is called a cell phone and we mostly use it to contact each other in our world. It won't work that way here, but it still holds some of the power from our world, and so I can make it produce the light. When the power is used up, it will not work again until we get back to our world."

"There must be many marvelous things in your world," the prince mused. "I should like to go there some day and see them."

"Can you do that?" Emma asked. "I thought we just came through because we are Angeluscustos and you needed us."

"I suppose you are right," the prince sighed, "but I can dream!"

They had arrived in a small, room, and the prince held out his arm to stop them. "Careful. We mustn't fall through the slide before we are ready to. It should lie just to the left of this doorway and towards the back."

Hannah swung the light in the direction that he indicated and a gaping, black hole appeared in the floor near the wall.

"Ah, yes. There it is!" the prince murmured in a satisfied voice. He moved to the hole, reaching up and to the right of it to tug down a coil of rope. "This is where my ancestors used to hang criminals," he explained. "They would fasten a rope to the iron ring up there," pointing to the ceiling, "and put a noose around the man's neck. Then they pushed him over the hole and his neck was broken. When he was dead, they just cut him down and his body would slide down the rocks into the lake below."

"If there's a lake below this, how will we get away?" Hannah asked. "It must surely be too cold to swim in."

"Oh, the lake water only reaches below us here in the spring when the snow from the mountains has melted and runs down to fill it. Now there won't be more than perhaps some mud. We used to swing out on the rope and drop into the mud as boys, my friends and I, until my tutor caught us one day. Then we weren't allowed to play here any longer, but thankfully, no one moved the rope."

He had uncoiled the rope as he talked. "We can tie this around under your arms and lower you to the ground. Then I'll come down hand over hand. I've done it before, you see."

"Then Emma first," Hannah insisted, holding the light as the king wound the rope around Emma and knotted it in the back.

"This is a slip knot. When you get down," the prince instructed, "slide out of the rope and tug it three times so we know to pull it up again. Then just wait. We will follow close behind. Now, step over to the hole, sit down and slide in. I'll play the rope out slowly so you don't descend too quickly."

Emma wasn't wild about this plan, but she moved to the hole and rock slide as the king instructed, pushing herself into the slide before grasping the rope above her head with both hands. The prince had swung the rope around a nearby stone pillar to serve as a brake and began to slowly play out the rope as Emma disappeared from sight. When he rope reached its end, he eased it from the pillar to give it another foot of length. Then they waited. They could see the rope wiggling and finally they saw three firm tugs. The prince hauled the rope up quickly, secured it again around the pillar, and slipped the loop over Hannah's head. She tried to hand him the cell phone, but he shook his head.

"No. You keep it. I can manage."

So, Hannah shut it off and carefully secured it back in her backpack before following Emma down the black hole. In a surprisingly short time, she had dropped free of the rock tunnel and reached the end of the rope's length. She heard Emma just below her and felt arms catch her legs and guide her feet to the marshy ground.

"It's kinda wet," Emma commented.

"I guess!" Hannah agreed, her feet squelching in the mud as she pulled the rope over her head and gave it three hearty pulls. Quickly the rope disappeared from sight. Hannah dug for the flashlight again to give the prince light as he descended through the tunnel, and then she stopped. The prince said he had done this before. She had better save the light. They might need it later. At that moment, the rope dropped again and then began to twist as the prince descended. As Hannah and Emma watched, he lowered himself along the rope, hand over hand.

"Hannah," Emma whispered. "He's not wearing any shoes!"

"Nor a coat, either," Hannah agreed. "No wonder he was huddled on that cot! He must be freezing!"

Suddenly the prince seemed to lose his grip on the rope and begin to slide more quickly.

"Look out!" Hannah cried. "Grab him!" And she and Emma reached for the prince as he literally fell into their arms, tumbling all three of them onto the muddy ground.

"Yuck," Emma said, untangling herself and wiping her muddy hands on her pant legs.

"I'm sorry," he whispered in a weak voice. "I thought I could do it, but I am weaker than I thought I was."

"How long has it been since you ate something?" Hannah asked suspiciously.

"I don't know. Not since I got to the dungeon . . . three days, maybe. Before that it was only broth and some oatmeal," he answered.

"We have some food," Emma said. She dug in her bag and produced two protein bars that she unwrapped and handed to him. "Try them, they are pretty good."

"And your shoes and coat?" Hannah asked as he took the bars, tasted cautiously, and then gobbled them down. "Where are they?"

"They took them away from me," mumbled the prince around a mouthful of protein bar.

Hannah clicked her tongue in disgust. "Well, I don't have any shoes for you, but I do have some knitted booties that I got for Christmas last year. They should stretch enough to fit you and will give your feet some protection." And she dug a pair of red and green knit slippers from her backpack.

"Wait until we get to dry ground," the prince suggested, struggling to his bare feet. "I feel better now and we need to get to better cover."

"Where will we go," Hannah asked, looking at the marshy ground that ended in the lake to their left and the high castle wall to their right.

"Along the castle wall a ways and then through a sort of tunnel that leads into the woods. We'll be out of sight there and we can find a place to hide until dark." And with that the prince began to follow the castle wall, bracing his left hand against the stones to give him balance on the wet ground. The girls followed, Emma wincing at the mud that was caking on her pretty boots. When they could see the square of a watchtower just ahead of them where the castle walls turned back away from the lake, the prince bent to shove at a rock that leaned against the foot of the wall.

"I'm sorry," the prince sighed, "but perhaps you can help me push this. I just don't have the strength to do it alone."

The girls started to push, but Emma, who was next to the wall, leaned against it and disappeared from sight. She reappeared nearly as quickly and said, "We forgot. Just take my hand. This will be way easier." And, with the prince and Hannah holding her hands, she pulled them through the stone and into another dark tunnel. Once again Hannah pulled out the cell phone, dug for the slippers, and handed them over to the prince.

"No," he objected, "I'll be okay."

"Try them," Hannah insisted. "They won't do much good, but they may help a little."

So the prince sheepishly took the slippers, scraped as much mud off his feet as he could by rubbing them on the stone floor, and then pulled on the slippers.

He grinned at Hannah. "I admit they are soft and warm! Thank you!"

"And aren't you cold?" Emma asked.

"I'll be fine," he assured them, "so don't even think about offering me one of your coats. A gentleman doesn't take a lady's coat from her."

"Humph!" Emma commented, but Hannah only blushed.

And so, they started off once again. By the light of Brennan's cell phone, they made quick time through the tunnel, which led gradually upward as they walked. The **prince** seemed to have recovered some, and when they were suddenly faced with a blank stone wall, he simply said, "Straight ahead," and Emma took their hands and walked through the wall and into the woods.

8 JULIA MEETS ARABELLA

Brennan and Julia hurried after Bruno and the false prince, carefully not looking back at Hannah and Emma, and so neither one of them realized when the two girls slipped off into a side corridor. Brennan wondered how long they would be able to go before Bruno or the prince realized that the girls were gone. Julia, however, decided to help things along. She hurried up to the two and inserted herself between them, linking her arms in theirs and chatting excitedly.

"I've never met a real prince before! This is soooo exciting! And the dungeon is so spooky! I just love it!"

The imposter harrumphed. "You wouldn't think it was so great if you had been locked in down here!" He attempted to pull his arm free, but she squeezed her arm tight to her body, making it impossible for him to detach himself without being brutally rough.

"Oh, I suppose you are right," she agreed. "I think you have been so very brave."

Turning to Bruno, she added, "You were very brave also, Bruno. I mean, fooling those guards and stealing their key, not everyone would have done that. I hope the king rewards you." And she looked back at the frowning imposter.

"Oh, I expect I will be rewarded," Bruno commented, not hearing the faux prince mumble "Not if we don't get out of here soon!"

"Do we have much farther to go," Julia asked. "I'm starting to get chilly. It is so cold and damp down here!"

"Almost there," Bruno assured her, stopping before a seemingly blank wall. Raising the torch high and pulling his arm free of Julia, he bent to feel along the floor until he found some sort of lever, which he pulled. With a creak of stone on stone, a narrow section of rock swung inward to reveal a low doorway. As Bruno turned to usher them through, he suddenly realized that Hannah and Emma were no longer with them.

"Where are the others?" he demanded, his voice rising with panic.

"What?" Brennan asked, turning to look behind them. "Hannah? Emma? Hurry up, we're waiting for you!" he called.

But of course, no one came and no sound of footsteps echoed down the hall.

"Where are they?" the false prince hissed angrily.

"Maybe Emma had to go to the bathroom again," Julia suggested helpfully.

"I'll go look for them," Bruno said hurriedly, looking nervously at the prince. "You three go through here. This opens into a small cave and the light from the opening should give you some light. I'll take the torch and go find the girls. They must be frightened in the dark."

"Yes," the imposter agreed. "You go find them." And with that, he ducked through the opening. Brennan glanced at Julia and then pushed her towards the cave before following her. Bruno moved the lever again, closing the door behind them and then hurried worriedly back down the hallway, disappearing the way they had come.

Bruno was undoubtedly right that this was a cave, Brennan thought as the door closed behind him, but he was not so right about the light from the opening. He blindly reached out his hands and touched someone. "Julia?" he questioned.

"Yes. But I can't see anything. Are you still here, your Highness?" she asked, feeling ahead and around her.

"Come ahead about ten steps," answered a disembodied voice. "The cave turns and you'll be able to see the way out."

Brennan, who had grabbed Julia's shoulder when he realized it was she who stood in front of him, hung on to her as she stepped cautiously forward. In a few steps they could indeed see a rough circle of light off to the right, framing the silhouette of the faux prince. Brennan wondered what on earth they were going to do with him, and why Bruno had led them to him to begin with.

Obviously Bruno knew he wasn't the prince, and equally obviously this guy was in on the masquerade since he had readily answered to "your highness." Just as he thought he had it figured out, Julia whispered to him, "They must expect us to lead them to the Gwencalon or to the others who are loyal to the real prince."

"Yeah," Brennan agreed. "And we need to be sure not to do that."

"How?"

"Lead them somewhere else," Brennan shrugged. "Play it by ear, I guess."

"Are you coming?" the faux prince called. "We should get going before someone realizes that I am gone."

"Coming," Brennan answered. "We were just wondering what to do now," he explained truthfully.

"We need to get to the Gwencalon," the prince said, as they reached him at the cave's mouth. "He'll know what to do next."

"The Gwencalon?" Julia repeated. "But. . . ."

"Haven't you heard," Brennan interrupted. "The Gwencalon is dead. Drowned."

"No, no." The faux prince shook his head. "He can't be dead or you wouldn't be here. You are Angeluscustos, aren't you? He had to send for you."

"How did you know who we are?" Brennan asked suspiciously. "Bruno didn't introduce us."

Julia, afraid that Brennan was sounding too suspicious, interjected. "Apparently the Gwencalon sent for us before his boating accident. So sad, really, and now such a problem for us."

"Yes," Brennan agreed, recovering his poise. "I suppose you were expecting us since you were in trouble. But we were delayed elsewhere and when we arrived, we discovered that the Gwencalon was dead. He sent us some instructions, but they are incomplete."

The prince seemed to accept this, but still asked, "But how did you get into the castle."

"We are Angeluscustos," Julia answered simply.

"Now," Brennan continued, starting down through the trees, "we need to get away from the castle."

"But where are we to go?" the prince asked.

"To Meerwald," Brennan answered, coming up with the only name he recalled from the conversations with the Gwencalon.

"To Meerwald!" the prince exclaimed in a shocked voice. "But my fa. . . er . . .uncle the Duke is from the east of Meerwald. Aren't all the people loyal to him?"

"Surely you know," answered Julia, backing up her brother, "that someone will always choose the prince over a local lord."

"A traitor, uh I mean a loyalist in my uncle's own territory?" asked the fake prince incredulously.

Brennan answered, "How could we find a better place to hide you than right under the Duke's nose? He'd never think to look for you there!"

Julia smirked as she turned away. That would give the faux prince something to think about! He remained silent as he followed Brennan where he was working his way down the thickly wooded mountainside.

Julia trailed after the pretend prince, noting his thick sweater and his wool pants and boots. He was dressed awfully well for the cool weather, almost as if he had planned to be out hiking through the woods. She shook her head. They sure must have thought that she and her siblings were really stupid. No one locked someone in a dungeon dressed for the out of doors. His clothes alone would have made them suspect him.

Brennan, on the other hand, was thinking how fortunate that Hannah had had that dream so that she could tell immediately that this wasn't the real prince. Otherwise, he mused, he and the girls would probably have simply accepted him and led him straight to Lord Bernald or even to the Gwencalon. He wondered if Hannah and Emma had been able to locate the real prince and get him out of he castle. So far, God seemed to have things well under control, so he supposed he should stop worrying, although what they would do when they reached Meerwald, he did not know.

They broke out of the trees into a high, fenced meadow, lined on one side by a shallow, fast running stream. Several horses grazed placidly on the lush grass. The prince suddenly snapped out of his reverie and pointed to the horses.

"Those are horses from the castle stables. Let's catch some so we don't have to walk anymore."

"But they don't have saddles on," Julia objected.

"No, but the grooms usually keep some in that hut over there," the pseudo prince insisted. "Come on." He hurried along the edge of the pine trees to a small, wooden structure made out of the same dark, almost black wood as the houses of the village below. As Julia and Brennan reached him, he began tugging on the door.

"Here, help me open this," he said, struggling.

Julia rolled her eyes at Brennan, but they each grabbed at the edges of the door that had opened an inch or two at the fake prince's pulling. With their combined strength, they yanked the door open and Julia and Brennan looked, dumbfounded, at a row of five saddles and bridles. The fake prince swung a saddle onto his shoulders and started out, bridle in the other hand.

"Are you thinking what I am thinking?" Julia asked.

"Pretty sure I am. Five horses in the pasture, five saddles, four of us plus the fake prince. They were all ready for us," Brennan answered. He looped a bridle over each of two small saddles and picked one up in each hand.

Julia followed him out, shoving the door. "But how stupid do they think we are?"

"Pretty stupid, I'd say," Brennan answered her.

"Here, girl," the prince called. "Take this mare."

"The name is Julia," Julia said through clenched teeth, but the prince paid no attention to her. She walked over to where he held the horse, a lovely, soft cream with dark mane and tail. Brennan dropped the saddles and then hoisted one onto the buckskin's back, watching the ripple of muscles as she reacted to the weight.

"Do you remember how to saddle her?" he asked Julia. The prince was busy saddling his own horse, a muscular bay, and was paying no attention to them.

"I remember," Julia replied. "Who knew that all that money mom and dad spent on riding lessons for us would come in so handy in a practical way."

"Don't you suppose that's why dad made sure we got them, just in case?"

"I guess," Julia responded, tightening the cinch.

"Come, boy," the prince called to Brennan. "Here's a horse for you."

"I'll find my own," Brennan announced, picking up the other saddle and walking towards a stocky grey. "May I ride you?" he whispered to the horse.

The horse looked at him for a moment, and then tossed his head, standing quietly while Brennan saddled and bridled him.

Julia, in the meantime, had stroked her horse's velvety nose and inquired. "What is your name, you beautiful girl?"

"Arabella," answered the horse. "You'd better get on before that rude young man decides to leave. He won't want to wait for you."

"I know," Julia sighed.

"Tell me," Arabella asked, as Julia mounted her. "Who are you?"

"My brother and I are Angeluscustos, called by the Gwencalon to protect the prince until his birthday."

"That's why you can understand me, hmm? Lord Gabin can't, ignorant young man! And what are you doing with Lord Gabin?"

"Lord Gabin? So that's his name. He's pretending to be the prince."

Arabella snorted and shook her head. "That one is no prince! He's Duke Ferigard's son and just as nasty as his father! So why are you with him?"

"We're pretending to believe he is the prince while our sisters save the real prince from the castle dungeon."

"Tsk!" said Arabella. "I had heard the dungeon rats were saying he was down there, but you never know if they are telling the truth or not. So what are you going to do?"

"I don't really know," Julia admitted as she turned Arabella and started to walk her towards the fake prince. "Right now we are just buying time for Hannah and Emma to find the real prince and get him to safety."

"I was the queen's horse," Arabella confided. "She was nothing like her pig of a brother! I will do anything I can to help her son. Just let me know what you need."

"Thank you," Julia said, "We really may need your help."

"Julia," Brennan's voice called. "Come on, we need to go before someone sees us."

"Coming," called Julia. "Let's be off, Arabella," she urged, and Arabella started to join the others as the prince suddenly set his mount to a canter and sailed across the rough wooden fence surrounding the pasture. Brennan urged his grey forward and followed him over.

"Can you do that, Arabella?" Julia asked, leaning over her neck.

"I can if you can," Arabella answered, dancing in a circle.

"Then let's go," Julia cried, setting Arabella at the fence. They sailed over it and caught up with the others who had slowed to a walk as they picked their way through the trees.

.

9 THINGS PROGRESS

Prince David led Hannah and Emma up into the forest of towering pines, brushing aside low hanging branches and circling the occasional boulder until at last he stopped in a small clearing. A thick stand of pine whose branches dipped to the ground edged the upward slope, and it was to these that the prince moved. He held aside some thick branches, revealing a rocky overhang.

"In here," he instructed. "I have been stashing things here for weeks."

The girls crawled inside, followed quickly by Prince David. As the branches settled back into place, Hannah saw that although the darkness of the overhang had hidden this small cavern, the light that filtered through the branches of the pines was enough to see by. The cavern, although shallow, still must be a good eight to ten feet deep, she estimated, and about as wide. As she moved deeper into the cavern, she discovered a pile of blankets and a couple of leather bags.

"Did you bring all this stuff here?" she asked the prince.

"I did," he confirmed. "I figured out some time ago that my uncle was getting too fond of ruling Serenia. When I overheard him talking with envoys from Kummer, that's the neighboring country that my father had just defeated when he was killed, I began to think he was plotting to be rid of me also. So, I started smuggling supplies out here, thinking I would hide out here until I could get away to some loyalists. But," he admitted ruefully, "I waited just a day too long. I guess he thought I was suspicious, or maybe it was just too close to my birthday, but I suddenly found myself locked in my chambers. Then a few days ago, he had me moved to the dungeon."

As he had been speaking, Prince David had dug through his supplies, pulling out a wool coat, some boots and socks, and a bag of apples. He bit into a juicy red apple and then offered the sack to Emma and Hannah.

"Want one? I'm sorry I have forgotten my manners, but I am still hungry," he apologized, crunching appreciatively.

Hannah turned the apple down, but Emma took one, handing the bag back to the prince. "What else do you have stashed here?" asked Hannah curiously.

The prince was holding the half eaten apple in his teeth while he shrugged into the black woolen coat. He waited until he had it on and then pulled the apple from his mouth to answer her with a mischievous smile.

"Oh, a few things they might be wanting such as the royal seal, my father's ring of State, and the scepter that is used in all official ceremonies." He took a last bite of the apple, chewed, and then swallowed before continuing. "They can't really run things without those, at least not legally. I don't think the Landsgemeinde would allow it."

He pulled off Hannah's knitted slippers, exchanging them for some old grey socks and a pair of well-worn boots.

"These aren't as good as the boots they took away from me, but I'm sure glad I thought to hide them here."

"Why did you?" Emma asked. "If I thought I had to run for my life, I would think of food and a warm coat and some money, but not an extra pair of boots!"

"I didn't know how far I would have to go before I found someone who was still loyal to me," the prince explained sadly. "My uncle has ruled for nearly ten years now and most of that time he has kept me pretty well away from everyone. If it weren't for my godfather taking me out for rides, I don't know if anyone would even remember me." He lloked sheepish.

"That's the real reason I brought the royal seal and my father's ring of State, to help prove who I am."

"But wouldn't your godfather be able to identify you?" Hannah asked.

"Yes, of course. But I just don't trust my uncle not to try to kill him as well as me . . . or, I don't know," he finished stubbornly. "It's probably illogical, but I just don't trust him!"

"After the way he has treated you, I don't think that is at all illogical" Hannah retorted.

"And Hannah saw you in a dream," Emma explained artlessly, "so she knew who you were right away. That's how we knew that other guy wasn't you."

"You had a vision of me?" the prince asked Hannah, who squirmed uncomfortably at the casual way that Emma had brought it up.

"Yes," she replied. "I saw you in the dungeon cell. You were praying for help. I didn't mean to eavesdrop, but I couldn't really help it. We had already gotten a letter telling us to come here, but we weren't sure what to do. When I told my father about the dream, he said we had to come right away."

"And so we did," Emma finished.

"Then the Holy One sent you in answer to my prayer," the prince said wonderingly.

"No," Hannah corrected. "I think He had sent for us even before

91

you prayed. He does that, you know, answers prayer we even know what to pray for."

"Hannah," Emma interrupted. "I hear something,"

Prince David and Hannah stopped talking to listen. In the distance, they could just hear the excited barking of a pack of dogs.

"They brought the deer hounds out," Prince David explained in dismay. "I didn't think of that." He began hurriedly putting on a hooded cloak and dropping the straps of two leather bags over his head, one on each side. Then he pulled apples and pears from another bag, splitting them between the three of them.

"Put these in your bags and bring them along. We need to move. Deerhounds are not trained to track people, but I've played with those dogs. They will recognize my scent if they get close."

The three of them crawled out o f the cavern and stood up. As the prince started off to the west, Hannah thought ruefully that the cavern would have been a cozy place to wait for nightfall, bundled in the blankets and munching on apples. But they had had to leave the blankets, and because of the dogs, they were moving farther and farther from the castle's secret exit where Lord Bernald would be waiting for them. How on earth were they to find him or get word to the Barbegazi to collect them even if they could still get to the far valley undetected. God certainly allowed things to get complicated, sometimes!

The prince interrupted her thoughts, turning to talk over his shoulder. "There's a creek about a kilometer away. We can walk down the mountain in the streambed. Hopefully the moving water will dispel my scent."

"How have they found our trail so quickly?" Hannah wondered.

"I don't think they have, yet. I would imagine they are walking the dogs around the castle walls, searching fora hit on my scent." The prince explained. "But I don't want to stay around until they find our trail. Try to walk right behind me," he instructed. "The mix of scents may confuse the dogs, too."

Emma and Hannah followed swiftly after the prince as he moved off, crossing the mountainside. The trees were thick enough to offer them cover as they hurried, but the barking of the dogs, which at times faded, and at other times increased in volume kept them anxious. They heard the sound of water gurgling over the rocky streambed long before they reached it.

"This is going to be icy cold," Prince David warned, "but I think it's the only way to avoid the dogs."

"Okay, then," Hannah agreed. "Let's do it!"

She and Emma followed Prince David into the shallow, Swiftly moving water, finding it not only frigid, but also tough going. The rocky bottom was slippery, and the stream wound its way downward which made the footing unsteady. Emma almost fell twice and Hannah nearly lost her balance as well. Finally, the prince took one girl on either side and with arms linked, they found the going easier. Soon the sound of the dogs came more directly above them, and despite the cover of the trees, and the potential scent-masking water, the three increased their speed. Moments later they broke out of the trees and into an open meadow, startling two horses that were grazing nearby.

"Horses," Emma cried, pointing. "That will kill our scent!"

"Can you ride?" the prince asked, a hopeful note creeping into his voice as the three waded out of the water.

"We better know how," Hannah answered. "We've been taking lessons for years."

"There may be bridles or at least halters in that shed over there," the prince advised, hurrying toward a squat, dark wood building with a door standing ajar. Emma called to the horses as Hannah followed the prince to the shed.

"Hi, how are you doing, you pretty horses? We need a ride. Would that be okay?"

Both horses walked slowly towards her, and one of them, a sorrel gelding with a white blaze answered. "We'll give you a ride if you tell us who you are."

"We are Emma and Hannah and that is Prince David," Emma answered.

"Nope. Not even close," the gelding said, tossing his mane. "We know the prince is too sick to leave his chambers. Besides, we would know the prince. We are horses from the castle stables. So who are you, really?"

"Look," Emma said, exasperated with the snooty horse, "I am Emma, and they," pointing to the shed where the others had gone, "are Hannah and Prince David. Hannah and I are Angeluscustos and whatever you think you know, he is the prince!"

"Okay, maybe he is the prince, though I haven't gotten a close enough look to tell yet," the horse conceded, "but anyone can call themselves an Angeluscustos. How do I know you are telling the truth?"

"I'm talking to you, aren't I?" Emma snapped back.

"Oh, I guess you are," the horse admitted.

"Blaze, you old fool," the other horse said, nudging the sorrel with his head, "give it up." And to Emma, "I'm Rascal, at your service." He bobbed his head in a bow. "Of course you can ride us. Don't mind him, he's just annoyed that the others didn't pick him to ride."

"Others? What others?" asked Emma quickly.

"Two young men and a girl, dressed a lot like you. They saddled up and started down the mountain." Rascal responded. "They left here, oh, let's see, while I was eating that patch of clover by the shed. Then I went to get a drink from the stream, and then you came. Not long."

Emma, excited, motioned the horses to follow her, and ran to the shed. She found Hannah and the prince inside, holding a saddle between them.

"Hannah!" she exclaimed. "Two guys and a girl just saddled up and rode away down the mountain. It must have been Julia and Brennan and the fake prince! If we hurry, we might be able to catch up with them!"

"We can't go looking for them," Hannah disagreed as she and the prince moved past Emma with the saddle. "Remember what our mission is. Maybe we will catch up with them, but that is not our purpose right now."

Emma frowned in disappointment, but recognized the validity of her sister's argument. She grabbed the bridles that were lying on a wooden bench, and followed the others out.

The prince helped Hannah swing the saddle onto one of the horses that were once again peacefully grazing outside the shed. As she began to tighten the cinch, he turned to Emma and said, "I don't mind at all going after them. I feel infinitely sorry for anyone who has to put up with my cousin for long, so I think we should rescue them. But, we won't be able to move fast enough to catch up to them until we get into the valley, and then it will depend on whether or not we can figure out which way they have gone."

"I know," Emma admitted. "I just hate being separated from them in a strange place." She handed Hannah the bridle as the prince went back for the other saddle.

"Help him," Hannah hissed. "He is still pretty weak."

Emma hurried to the shed and grabbed one side of the saddle as the prince struggled to lift it. In only a few moments they had the second horse saddled, and Emma turned to the prince.

"Why don't you take the sorrel, your highness. His name is Blaze and he is unhappy because none of the others chose to ride him."

"Yes, his name is Blaze," the prince said. "I recognize him from the stables, but how did you know his name?"

"I asked him," Emma smiled.

"Emma," Hannah called, having mounted Rascal. "You will have to ride behind me. Come on, give me your arm and step into my stirrup. I'll pull you up."

As Emma mounted behind Hannah, wrapping her arms tightly around her sister's waist, the prince walked Blaze over to the gate in the fence and leaned down to open it. Once through the gate, he started Blaze along the fence with the girls beside him.

"There's an old hunting trail over this way that we can follow to the valley. It will be easier going for the horses and will keep us away from the main road. But first, let's walk the horses in the streambed to disguise the way we have gone," the prince suggested.

"You are pretty good at evading pursuers," Hannah praised. "Was this part of your training as prince?"

"Actually, it was," the prince answered as the horses stepped cautiously into the streambed. "My father had me spend lots of time with his head tracker when I was very young. He used to bring me out onto the mountain nearly everyday, and I loved it. Apart from being outside rather than cooped up in the castle, it kept me away from boring studies with my tutor."

His face clouded. "My uncle pretty much put a stop to that when I was about ten, but I still crept out whenever I could to follow Jules around." He looked around him. "I think we can risk getting out here. The ground is rocky enough not to leave prints. We'll head for the hunting trail just beyond that clump of trees."

They hadn't heard the dogs for some time, but the prince still urged Blaze into a trot as soon as they reached the hunting trail, and Emma, who despite her age had taken to horseback riding with great enthusiasm, found trotting behind her sister rather than in the saddle to be a challenge.

The girls found descending to the valley much more enjoyable than coming up to the castle in the wagon's secret compartment had been. Even concerned as they were about the searchers, they could still enjoy the smell of autumn in the air and the crunch of the pine needles and fallen leaves beneath the horses' hooves.

Birds occasionally flew over head, calling to one another, and from time to time a squirrel would chatter at them as their passage disturbed his tranquil hunt for nuts. After some time, the prince slowed Blaze to a walk again, and Hannah was able to pull Rascal alongside him. The shadows were lengthening and her stomach reminded her that she had skipped lunch and now it was mealtime again. She pulled one of the prince's apples out of her Schulmappe and offered it to the prince. He reached across to take it, but then passed it back to Emma.

"Don't you want one?" Hannah asked, thinking he must surely be hungrier than she was.

"Sure, but ladies first, my mother taught me," he laughed. "She would say that being a prince doesn't give you an excuse to forget manners!"

"Obviously she didn't raise your cousin," Emma said tartly between bites of apple. "He was pretty rude when we arrived to 'save' him."

Hannah had handed another apple across to the prince and bit into one herself as he answered, "No, my mother always did think he was spoiled. She and my father taught me that a lord has responsibility to his people and part of that is treating them with respect."

Hannah suddenly gasped, pulling the half-eaten apple from her mouth. "Oh, no! In the excitement of escaping I totally forgot! We are supposed to meet Lord Bernald at the entrance to the secret passage into the castle at dark. It is nearly dark now, and we don't dare go back to the castle because of the men with the dogs! What if they catch him? How can he explain what he is doing lurking on the mountain in the dark?"

"Lord Bernald will think of something. He was a good friend to my father and often hunted with him on this mountain. He will be able to evade them, I should think." He shook his head. "I too have been remiss. I was so eager to get away from the castle that I did not ask if you had a plan of escape. We still have several days to get through before the Landsgemeinde and my birthday. Until Wednesday, my uncle is still my guardian, and without firm proof that he is trying to usurp the throne, there is nothing we can do. Lord Bernald will hide me at his manor, I am sure, but my uncle has many men at the castle to send after me if he suspects I am there."

"The plan," Hannah explained, "is to get you up to the Barbegazi where the Gwencalon is hiding. You will be safe there until the Landsgemeinde."

Emma piped in, "But we don't know how to get to the meadow

97

where the Dragons de Neige left us."

"It was the Meadow of the Larks," Hannah remembered, "in Nidwald."

"Not so much of a problem, then," decided the prince, "but we will need to find a place to shelter for a few hours. There is an old hay barn near the foot of this trail. It's far enough from Charlesville that the town dogs won't hear us and bark. We can rest there for a few hours and eat the rest of our apples," he grinned.

"I have some more granola bars," Emma added, "and a package of Fig Newtons."

"I won't even ask what 'Fig Newtons are," the prince responded. "As long as it's edible, I'll be happy to eat it!"

"I have a couple of bottles of water, too," Hannah added.

"Okay then," the prince smiled. "You have thought of everything!"

Hannah blushed and looked away. When she looked back, the prince was watching her with a rather intense expression on his face, but he said nothing, instead, kicking his horse into a canter as the trail flattened out.

They could see the valley now, spread out before them like a patchwork quilt of houses and farms, edged by a wide green swath of uncut alfalfa. The hay barn sat fairly close to the trees and they reached it quickly, dismounting to lead the two horses inside the dark, wooden structure. The prince unsaddled both horses, as Hannah and Emma piled some hay at one end of the barn for them. Both horses immediately began pulling at the hay, munching it hungrily.

The prince had seen a wooden bucket outside that the farmer probably used to water his own horse when he cut the hay. Grabbing it and telling the girls where he was going, he started back into the trees to find the stream that had paralleled them down the mountain. While he was gone, Hannah and Emma used handfuls of hay to wipe down the horses and then gathered more loose hay on the barn floor into three heaps to serve as beds.

When the prince returned, he placed the bucket where the horses could reach it and joined the girls on one of the piles of loose hay. By the light of Brennan's cell phone, Hannah and Emma had set out three more apples, the granola bars, the Fig Newtons, and the two bottles of water and the three of them dug in.

"I didn't see anyone while I was filling the bucket," the prince reported, "but I did hear some kind of commotion to the east, maybe by the road to the castle. Still, it is getting pretty dark and I don't expect them to continue hunting us tonight."

Emma felt her stomach clutch as she wondered if the commotion had something to do with Julia and Brennan. Hannah, understanding her fear, whispered, "I'm sure they will be fine."

10 BRENNAN DISCOVERS HIS GIFT

Brennan and Julia had followed Lord Gabin, the false prince, as he led them to the same castle road they had climbed up that morning, hidden below the bed of the butcher's wagon. Once there, he had insisted, with all the arrogance of a real prince, that they follow the road to the valley and then look for a place to spend the night.

Lord Gabin insisted that they could stay at the local inn if Brennan bespoke the rooms while he and Julia waited with the horses. They could sneak in later, he argued, with no one being the wiser. Brennan had pointed out that he and Julia had no money and that it was stupid to run the risk of someone recognizing the prince when they could simply find a barn to sleep in. Julia countered Lord Gabin's argument that they needed food as well, by pointing out that she and Brennan had brought food with them in their Schulmappes.

Failing in those arguments, Lord Gabin tried to convince Brennan to tell him exactly where they were headed. Naturally, since Brennan had no idea where he was taking the false prince, he had to continue to stubbornly refuse to answer. He figured he and Julia would try to creep away from him while he slept. Then he and Julia could go back to the meadow to meet the others without worrying about leading the Duke's men there. So he met every pleading argument of Lord Gabin's with, "It is better you don't know where we are going."

At long last, Lord Gabin had given up asking and gone back to arguing for a more comfortable night than one spent in a barn. He had money, he volunteered, enough to pay for a room for them and some food. It was silly and unnecessary to sleep in a barn when they could be safe and comfortable in an inn. Julia found that she agreed with him, but when she tried to agree with him, Brennan met her suggestion with a scowl and so she subsided, figuring that he had a plan. Then it occurred to her to wonder why he should volunteer that he had money. Was there a particular reason that he wanted them to stay at an inn, or was he just too spoiled to sleep in a barn? Maybe Brennan wasn't wrong in refusing to go along with the faux prince's plan.

Finally, Lord Gabin pouted in silence as they continued to decend toward the valley in the gathering dusk. Suddenly, Arabella warned Julia, "Several horses are following us. I can smell them and hear them." Julia moved Arabella up close to Brennan to warn him, but at that moment, Lord Gabin cried, "I've had enough of this stupidity!" and putting two fingers to his mouth, whistled shrilly.

Immediately they all heard the sound of galloping hooves above them on the mountain road and could see the flash of horses and riders through the trees. Brennan swung Blaze around to face the danger, calling "Julia, go!" as he did so. Julia hesitated and so saw what happened next. As the group of horsemen swung around the last bend in the road, breaking from the trees, Brennan automatically raised his right arm above his head and shouted, "In the name of the Holy One, come no farther." Then, as the horsemen slowed partly in astonishment and partly to avoid plowing into the threesome in the road ahead of them, Brennan brought his arm down in a wide arc and the road between the horsemen and him suddenly erupted into flames.

The horses the men were riding stopped so quickly that several of the riders were tossed to the ground. The rest fought to control the terrified animals that bucked and lunged away from the flames. Their own mounts quivered with fear, but were far enough from the flames not to be so panicked as the others. Brennan pulled Blaze around again and started forward, past Lord Gabin, but the false prince had pulled a knife from his clothing and struck out at Brennan as he passed, cutting a long gash in his left arm. Immediately, Brennan's concentration broken, the flames died down, and those men who had retained some control of their horses were able to leap across the patch of coals or pick their way through the trees on either side of the road.

"I said go, Julia," Brennan called, gritting his teeth against the pain. Again he tried to urge his own horse forward, but Lord Gabin easily blocked his way, grabbing for his reins. Julia wanted to go to Brennan's aid, but Arabella, her wits not clouded by emotion as were Julia's, got the bit between her teeth and plunged off the road and down through the trees, recklessly risking injury in her attempt to save Julia. Julia was forced to cling to Arabella's neck, crouched low to avoid being brushed off by branches.

They crossed downed trees and skirted tall pines until eventually they reached the road where it curved back upon itself, and Julia thought Arabella would shift to the road where the going was easier. But Arabella plunged across the road and into the trees once more, jumping and sliding and dodging her way. Finally Julia simply shut her eyes and hung on, trusting the horse to pick her way down the mountain.

Eventually the shouts from above died away and the only sounds she could hear were the snapping of twigs and the crunch of dried vegetation that heralded Arabella's passage. Soon she realized that Arabella was no longer lunging and sliding, but had settled into a steady gait on more level ground. Julia opened her eyes and found that the trees grew farther apart here, and that to her right she could catch glimpses of meadowland.

Looking to her left, she saw that they were rapidly skirting the foot of the mountain, moving swiftly away from the road. When they reached a shallow stream, Arabella came to a stop, her flanks heaving, to take a long drink of the chilled water. Remembering her equestrian lessons, Julia leaned over her neck and cautioned, "Not too much, Arabella. You are overheated. Let's walk a ways."

Arabella allowed her to slip the bit back into place and guide her away from the water.

"I need to thank you for saving me, Arabella," she said. "But they hurt Brennan! He needs me! As soon as you are rested, we need to go back!"

"You can't help him by being caught yourself!" Arabella insisted. "The Duke will want to question him, so the most they'll do tonight is put him in the dungeon. As for the injury, they have to bind it up. Dead men can't talk!"

"Dead. . . . Thanks, Arabella," Julia responded tartly. "That was reassuring!" She sighed. "I guess you're right, though. Let's find a place to hide and rest for a while, and then we can start back up to the castle."

Arabella bobbed her head in agreement. "There are hay barns scattered between the village and the foot of the mountain. If we move away from the road, we should find one where we can shelter for a few hours."

"Okay, Arabella," Julia agreed. Lead the way!"

Arabella turned back to step gingerly through the stream, heading west again. Although the stars had come out, the moon was only a sliver in the black sky, giving very little light for the girl and her horse. Still, as they moved out of the trees and across a field of thick, tall grass, Julia soon could just make out the darker mass of a barn a little bit ahead of them.

"There! Is that a hay barn?" she asked, pointing.

"Yes," Arabella responded, suddenly stopping as an answering whinny sounded from the barn. "That's Rascal! We left him in the pasture by the castle!"

"Oh, hurry! It must be Hannah and Emma with the prince!"

Arabella broke into a run, covering the ground in a few long strides. As she came to a halt at the door to the barn, Julia slid quickly off her back and ran to pull the door open. The interior was dark, but the smell of horses and the rustle of the hay on the floor as the horses stirred at her entrance greeted Julia.

"Hannah, Emma?" She cried. "Are you in here?"

"No, Julia. We're out here," answered Emma from behind her, causing her to jump.

"You scared me!" she accused, hugging first Emma and then Hannah as she and the prince appeared around the side of the barn. "What are you doing out here?"

"We heard your horse," Emma explained, a mischievous look in her eyes, "so we went out, ah, another way, to hide until we saw who you were."

"Where's Brennan?" asked Hannah, looking around for her brother.

Julia's eyes teared up and her voice quavered as she answered, "We were ambushed. The fake prince cut his arm with a knife and they captured him and Arabella ran away with me and brought me here. She said I couldn't help him if I was captured too!"

"Were you followed?" the prince asked anxiously.

Arabella shook her head vigorously and Julia answered. "Arabella says no, and I didn't see or hear anyone. I think they were just happy that they had Brennan," she concluded in a teary voice. Then she brightened. "But oh, Hannah! You should have seen it! Brennan's gift! He ordered the soldiers to stop and swung his arm and the road burst into fire! It was so cool!"

The prince shook his head. "You Angeluscustos continue to amaze me! You carry on conversations with animals, order people to do what you say and they obey, walk through walls, call down fire. . . . I'm really glad you're on my side!"

"Who walks through walls?" Julia asked.

"Me," answered Emma. "That's how we got out here, through the wall. Hannah orders people around. What do you do, Julia?"

"Um, I don't know. Nothing yet," Julia answered, feeling somehow ashamed.

"We'll find out when we need her gift." Hannah assured her sisters.

"Have you eaten anything, Julia?"

"Nope. Haven't had time. I have some granola bars, though and some water."

The prince laid a hand on Arabella's sweaty withers. "Let's get this lady rubbed down and fed, too. Then we can talk about rescuing, what was his name, Brennan?"

"Yes, our brother, Brennan," answered Hannah. She ushered the others into the barn and turned on the flashlight app once more, but the light flickered and then died out. "Rats! I think the battery is finally dead," she mused, dropping the phone back into her Schulmappe.

"Never mind," the prince said. "I can rub Arabella down by feel. She was my mother's horse, you know. My mother loved her!"

"She's a great horse," Julia piped in. "She saved me because I would never have left Brennan, and they would just have caught me, too." She dug a granola bar from her Schulmappe, unwrapped it, and began chewing hungrily.

"So how do we rescue Brennan?" Emma asked.

"Our first order of business is to get the prince to the Gwencalon," Hannah answered. "We just have to trust The Holy One to take care of Brennan."

The prince paused in rubbing down the horse and mused, "It's too bad we don't have someone inside the castle that we can trust to tell us where your brother is. Then you could rescue him like you rescued me."

Julia, suddenly stopped eating and addressed the horse. "Arabella, didn't you say the dungeon rats told you where the prince was?"

"Yes," Arabella answered.

"Can't trust those rats, though," Blaze added. "They lie."

"Are there any other animals that we could trust that roam freely through the castle?" Julia pressed.

106

"What about Hobo?" asked Rascal. "The poor old fellow might enjoy something to make him feel useful again!"

"Hobo?" Hannah asked. "Who's Hobo?"

"Poor old Hobo was supposed to be my father's hunting dog," the prince explained, "but he broke a leg that never healed properly, so he just became a castle pet instead. He is getting pretty old, though. He must be all of twelve years old."

"Pooh, that's nothing," Arabella scoffed. "Rascal is right. No one pays any attention to Hobo. He can go anywhere he wants and I know he will help us!"

"Then," Hannah began, "we will get the prince to the Meadow early tomorrow morning and then return to the castle for Brennan afterwards."

"How will we contact Hobo," Emma asked.

"Through the mice," Blaze answered. "There are always mice around and unlike the rats, they don't lie."

"We'd be safer using Mouser, the cat," Arabella objected. "Otherwise, she just might catch and eat the very mouse that was carrying our message to Hobo!"

"Hem, maybe so," Blaze agreed, munching some more hay.

The prince had finished rubbing down the mare, and so he cautiously moved to where the girls were sitting, bumping into Julia in the dark. "Oh, sorry," he apologized. "I couldn't see you there."

"It's okay," Emma assured him. "Anyway, Julia is sitting in your spot. Move over here by me, Julia," she instructed.

Julia scooted across the hay, settling close to Emma's voice. "It's kind of spooky in here in the pitch black!" she commented. "Except for a few slivers of light here and there between the boards in the walls, it is totally dark. Don't they keep lanterns or anything out here?"

The prince made a sound of disgust. "Lanterns! Why didn't I think of that? If we are lucky, they may be one hanging over by the door." He got to his feet and the girls heard the rustle of dry hay as he carefully moved across the barn. "Yes, here is a lantern!" he cried, "but I have no flint to light it with, and I can't feel any box of flints here along the wall."

"Doesn't matter," Julia commented, taking another bite of granola. "I have matches in my bag."

In short order the prince had worked his way back across the dark barn with the lantern, which from the sound of it, had only a little fuel left in it. Hannah had found Julia's matches and only wasted two before managing to light the wick of the lamp. A soft, warm glow surrounded them as the prince swept clean a spot on the floor and set the lantern between them.

"You know," he said casually, returning to their earlier conversation, "I grew up in the castle and I know most of its secrets. You need me to help you rescue your brother. Please let me help."

Hannah wished she could see him better in the light from the lantern, but with the light on the floor his face was still in shadow. So she reached out to lay a hand on his arm. "I can't let you do that, Prince David. It is our job to rescue you and keep you safe. Brennan will be fine until we can get back to him. We cannot chance your being recaptured before your birthday, don't you see? Your duty to your country must come first as must our duty to do the will of the Holy One."

The prince sighed. "Yes, I suppose you are right. But I still don't like it. My uncle can be vindictive and cruel! I don't like leaving your brother in his control any longer than necessary!"

"We won't be leaving him there at all," Julia said. "Hannah will take you to the meadow to meet the Barbegazi, and Emma and I will go after Brennan."

"Julia, I can't let you two go off on your own like that, especially back to the castle!" Hannah argued.

"Of course you can. In fact, you have no other choice. We wouldn't have been brought here if we weren't capable of doing what we have to.

We can do it, can't we, Emma?'

"Sure," Emma answered, confidently.

"Especially with Arabella and the cat and Hobo helping us!" Julia concluded.

The prince wisely stayed out of the discussion, allowing Hannah to make up her own mind. She had always felt responsible for her brother and sisters, and now she had the added responsibility of the prince. If something bad happened to Brennan, that would be bad enough, but what if something bad happened to all of them. "God," she prayed silently, "what do I do? Should I take the prince to the meadow alone, or should we all go after Brennan?"

Suddenly from outside came a high-pitched squeal followed by a series of equally shrill chirps. It sounded again, and then died away.

"What was that?" Emma asked, fearfully.

"It sounded like an eagle," the prince answered. "Don't worry," he continued jokingly. "It's looking for mice and other small creatures. You're too big to interest it."

An eagle's call, Hannah thought. An eagle was watching for them in the meadow where they were to meet the Barbegazi. That was surely a sign, an answer to her prayer.

"Okay," she said, finally. "Julia, you and Emma will go after Brennan on Arabella, and the prince and I will go to the meadow."

"Good call," Julia agreed smugly.

"Then let's get some sleep," the prince suggested. "We need to wake up before dawn, though."

"What time is dawn," Emma asked. "I can set my watch. It has an alarm."

"What's a watch?" the prince asked, puzzled.

"Something that tells time, like a sundial, except without the sun," Hannah answered. To Emma she said, "Just set it for five hours. That should work."

And so the four of them rolled themselves in their cloaks and snuggled into the hay, listening to the rustling of the horses in their corner until at last they all slept.

11 BRENNAN MEETS THE DUKE

As Julia's horse plunged down through the trees, carrying Julia toward safety, Brennan fought to wrench the reins of his horse back from the false prince's control. His right arm burned ferociously and he could feel the blood running down onto his hand. Still, he knew he had only a few seconds to react before the others would reach them.

Grabbing the reins and the pommel in his left hand, he kicked his right foot free of the stirrup and slid to his left until he was nearly standing in his left stirrup, balanced by his hand on the saddle. Then, using every bit of strength and agility built up over summers of soccer games, he raised his right leg and kicked the false prince in the chest.

Unprepared for the onslaught, the prince lost his grip on the reins, tumbling from his horse as in one continuous movement, Brennan regained his seat and pulled his horse to the high slope, away from where Julia had gone. Kicking the horse in the ribs, he started it up the hill in a giant leap, just as the first of the horsemen reached the fallen prince.

"After him," their leader called. "Never mind the girl."

And so the race was on. Unfortunately for Brennan, some of the horsemen had turned to follow the road, a much faster and easier ride, and so by the time his horse reached the switchback above and he could turn onto the road to the castle, the others were close behind him. Still, his horse knew the road and was sure footed enough to make good speed even in the increasing darkness. It would truly have been a race except for two factors. Brennan had really no place to go except to the very place he wanted to avoid, and his arm continued to bleed freely, soaking through his shirt and jacket and running down his arm. He crossed his arm painfully across his chest, grabbing the left side of his collar, trying to elevate his arm somewhat to slow down the bleeding, but he found he could not maintain the position. Gradually he let the arm drop to his side, let his horse have its head, and slumped half conscious over the horse's neck.

Later, he could neither say when they caught up with him, nor how he arrived back at the castle. He had a vague notion of being pulled from the horse and dragged between two men into the building. Then nothing until he awoke to a dark room and a pretty angel, her dark hair haloed in the light of a lantern, as she bathed and bandaged the gash on his arm.

"Are you an angel?" he asked. "Am I dead?"

"No," she laughed. "You've got a nasty wound on your arm and you are weak from loss of blood, but you aren't dead. And I'm no angel. I'm the castle's apothecary. I've put a paste of sugar and honey on the cut to draw out any infection and to help the wound heal. I've also given you something to help with the pain. I'll be back in a few hours to change the dressing for you. In the meantime," she glanced back over her shoulder, "you need to rest. The guards have been warned to leave you be until I've checked you in the morning, and if they don't, they will suffer for it." She looked back at him. "The Duke can't question someone who is unconscious."

Brennan had the strange feeling that she was trying to convey some message to him, but his eyelids felt so heavy that he let them drift shut. He would think about her message later.

The apothecary continued talking softly to him. "I've sent to the kitchen for some good beef broth and wine to build back your strength. Finish it all when it comes." She began gathering her clean cloths, her jars, and her tools. "Get some rest, now." And then she was gone with a clanging of metal and the squeak of rusty hinges.

"I must be in the dungeon," Brennan thought as he drifted off to sleep.

Only moments later, it seemed, he was being gently shaken awake and a warm, watery broth was spooned into his mouth. Hunger and lassitude caused him to accept all of it and the tart wine that followed. Then the cook, for it had been the cook herself who had tended to him, allowed him to lie back as she, too, was ushered out of the cell.

Brennan suddenly started awake to find himself staring into two small red eyes. He struggled to get up, forgetting his injured arm and sank back with a groan when it wouldn't support him.

"Hey, lie still," a voice said. "We aren't going to hurt you."

"We?" Brennan questioned.

"Yeah, my men and me," answered the voice.

Brennan's eyes were becoming accustomed to the semi-dark of the cell and by the feeble moonlight that fought its way through the bars of the high window, he could just make out the scrawny outline of a rat, sitting squarely on his chest, and on the floor beside his cot, the slightly darker silhouettes of a half dozen more.

"You're an Angeluscustos, right?" questioned the rat. "I'm Duke Topo, at your service." And the rat performed a courtly bow.

"Brennan," Brennan answered, wondering why he was carrying on a conversation with a rat.

"We saw them bring you in earlier," Duke Topo continued. "I guess you know the guy you were rescuing wasn't the real prince."

"Yeah, we knew," Brennan answered. "Who was he? One of the servants?"

"Heck, no. That was Duke Ferigard's son, Lord Gabin. They wanted you to lead him to the Gwencalon. They don't really believe that he is dead."

"Really?"

"Yeah. We know he is still alive, you know." Duke Topo explained. "The animal network spreads news pretty quickly. We get the news last down here, but we get it. And we kept telling them that the prince had been brought down here, but no one would listen to us."

"Yeah," piped up another rat. "They think we lie to them."

"Well," giggled another one, "usually we do!"

"Quiet, Fats!" bellowed Duke Topo. Turning again to Brennan, he continued in a wheedling voice. "You're an Angeluscustos, so we know you have some magic powers. We thought maybe we could work out a deal, see? We pass the word that you are down here and you conjure up some food for us."

"Hey, I'd like to help," Brennan assured him. "But all I can do is talk to you and create a wall of fire." He thought for a minute. "I do have some granola bars and a Milky Way bar in my Schulmappes."

"Ah, that's no help," Duke Topo said, waving away that suggestion. "They never brought your Schulmappe down here."

He paced back and forth along Brennan's chest and midsection. "We're starving down here. Used to be in my father's day there were lots of prisoners down here and we could steal food from them and from the guards. Now, we have to sneak up to the larder and fight the mice for everything we get."

"Yeah," Fats added. "And that dratted cat, Mouser, sleeps by the larder so one of us has to draw him off so the others can grab some food. Mighty dangerous work, that!"

"Yup," agreed the Duke. "We lost my cousin Cheesy that way just last week, may the Holy One rest his soul!"

"Amen," chorused the others.

"Well, look" Brennan suggested. "If you pass on the word that I am locked up down here, the Gwencalon will send my sisters to rescue me.

114

When they do that and the prince becomes king on Wednesday, I will see that he supplies you with lots of food."

"Hooray!" cheered the rats.

But Duke Topo was less trusting. "How do we know that you aren't lying to us?" he asked suspiciously.

"I'm an Angeluscustos, remember. Angeluscustos don't lie."

"He's right."

"Yup, he's got a point!"

"I believe him!" "Me too." "I say trust him!" chorused the other, obviously hungry rats.

"Okay, I guess it can't hurt to give you the benefit of our trust," sighed the Duke. "Put her there," he admonished, holding out a paw to shake with Brennan.

Brennan gingerly stuck out a finger from his right hand for the rat to shake.

"We'll get right at spreading the word," Duke Topo said, turning to leave. "Oh, and you might just offer some proof of your word by leaving a little of your breakfast for us to clean up. Just slide it under the cot. We'll find it." He winked at Brennan, hopped off his stomach onto the cot and then to the floor, where, followed by his men, he strode purposefully out of the cell.

Brennan wondered how long it would take word to get all the way to the Gwencalon. He was very much afraid that he wouldn't have the days that it might take for rescue to come. Julia would know, of course, but what could she do all by herself? "God, I know you brought me here for a purpose, but I'd really like to be able to get out of here once the prince is safe," he prayed. Then he purposefully tried to sleep once more, but the fight on the mountain and thoughts of how he might handle Duke Ferigard's questioning swirled around in his mind.

All too soon, the light through the high window became stronger and Brennan was startled again, this time by the sound of heavy footsteps outside his cell and the rasp of a key in the lock. Remembering the apothecary's hint about being unconscious, he lay still with his eyes closed. Someone laid a cool hand on his forehead and then began unwinding the cloth wrapping his arm.

"Ah," said the pleasant voice of the apothecary, "this looks much better. No infection." She wet a cloth in a bowl of water and gently sponged off the long wound.

Brennan opened his eyes, but she lay a hand on his lips before he could speak. "It's too bad you haven't gained consciousness yet, but sometimes the loss of blood and the shock of a wound like this can cause that. Your body is trying to heal itself while you sleep."

She patted the wound dry again and, opening a small container, began to smooth the sugar and honey mixture onto the wound again. Whispering, she said, "I'll get you a few more hours, but that's the best I can do. I hope someone realizes you are down here and comes after you by then."

Aloud she said, "I'll have the cook send down something to eat in three to four hours. You should have regained consciousness by then. In the meantime, the rest can only do you good." She finished winding a clean wrapping onto Brennan's arm and then fashioned a sling for him, tying the wounded arm high across his chest to stabilize it. Finally she gathered her things to leave, whispering "Good luck!" to Brennan as she did so.

To the guard she called, "You can let me out now. He hasn't regained consciousness yet, but the wound looks clean."

"Well when do you think the duke will be able to question him," the burly guard asked, opening the cell door for her. "He is anxious to find out what this kid knows."

The apothecary appeared to think for a moment and then responded, "I think another four or five hours and he should be awake. He'll still be weak, though," she warned, "so I don't know how many questions he'll be able to answer."

"So long as he is conscious so I can take him up to the duke."

"I'll tell the cook to bring him some food later. That will increase his strength," the apothecary responded as she and the guard moved down the hall.

Brennan listened carefully, but the guard did not come back down the hallway. Cautiously he swung his feet to the floor and used his left arm to ease himself from the bed. Stiff and sore muscles protested loudly, but although his arm still ached, the searing pain of the previous day was gone. Gingerly he slipped it from the sling and moved it, biting off a gasp at the pain that shot through it. The knife must have cut deeply enough to tear into muscle, he thought ruefully. A fat lot of good he would be with a sore right arm!

He wondered if he could call down fire with his left arm. He rather thought he could if the situation called for it, but until he had a clear route of escape, a wall of fire wasn't going to do him much good. Then he recalled that the Gwencalon had said that the gifts were only to be used for the aid of others, not themselves. So, it didn't look like he could save himself, at least not until his arm was better.

Still, he'd better be ready just in case the opportunity arose, he thought. So as quietly as possible, he stretched his legs and his left arm, moving around the cell to stir up his blood. It was chilly down there, and the apothecary had removed his jacket and cut off the arm of his shirt in order to treat his cut. His cloak that someone had pulled over him on the cot had helped while he was unconscious, but now he needed to get that coat back on.

Carefully, he slid his arm from the sling again, wincing at the pain, and guided the arm slowly into the slashed sleeve of the coat. Amazingly someone had washed some of the blood off it while he slept and roughly stitched up the cut. It wasn't perfect, but he could get it on. Sliding the arm back into the sling, he moved the sling on top of the coat and then shoved his left arm into that sleeve. Buttoning it up with only his left hand was tough, but eventually he managed it, collapsing onto the cot to rest.

He must have fallen asleep again, because the rattling of a key in the lock and the screech of the hinges brought him awake with a start, and he sat bolt upright on the cot. This time a young girl entered, carrying a wooden tray of food for him. Too late to pretend to be unconscious, Brennan thought ruefully, as he thanked the girl for the breakfast. She set it carefully on the edge of the cot and scurried back out of the cell, sliding past the guard, who leered at her. Brennan deliberately coughed to draw his attention from the girl, and it worked as the guard swung back to Brennan as he pushed the cell door shut and turned the key again.

"Awake at last, I see," he commented. "The duke will be more than happy to hear that bit of news! If I were you I'd eat quickly. He's sure to send for you soon!"

He laughed uproariously at his own comment as he lumbered back down the dungeon hallway in the direction that the serving girl had gone.

Brennan felt sure that any discussion with the duke would no doubt include Lord Gabin and was sure to be unpleasant. Still, he knew he should eat to keep up his strength, especially since simply putting on his jacket had cost him so dearly. Remembering his pact with the rats, however, he carefully tore the thick bread in half and slipped half of it under the cot along with most of the unidentifiable meat. The rest he forced down with the bread. He sniffed the cup, decided it simply held cider, and drank it all to wash down the dry meat and the unbuttered bread.

Then he looked around carefully, wanting to be sure he could find no means of escape. The room held only the cot, a high window too small for him to crawl out, even if he could reach it, and a bucket for personal needs, which he promptly made use of. He even looked under the cot, thinking that perhaps a previous guest of this cell had dug a passage out and hidden it with the cot. No such luck, however. He was stuck until someone let him out, whether foe or friend.

Unfortunately for Brennan, it soon became obvious that his release would come by way of his foe, as the guard and two other men came down the hallway. The guard unlocked the cell door, calling cheerfully, "I told ya, didn't I? They've come to get you, they have!"

The two men pushed him aside and strode into the cell to grab Brennan's uninjured arm and usher him out. They hurried him down the hall and up the stairs that Bruno had led the four down was it only yesterday? Then they traversed another long hallway, this one paneled in wood, and up a wide stone staircase and into a large room, empty except for a throne at one end on a slightly raised dais. The room itself, like the hallway below, was paneled in a wood, much lighter than the wood of the houses in the village below the castle.

On both sides of the room between the many paned mullioned windows hung shields representing the various noble families of Serenia, many surmounted by crossed swords. A thick woven carpet ran the length of the room in the center, leading from the door to the dais and the throne. Behind the throne itself, the wall was draped in deep purple curtains, meeting at a point directly behind and above the throne and held back on either side of it by carved wooden rings. The throne itself was ornately carved wood of a darker hue than the walls and upholstered in purple cushions that matched the draperies behind it. All this Brennan observed as he was led to a spot before the throne to stand before its occupant who must surely be Duke Ferigard.

The duke bore a striking resemblance to Lord Gabin, who stood beside him, one hand resting casually on the top of the throne. Like his son, the duke's hair had obviously once been blond, but had now turned into that sort of faded yellowish-white of a blond man past his prime. He had no doubt once been a handsome man, but his face now was ruddy and puffy and he had the paunch around his waist that Brennan had heard people at home often describe as a "beer belly."

His clothing was rich and well tailored, but somehow did not help make him look the least bit dignified. He reminded Brennan of someone not born to a cultured family who was desperately trying to appear wealthy and refined and failing miserably. The duke rose to his feet as Brennan approached, and Brennan realized that had the duke not been standing on the dais, Brennan would have towered over him. As it was, he looked directly into the man's cold, blue eyes.

"Ah, at last," the duke murmured appreciatively, "the Angluscustos I have heard so much about. You, my boy, are going to tell us where to find both the prince and the Gwencalon!"

"I've been told the Gwencalon is dead," Brennan answered truthfully. "And I have no idea where the prince is."

"So you say now, " the duke smirked. "But I feel sure you will soon change your mind! Bring her in!" he called, and suddenly two more guards entered, pulling Emma in between them.

12 THE JOURNEY

Emma's watch alarm rang after what seemed to Hannah to be just a few minutes of sleep. Still groggy from sleep, the girls and the prince divided up the last of their food, gathered their belongings, and led the horses out to be saddled in the waning light of the moon. Then, after hugs all around, the prince tossed Emma up behind Julia on Arabella's back, and he and Hannah mounted Rascal and Blaze, who grumbled a little at the early hour.

Arabella started towards the trees at the base of the mountain where the hunting trail emptied into the valley. Knowing all the trails from years of rambling across the mountain with the Queen, she was to take the girls secretly to the castle to rescue Brennan. Hannah and the prince turned their horses toward the township, hoping to pass through the village before many villagers were stirring.

Although it must surely be nearing dawn, the sky had not yet begun to streak with light, the tall mountains hiding the rising sun from their view. Hannah and the prince walked their horses through the meadow, skirting the village houses until they reached the main road. Then, pulling up their hoods, they turned onto the road and began to move through the village.

A few lights burned in windows, indicating the early rising farmers preparing to head to their fields, and the housewives, starting their baking

121

for the day. On the street itself, no one seemed to be yet abroad and they made swift and silent progress to the outskirts of the town. But it was here that the trouble began. By now the first light of dawn was coloring the eastern sky above the ragged peaks of the mountains, casting a lighter glow across the sky. They were nearing the last buildings in the village when the whinny of a horse off to the left brought the prince to a halt. Hannah stopped as well, asking "What's wrong?"

The prince shook his head. "I don't know, but a horse is behind that building where a horse wouldn't normally be. Let's go back." But before he could turn his horse, two men with lanterns stepped from the shadow of the last house to hold them up.

"Halt you two," one of the men ordered them, moving forward to hold a lantern high as he grabbed Hannah's reins. "Where are you headed?"

"To our aunt's farm," Hannah answered quickly, answering in a gruff voice from the shelter of her hood. "She's ill. We're going to help her with the chores until she is well again."

"Who is your aunt?" the man demanded suspiciously.

But at that moment, the other man who had been circling them slowly charged, "Hey, they are riding horses from the castle. See here," he cried, "holding up his lantern, "the royal brand!"

Reacting swiftly, Prince David drove his heels into Blaze and slapped Rascal hard on the rump as Blaze lunged past him. Rascal reacted by plunging forward, tearing the reins from the man's hands and nearly unseating Hannah. Blaze shouldered into the man, knocking him down and sending the lantern rolling across the road, spilling oil and flame as it rolled. The second man kicked it away from the house towards the center of the road and then ran for their tethered horses as the first man scrambled to his feet.

Blaze and Rascal galloped freely now, eating up the yards of road beneath their powerful legs. At first Hannah could only hear the pounding of their hooves, but as the road circled back from the fields to skirt the woods at the foot of the mountains, she heard the prince call to her and motion towards the trees. He pulled his horse up and urged him into the trees, Hannah following close behind. They had to lean close against the horses' necks to avoid low hanging branches, but soon they had reached an area of thick pines whose branches swept the ground. Prince David quickly dismounted and led Blaze behind the trees, holding his nose to discourage him from whinnying. Again Hannah followed his example.

"We can't out run them," the prince explained. "Our horses are faster, but they will tire out all the same. We've got to hide and stick to the woods as much as possible until we get to the pass."

"But won't they realize we are hiding in the trees?" Hannah asked.

"Yes, eventually. But they'll have to hunt through the trees while I know of an old road that I hope they aren't aware of." He paused.

"Shush. Hear them coming?"

And indeed she could hear the sound of their horses growing louder and then softer again as they galloped down the road, well past their hiding place.

"Now we move," the prince instructed, leading them farther into the woods. Here the limited amount of sunlight that filtered through the trees had caused the lower reaches of the trees to be relatively free of branches, allowing them more freedom of movement. Soon they reached a narrow road through the woods and Prince David and Hannah were able to mount and walk their horses side by side.

"Lady Hannah, what's it like to be an Angeluscustos?" the prince asked.

Hannah was startled by the unexpected question. "Terrifying!" she finally answered with a laugh.

"What? But you have those extraordinary powers. What do you have to be afraid of?"

"We're rather new to this," Hannah explained. "This is our first mission and we had no idea what our powers were until we got to your country. So it's been a bit daunting, not really knowing what we can and cannot do."

"I don't really understand about Angeluscustos, actually," the prince confessed. "I know that members of your family have come from your world to help us before, but I was only eight years old when the last one was here. I only remember that my father was killed coming back from a battle and that my mother and I were saved by the Angeluscustos. "

"She had gotten the news of the victory," he continued, "and taking me, rode out to welcome the conquering army home. We were ambushed in the pass between Oberwald and Unterwald. The Angeluscustos spirited us away somehow. Then he left to go back to his world and my uncle came to comfort my mother. She had him appointed my co-guardian shortly before her death, and my uncle has reigned in my stead since then."

He was silent for a moment, thinking of his lost parents and how much he missed his father's camaraderie and his mother's gentle smile. Then he asked, "Are your parents still alive?"

"Oh, yes." Hannah answered. "I think my mom didn't really want us to come. She kept fussing over us, but Dad said we had to." She paused. "I miss having them here with us to give us advice. You must really miss your parents."

"I do," Prince David confessed. "I was pretty young when they died, but my father still took me hunting sometimes and my mother, she was just so kind to everyone. I really didn't know my uncle, and my cousin, Frederick, you know him as Lord Gabin, was always jealous of my position. We've never got along very well, even though we shared the same tutor and were expected to play together."

"That's too bad," Hannah said. "I don't see my cousins as often as I would like to, but we always get along well. We love each other, family, you know."

"Yeah, well, family to a royal can mean more danger and jealousy than love!" He changed the subject. "Do you have Angeluscustos in your world? I mean, besides yourselves."

"Yes, I think so. We call them guardian angels," Hannah answered, "but we never get to actually see them. And when we are not in your world, we are just ordinary people, not Angeluscustos."

"Really? And so you don't have special powers there? That's strange!"

"I know, but I guess that's how it works. Dad says it's to keep us from getting big heads."

"Big heads?" The prince was baffled. "Your heads would swell up?"

Hannah laughed. "Only figuratively. That means 'thinking we are more important than we really are.'"

"Oh," Prince David laughed, too. "Like my uncle and cousin Frederick!"

"Exactly!"

The trees were beginning to thin out again and the prince turned back away from the mountain and toward the road again.

"We're almost at the pass. We have to rejoin the road. It's the only way over," Prince David explained.

"Here's hoping those men aren't still out there!" Hannah said.

"Oh, they're out here somewhere. This time, if we see them, you might try putting them to sleep like you did the guards in the dungeon," the Prince suggested.

"I guess I'll have to try," Hannah replied.

The reached the road which was empty in both directions as far as they could see, to the left to where it emerged from the woods and to the right where it began to climb until it became lost between the shoulders of the mountains. They turned their horses to the right, and still at a walk, began the climb up and over the pass. It wasn't until they reached the very summit of the pass where the road was the narrowest that they once more encountered the men who had been chasing them. One man jumped down from the rocks to their right and leveled a gun at Hannah, once more ordering, "Stop and dismount!"

"Don't even think about running," a second voice said from behind them. They both turned to look at the angry man who also had a gun trained on them. As they slid from their horses, the prince looked meaningfully at Hannah, but she needed the men together, she thought, so she ignored him and focused instead on the two men.

"So, it is you, your Highness," the first man said. "I thought as much." He looked at Hannah. "And this must be one of the famous Angeluscustos." The other man had moved between the horses and taken the reins from their hands, nudging them together as he joined his compatriot.

Hannah decided now was the time to act. "Yes," she answered. "I am an Angeluscustos, and you will sleep now. When you awake, you will forget you have seen us."

The first man dropped instantly to the ground even as the second man, who had been watching the prince, began to laugh. His laughter died at the sight of his friend, asleep, gun dropping from relaxed fingers. He looked swiftly at Hannah, taking a step back toward the horses whose reins he still held, but at that moment Hannah, looking him in the eye ordered, "Sleep!" and he, too, slid to the rocks, dropping both the gun and the reins as he closed his eyes.

"Quick," Hannah instructed. "Let's go! I don't know how long that lasts!"

She and the prince quickly mounted their horses and moved them carefully around the two sleeping men and on through the pass. As they descended the far side of the mountain pass, Hannah began to wonder where the two had left their horses. The rocky pass left no hiding place for animals that large and they had seen no sign of them before they entered the pass. Soon the rock walls, sprinkled here and there with scraggly shrubs and grasses that somehow found enough dirt to anchor their roots, began to give way to more and more vegetation, and suddenly the road leveled out, spilling into another wide valley. To the right of the road, in a small copse of trees, two brown horses grazed placidly.

"Let's get their horses," Hannah suggested, nudging her horse toward the others. "We'll make them walk back to the castle!"

"They'll just take horses from some local lord," the prince commented, "but at least that will slow them down."

Moments later, they had untied the horses, and leading them behind them, the prince urged them into a canter along the main road. By now the sun was well up in the sky and Hannah was beginning to get really warm in her hooded cloak. Farmers were working in their fields now and they passed an occasional donkey cart on the road. None of those they passed were as heavily cloaked as they were, and she considered that they might be less conspicuous without the wool cloaks.

"Let's get out of these cloaks," she called to the prince. "It's too late in the day and we are drawing more attention with them than we would without."

"Right," the prince agreed, and they reined in their horses to shrug out of their cloaks. Suddenly they heard the sound of horses behind them and swung around in their saddles to look back. A large group of horsemen were galloping towards them, a red and black banner flying above them.

"Oh, no," Hannah moaned. "I can't be sure of putting that many to sleep!"

The prince laughed. "You won't need to! That's my godfather, Lord Bernald, the one you were supposed to meet after you rescued me from the castle. We are fine!"

"Thank goodness," Hannah sighed. "I was so worried that something had happened to him!"

"Not my parrain!" the prince chuckled. "He is very capable of taking care of himself!"

"Parrain?"

"Parrain, godfather. You know. He was my father's best friend, and I would have been much better off if he had been named my guardian, but my mother wanted her brother near her after my father's death. That made it easy for him to convince her to have him named guardian instead. But Lord Bernald has never abandoned me. He's the one who began to complain to the Gwencalon that I was being kept away from not only him, but everyone else as well."

"Filleul," a voice called, as the horsemen reached them, enclosing them in a happy circle. "My prince, it is really you!" Lord Bernald pulled his horse close to Blaze, clapping Prince David heartily on the shoulder. "And you, my Lady," he said to Hannah, "you have done well. Those two men we rode by in the pass? That was your work?"

Hannah blushed. "Yes, and here are their horses. We thought they could walk for awhile."

Lord Bernald laughed. "They will be well rested, those two. A walk will be good for them! Come, let's get to the meadow to wait for the Barbegazi. They won't come until after dark, but we can make camp in the woods and discuss matters while we wait." He laughed again and Hannah was amazed at the change in this man who when they met him earlier had seemed so taciturn. "Besides," he continued, "it's almost time for the noonday meal!"

Now that the prince was safe with Lord Bernald and his men, Hannah's thoughts turned back to her brother and sisters.

"Lord Bernald," she began earnestly, "I should get back to the castle to help Brennan and my sisters. He was captured and they went back to try to release him. They may need my help."

"Nonsense, my Lady," Lord Bernald assured her. "We may need your help, but they certainly do not. Remember, you are not the only Angeluscustos!"

Stung by his answer, Hannah objected, "But I am the oldest. Emma is still a child and Julia is not much older."

"Yes, and no doubt you have looked after them all of their lives. I understand, but you must let them try their own wings." He reached over and patted her hand. "Don't worry. I have some of my men placed around the castle and the cook's son will keep them informed of what is happening to your brother and sisters. Besides, not even the duke is crazy enough to try to kill Angeluscustos. No," he finished, "you come with us. The Gwencalon will wish to talk to you and we may well need your powers before this is over."

Reluctantly, Hannah put aside her worries and turned Rascal to follow Lord Bernald and the prince. Two of Lord Bernald's men took the reins of the extra horses, and the nobleman insisted that Hannah and Prince David ride on either side of him as they traveled, to relate the events of their escape to him. Hannah, still concerned over not meeting him, apologized earnestly, but he assured her that it had turned out for the better that way.

"I spent the entire night in hiding waiting for you," he explained, "and I saw some things that I would not otherwise have seen. Some very sobering things. But, because I saw them, we will be prepared and it will be Duke Ferigard who is surprised, and not us!"

The rest of the ride through the valley was very different from the journey they had taken just four days earlier. The people they met along the road doffed their hats or bowed to them as they passed, and in each village, one of Lord Bernald's men stopped to speak with the villagers before catching up with them later. Hannah wanted to ask what was going on, but Lord Bernald, seeing her inquisitive look, simply said, "Patience, my Lady. When we make camp, I will explain everything to you."

When finally Lord Bernald indicated that they had arrived, Hannah found nothing that seemed remotely familiar to her. If this were indeed the Meadow of the Larks, nothing here seemed to distinguish it from any of the other meadows they had ridden through on their way here. Nonetheless, she followed Lord Bernald as he led them to the trees at the edge of the meadow, dismounting to lead his horse into the woods.

As she moved to follow him, Hannah heard a familiar cry and looked up to see an eagle wheeling above them in the sky. He circled once, twice at a fairly low altitude before rising and sheering off across the valley to the mountains on the other side. That must be the Gwencalon's eagle, she thought. So their arrival had been marked and surely by nightfall, the

Barbegazi would come for them with their Snow Dragons.

As the horses were dealt with, Lord Bernald, the prince, and Hannah sat beneath the trees, eating bread and cheese that one of the men had produced for them, washing it down with the ubiquitous cider. The other men soon joined them, sitting a little apart. Two of the men disappeared through the trees and Hannah assumed they were going to keep watch. Finally, Lord Bernald began to talk of the matters that concerned them.

"So, my Filleul. Your uncle is determined to become king any way he needs to. As we now know, it was his plan to be rid of the Gwencalon, and then have you mysteriously die of this unknown illness you were supposed to be suffering from. If you hadn't eventually succumbed to the lack of food and heat in the dungeon, I think he might have helped you along."

"Killed me, you mean?" Prince David asked.

"Yes, Filleul. He has gone so far as to forge an agreement with Kummer. They are digging a tunnel through the mountains into the western part of Meerwald, your uncle's land. He has agreed to allow them free access through their tunnel and across his land to the sea."

The prince nodded his head. "I am not surprised. I saw him talking with envoys from Kummer a few weeks ago. I couldn't hear what they were saying, but they seemed awfully friendly."

"Duffy was hiding in the secret panel behind the council room. He has been listening there and reporting back to me and through me to the Gwencalon. He heard every word. A group of Kummer soldiers waits just inside Serenia to the south to come to the Duke's aid. And what I saw while I was waiting for the two of you adds to the difficulty." He paused. "Last night about 50 soldiers arrived at the castle from Kummer. He is going to make sure that the Landsgemeinde names him king through force if not through choice!"

"So that's what he's traded for Kummerian access to the sea, their support for his kingship," the prince concluded grimly."

"That's what I believe. He's a fool to trust Kummer, though," Lord

Bernald commented, shaking his head. "They are still angry over their defeat when they tried to take Meerwald from your father."

"Parrain," Prince David asked. "What do you suggest that we do? Uncle has dismissed most of the army and all of the castle guards and replaced them with his own men. How can we stop them?"

"Ah, but you see," Lord Bernald explained. "I have sent men to all the villages and farms. The people will come armed to the Landsgemeinde and my men and some of the Barbegazi will try to disarm the Kummerians before the council begins."

He looked at Hannah. "And then, of course, we have you, your brother, and your sisters." He clapped the prince on the shoulder. "If everything goes as we hope, we will save the kingdom for you, Filleul."

"Lord Bernald, Lord Bernald," a voice called as one of the lord's men hurried towards them. "The Barbegazi have landed with the Dragons de Neige."

"What!" Lord Bernald exclaimed. "I thought they would wait until dark."

"Sachi said the Gwencalon thought it was vital to get the prince to safety immediately," the man explained. "And he has gathered all of the other Lords from the kingdom to a council. They are waiting."

"Right. Wait here for me with the men." Turning to Hannah and the prince he said, "Let's go, you two. We must hurry now. The Barbegazi will not wish to stay in the meadow long in the middle of the afternoon."

Lord Bernald, Prince David, and Hannah hastened to the meadow as the others climbed onto their horses and rode off. Sachi greeted the three, urging them to mount the Dragons de Neige. "We cannot wait here long, for fear one of the Duke's men will see us," he explained. As soon as they had mounted, the Dragons de Neige rose into the air, soaring towards the high, snow-crested peaks of the mountains. Below them, an eagle circled the meadow again, and then sank slowly to its nest on a craggy outcropping of the mountain, the valley still echoing with its solitary, satisfied cry.

.

13 EMMA, JULIA, AND ARABELLA HATCH A PLOT

Emma drooped with fatigue as she clung to Julia's back on the beautiful cream colored horse that Julia called Arabella. Julia, she thought, however, seemed awfully keyed up. Maybe she felt guilty for having left Brennan the evening before, Emma thought, but that was silly. For one thing, Arabella had apparently run away with her, and for another thing, what could she possibly have done against all of those men?

She worried about Brennan, too, and Hannah, but just because they were no longer all together. She also trusted that God would take care of them. She considered telling Julia that she should have more faith, but decided it wouldn't be politic. What Emma failed to consider was that Julia's extra three years of life experience had shown her that bad things can happen to good people. Julia had also seen Lord Gabin slash Brennan's arm and the quickly spreading blood. She worried about the pain he was experiencing, not really about the danger he might be in.

Arabella had carried them straight to the trail Emma, Hannah and the prince had descended the day before, and Emma hastened to tell Julia.

"This is the trail we followed yesterday," she explained. "It will take us very close to the meadow where we found Blaze and Rascal."

"This hunting trail will take us right up to the castle," Arabella corrected, "but yes, it does pass by the meadow where the grooms were told to leave us yesterday."

"So it was on purpose," Julia exclaimed. "Brennan and I thought so when we counted the number of horses and saddles. Just enough for the four of us and the false prince, we figured."

"Yes, they were ready for you," Arabella confirmed. "They hoped you would lead them to the Gwencalon."

"The cook told us that Bruno could be trusted," Emma told her, "but I think he told the duke that we were Angeluscustos come to rescue the prince."

Arabella agreed. "Yes, his loyalty lies with the current source of power always. What do you plan to do when we reach the castle?" she asked.

Julia had been considering exactly that. "I think you can drop us at the pasture and go on to the castle. Hopefully they will think you just got away and returned to your stall. Then maybe you can send word to us when you find out where Brennan is."

"Hmm. That should work," Arabella agreed.

"We talked about the dog, what was his name?" Julia asked.

"Hobo," Arabella answered. "He should be able to find your brother, and he could come meet you in the pasture if I'm stabled."

"Good. When we know where he is," Emma said, "we can go get him. I can pull us through walls and doors, so we only need to find a way to remain unseen."

Julia mused, "We may need to wait for night or try to get the dog and cat to help us create some kind of diversion."

"Even the rats may help," Arabella added. "They lie, as Blaze and Rascal said, but they can be bribed with food."

"Yuck, rats!" Emma exclaimed. "One ran over my foot when Hannah and I were in the dark in the dungeon. I about died!"

"I would have died!" Julia averred.

"I don't mind rats so much as mice," Arabella said, shuddering. "They are so small and they get everywhere. I just hate it when I stick my nose in the feed trough and up pops a mouse! Lucky for us, Mouser keeps the stables pretty free. I think most of them have moved into the granary."

The three sank into silence as they continued to wend their way along the hunting trail. The sun was rising and the early chirping and stirring of birds and other forest creatures followed their progress up the mountainside. Soon, however, the small scuffling sounds and the birdcalls fell silent and they could hear the sound of voices.

"I don't know why we have to be out here again," grumbled one voice. "If the prince had come this way, he is long gone by now."

"Hey, no one asked your opinion," another voice answered. "Why do you care how we spend our morning? It's kind of pleasant walking through the woods like this."

"Be pleasant on horseback." the first voice disagreed. "But on foot? No sir! Going down's not so bad, but we'll have to walk up again. I ain't used to this!"

"Oh no," Julia whispered. "Those men are sure to find us. Is there any place we can hide, Arabella?"

"I'll try to get behind some trees," Arabella answered, heading off the trail, "but if they look this way, I don't see how they can miss us."

As Arabella settled behind some trees, Julia saw that while the bare branches gave them some shelter, it would not be enough to protect them from sight.

"Oh, no," Arabella groaned. "They have the dogs. Hear them?"

Julia heard nothing, but she trusted Arabella's better sense of hearing. "If only there was some way to make us invisible to them," Julia mused aloud. Scarcely had the words left her mouth than Arabella disappeared and Julia and Emma were apparently sitting on air. She reached out to touch Arabella's neck and realized that while she could feel the horse's mane and neck, neither Arabella nor she herself were visible.

"Julia, what happened?" Emma whispered. "I can't see you or Arabella any more." She sounded panicked. "I can't even see myself! Are we invisible?"

"Yes, Emma, but shush! " Julia warned. "Here they come!"

In fact, the two men had come around a bend in the trail into sight, still squabbling good-naturedly, leading two dogs on leashes. One of the dogs suddenly threw up his head, looked in their direction, and began barking, joined immediately by the second dog. Both animals were straining at their leashes, their paws scrabbling on the trail.

"What is it?" asked the taller of the two men. "Do you see anyone?"

"Nah," responded the second, moving a little off the trail with the dog. "I don't see nobody."

"Then what are they fussing about?" responded the other.

"Probably some animal. They are deer hounds, after all." He pulled the dog back to the trail, ordering it to be quiet.

"Yeah, but we would have heard a deer running away," the first man objected.

"So, do you see anybody?" the second man asked. "Cause I sure don't. Come on Tracker."

Reluctantly and with a final look in the girls' direction, the first man called his dog to heel and continued down the trail after his partner. Once they were out of sight and the sound of their passage could no longer be heard, Emma said, "Make us visible again, Julia."

"Wait a minute, Emma," Julia said, reaching for a nearby tree branch. As soon as she took hold of the branch, the entire tree disappeared. "Wow!" she exclaimed, turning to an invisible Emma. "Did you see that? Apparently when I am invisible, everything that I touch is also invisible."

"Okay, Julia. Cool! But make us visible again so we can go!"

"Okay, just hang on," Julia, who of course had no idea what to do, replied. Tentatively she tried, "We want to be visible again." and was delightedly surprised when it worked and they were all back to normal.

"That really was cool, Julia!" Emma chortled. "Just like in Harry Potter! I guess now we know what your special gift is!"

"Yeah," Julia answered, thoughtfully. "Arabella, I think this changes things. Take us to the castle with you, but let us know before we are close enough to be seen, and Emma and I will dismount. We'll become invisible and just follow you in to the stables. We can talk to Mouser and Hobo directly and save some time."

"That'll work," Arabella agreed, picking her way carefully back to the trail. "Just beyond that bend is another trail that crosses back to the road. I'll take that. It'll be swifter."

The rest of the trip was uneventful, and Julia found herself enjoying the crisp fall air and the sights and sounds of the woods around them. Once again the birds chirped to one another as they flew from branch to branch. A black squirrel scurried across their path, a large walnut held firmly in his jaws and occasioned comment from Emma who had never seen a black squirrel before, only "normal" brown ones. In the distance, the rustle of dried leaves signaled the presence of a buck and two does, who watched them for a moment before crashing away deeper into the trees.

Emma wondered what they would do when they got inside the castle. She understood about getting in invisibly, but how would they get Brennan out? They became invisible, not bodiless, and if soldiers started shooting randomly or swinging clubs or swords, they could still be hurt or killed. She tried to ask Julia, but Julia just said, "Trust me. I have a plan, but we'll need help! I'll explain it to everyone at the same time."

"Who was the everyone that Julia was talking about?" Emma wondered. But she was quiet. Julia couldn't be pushed. She'd share her plan when she was ready and then Emma would have a chance to suggest changes.

All too soon, they had come to the secondary trail and followed it to the main road. They continued on until the towers of the castle walls loomed above them. Then Arabella stopped and the girls dismounted.

"Follow close but don't touch me," Arabella warned. "It wouldn't do for me to suddenly disappear from sight when I'm being led to the stables. Once we're in the stables and the stable hands have left, I'll find out who's about and we'll get word on your brother."

And so, Julia tied up Arabella's reins so she wouldn't trip on them, took Emma's hand and said, "We need to be invisible." And Arabella, who knew what would happen, started none the less, when the two girls disappeared from view and Julia's disembodied voice said, "Okay. Go ahead, Arabella. We'll be right behind you!"

A couple of more turns of the hunting path and they reached a small door in the castle wall. Emma was all for going through, but Julia nixed the idea and pulled her after Arabella who now followed the castle wall around to the road and the main gate. As she neared the gate, shouts heralded her approach and two guards moved to intercept her as she walked into the courtyard.

"This is one of the horses that was taken from the pasture!" one guard cried, recognizing her. "This was the queen's mare."

"I wonder where she came from?" the second said, gazing suspiciously down the road. "Hey, Roger. Do you see anyone out there?"

"No, no one," came the swift answer. "It's been quiet all morning. No one around but the guards out hunting the prince."

"Nothing on the saddle to show where she's been, either," the first guard commented. "Well, I'll take her to the stables and have someone unsaddle her. You'd better go tell the captain that she has come back."

The second guard took Arabella's reins and started toward a long, low building to the left of the gate. As they neared it, Julia and Emma saw a group of boys scooping hay off of a wagon and tossing it into a pile beside the building. The guard yelled at one of them.

"Hey, you, boy! Take this horse to the stable and rub her down."

The boy touched his forehead in obedience, hopped from the wagon, rested his strange, two pronged pitchfork against the side of the stable, and ran to take Arabella's reins from the guard, who growled, "Don't take too long doing it. Then get back to your job."

"Yes, sir!" the boy answered, before clicking to Arabella and running her to the stable door and into the cool darkness inside. Julia and Emma hurried to catch up, being careful to avoid other servants who crossed and re-crossed the courtyard in hasty completion of their various tasks. Once in the stable, the groom led Arabella into a large stall, poured grain into a wooden trough for her, and dipped a bucket full of water from a long trough in the center of the building. Then he removed her tack, rubbed her down as she grazed contentedly, then hauled her saddle and bridle out of the stall and left. The moment he was gone, the other horses, who had watched these proceedings with interest, began calling to Arabella.

"Hey, Arabella. Where you been?"

"Have you seen Rascal and Blaze?"

"Yeah, they're missing, too! Thunder came back last night, but not the other two."

"Hey, have you heard what the dungeon rats are saying now?" asked a piebald in the next stall. "They're saying the duke's got an Angeluscustos in the dungeon! Ha, Ha! What a laugh!"

Arabella tossed her head importantly. "Well, it so happens they are probably right!"

"What?" asked a rangy roan. "Those rats lie, you know that, Arabella. What would an Angeluscustos be doing in the dungeon?"

"He would be a prisoner!" Arabella snapped. "Look, I've met him, that Angeluscustos, and I saw the duke's men capture him. And I brought his two sisters here to rescue him!"

"Really?" said the piebald, impressed. "Hey, Mouser," he called to a grey and white cat who was cleaning his face industriously. "The rats are telling the truth."

139

"Rats never tell the truth," the cat replied, washing an ear.

"Well this time they are!" Arabella insisted. "Julia, time to show yourselves," she said.

"Let us be visible," Julia intoned, moving farther into the stable from an empty stall where she and Emma had taken refuge. Immediately they were visible again, to a chorus of excited whinnies from the horses. Mouser, interested in the goings on at last, leaped from the top of a box where he had been bathing and approached the girls to sniff curiously at their legs.

"So you are Angeluscustos. Sent by the Gwencalon, I expect," Mouser concluded. "I heard from Mr. Higgley that he was still alive."

"Mr. Higgley," Emma chimed in excitedly. "You have seen him? Did he get home safely?"

"I saw him this morning," Mouser answered. "He said he had met you. He also said you have come to save the prince."

"Save the prince?" echoed the roan, awed.

"Yes, well, we've actually done that already," Julia answered. "Our sister, Hannah, is taking him to the Gwencalon. We had to come back to get Brennan. He was injured by Lord Gabin, you see."

"Stupid, cruel young man," a black gelding commented. "He's a horrible rider and he always blames the horse. When he fell off jumping a ditch, he took a whip to poor Zephyr. Might have killed him, except Zephyr got away from him. I hear a farmer found him and took him to Lord Bernald. They've been keeping him hidden so Lord Gabin doesn't find out and get him back again. Course, now the rest of us have to put up with him!. Nasty boy!"

"I can believe that!" Julia answered. "The thing is, I have a plan for rescuing my brother, but we have to know exactly where he is, and we will need your help, Mouser, and maybe Hobo's too."

"Hobo?" Mouser shook his head. "Hobo's arthritis is getting him down these days. Don't know how much good he'll be, but his heart is brave. He will do all that he can for the Angeluscustos who saved the prince!"

"As will we all," added Arabella, to a chorus of snorts of assent from the other horses. "Mouser, can you bring Hobo to hear the Angeluscustos' plan?"

"Quicker than you can catch a mouse!" Mouser agreed, darting off towards the main castle building.

While they waited, Julia and Emma sat on the straw-strewn floor and Arabella told the other horses of the adventures she and Julia had experienced. Emma was called upon to describe the rescue of the prince, and then Julia insisted that Arabella tell about Julia's discovery of her special gift, invisibility. Everyone was duly impressed.

When Mouser returned, he was followed not only by Hobo, a sleek brown hound who walked a bit stiffly, but also by a large, but rather thin rat. "This is Duke Topo. He insisted on coming along to help." Mouser wrinkled his nose in distain.

"Have a deal, we do, the Angeluscustos and I," Duke Topo explained. "I'm going to keep my part of the bargain so he keeps to his!"

Hobo was introduced to both Emma and Julia and then they all settled in to hear Julia's plan. Duke Topo reported that Brennan had rested well and done some exercising that morning, news that cheered both Julia and Emma considerably. Hobo had been snoozing in the library when the duke had ordered Brennan to be brought to him as soon as the duke had finished lunch, which Mouser reported had been taken to him just as she and Hobo had crossed the kitchen on the way back to the stables, Topo having taken a more circuitous route since his presence in the kitchen would not have been appreciated.

"Then we must work quickly," Julia explained. "Emma," she began. "You are going to go to the front door of the castle with me and demand to see the duke. Then you are going to demand that he releases Brennan. I'll sneak in with you, invisibly."

"But even if I get to see the duke," Emma protested, "there's no way he's just going to let Brennan go! He'll just grab me, too!"

"Exactly!" Julia confirmed in a satisfied voice. "That is just what I am hoping for. Then listen," she motioned the rat, the dog, and the cat closer. "Here is what we will do next."

Arabella listened as well, as they were all sitting in her stall, but the other horses grumbled that they were missing most of what Julia was saying. But Julia, once she had explained the part that Topo, Hobo, and Mouser would play, explained to the horses that they too would have a role. When the three kids came out of the castle, they would need three horses to carry them away. They would saddle Arabella and two she chose before leaving for the main entrance of the castle. They would come out, mount, and gallop out the main gate. In order to do that safely, they would need the other horses to stampede out and cause a disturbance in the courtyard that would prevent the duke's men from catching them and following the three kids.

This plan introducedd a tough of excitement into what had been a dull day in the stabel and was greeted with enthusiasm by the other horses. So, the animals returned to the castle to get ready, Emma and Julia saddled Arabella and the two horses she picked out, unlatched all of the stalls, and finally, Julia took Emma's hand and said, "let us be invisible!" And the two girls left the stables and crossed the vast courtyard unseen and undetected.

14 GHOSTIES AND GHOULIES

Brennan's heart sank as he looked at Emma held between the two guards. Obviously the Duke was going to threaten to hurt Emma if Brennan didn't tell him where the Gwencalon was hiding. What was he going to do? He couldn't give away the Gwencalon's location because that would betray not only the Gwencalon, but also the prince. But, Emma? He couldn't possibly allow her to be harmed.

He still couldn't do much with his right arm and one of the guards had a tight hold on his left. He wouldn't be able to create a wall of fire, even if he could figure out how that would help them here inside the castle when no distance existed between them and their enemy. "God," he prayed silently, "I need help here!"

The Duke interrupted his thoughts by stepping down from the dais and strolling over to Emma, chucked her under her chin. Turning back to Brennan he commented, "It would be a shame for anything to happen to such a pretty little girl, now wouldn't it?"

"Leave her alone," Brennan ordered, struggling against the man that held him.

"It's okay, Brennan," Emma assured him. "Nobody's going to hurt either of us."

At that moment, the room erupted into chaos. First, out of nowhere, a spear came sliding across the floor to bang against the feet of one of the guards holding Emma. "What the. . . ?" the guard began, but his comment was cut short by a high pitched squealing which Brennan and Emma recognized as Duke Topo calling, "Let's go, men. Up their legs and bite them!" To the consternation of the guards, a dozen rats scurried into the room, followed by a yowling cat and a barking dog.

"Get those animals out of here!" shouted the duke, but before the guards could act, two things happened at once. The rats could not see an invisible Julia, and so, by chance, several of them raced right across her feet. Unfortunately for Julia, though she could not be seen, she certainly could see, and when she felt the rats, and looked down, the thought of those thin little rat feet on hers was too much to bear and she shrieked. The sound of a disembodied scream added to the rat attack proved to be too much for the guards holding Emma and they dropped her arms and ran, howling in fear.

"Ghosts!"

"The castle is haunted!"

"Run!"

They stumbled over Hobo who had veered toward them and deliberately tangled himself in their legs, picked themselves up and disappeared through the door. By then, the rats had reached the other guards, Lord Gabin, and the duke, running up their legs, nipping and scratching. The men guarding Brennan abandoned him to swipe at the rats.

Freed of restraint, Brennan reached for Emma, saying "Come on, let's run."

"No," she objected. "This way." And pulling him with her, she hurried onto the dais and past Lord Gabin. As he grabbed at Brennan, Lord Gabin suddenly found himself with Topo on his shoulder and Mouser clawing his way up his leg, hissing and yowling. He backed away, yelling, trying to brush the rat off his shoulder. As Lord Gabin got closer to the edge of the dais, Topo leaped from his shoulder to the duke's back with Mouser scrambling after him.

"Ayah!" the duke yelled to no one in particular, forgetting Brennan and Emma to swat at the clawing animals. "Get them off me!"

At that moment, Emma had reached the wall behind the dais, and with Brennan's hand tight in hers, placed her other hand against the wall and pulled Brennan through to the next room.

In the throne room, chaos still reigned. The rats had begun jumping from the men to avoid their flailing arms, but at Duke Topo's orders, they continued to run around the floor, followed by the cat and dog who managed never to actually catch one of them. Julia had quickly regained her equilibrium and had begun whacking the duke on his legs with the flat of a sword she had pulled from the wall. Shouting, he tried to move away from the blows coming from behind him, spinning to look behind him where he saw . . . nothing. Blows from unseen weapons and rats climbing on him were driving him crazy.

But then Topo scrambled up the duke's back and jumped from his shoulder, bouncing off Julia's back with a squeak of surprise, and she reacted with another shriek that sent the remaining guards scrambling along the floor, half crawling and half running, to escape, Lord Gabin hard on their heels. Julia dodged between them and the animals on her own way out of the room.

The animals, the guards, Lord Gabin, and the invisible Julia quickly scattered in opposite directions, leaving the duke staggering back to the dais to sink weakly onto the throne. Suddenly, he realized that he was alone, totally alone. In the midst of the turmoil, the two Angeluscustos had both escaped. Livid with anger, he slammed his fist against the arm of the throne and, suddenly reanimated by his fury, strode toward the hallway.

He had barely reached the door to the throne room when he was met by a bevy of guards and servants who had come running to investigate the shouts and commotion.

"Quick," he commanded. "Two kids, a boy and a girl. They are somewhere in the castle. Find them quickly and bring them to me! You two," he pointed at two men. "Guard the front doors and don't let anyone out! I want them caught, now!"

The guards hurried away to find Emma and Brennan, but of course, they were already too late. Hobo had met Emma and Brennan in the hallway outside of the adjoining room and led them quickly by the servants' stairs to an unused storage room near the kitchen where Julia, Mouser, and the rats met them.

Julia, who was once again visible, threw her arms around Brennan. "I'm so glad to see you! Are you okay?"

"Fine, Julia. The arm's a little sore, that's all."

"You guys were terrific!" Emma congratulated the animals. "We couldn't have done it without you!"

"Whoo hee, did you see those men jump?" chortled Duke Topo, slapping one of his men on the back.

"And Lord Gabin." Mouser's voice was smug with satisfaction. "I scratched him pretty good climbing up after you, Topo."

"Okay, everybody." Julia interrupted. "You did a great job! But they'll be looking for us. We have to get out of here."

"I'll take you to the stable the back way," Mouser said. "Come on!"

Brennan and the girls bid Hobo, Topo, and the others a hasty good-bye and followed Mouser as he scrambled out an open window in the storage room. Once in the courtyard, Mouser led them behind some stacked barrels and to a narrow, open door at the back of the stable.

"Thanks, Mouser," Emma said. "You're a great cat. I wish I could take you home with me!"

"You are pretty great yourself, Mistress Emma," Mouser replied. "But my place is here with my prince!"

"I know," Emma conceded, kissing him on the top of the head. "Bye."

"Emma," Brennan called. "Come on! Get your horse."

Emma realized that Julia had already mounted Arabella and Brennan was waiting to help her onto the black. She ran to the saddled horse and allowed her brother to hoist her up to the saddle, taking the reins as he climbed onto the roan.

"Remember the plan," Arabella called to the other horses, and they answered with various whinnies of enthusiasm.

"Got it!"

"We're ready!"

"Yeah, let's go!"

Arabella wheeled around and tore out of the stable, the other horses racing behind her. Julia lay flat against Arabella's neck and Emma and Brennan did the same as the herd of nearly twenty horses thundered across the courtyard. Fortunately for them, the guards inside had been too busy searching the castle proper to think of closing the front gate, so the horses stampeded out the gate, scattering grooms, the two gate guards, and a couple of servants. The air filled with the frantic shouts of the men, the excited whinnies of the horses, and the thunder of their hooves as they streamed through the gate and started down the road to the valley and the verdant meadows below.

The descent was wildly exciting. They careened around the bends in the road. They flew past workers on foot who shrank into the trees at the edges of the road. They sailed by horse drawn merchants' wagons, causing the startled dray horses to rear and plunge in their traces while their frightened drivers strove to calm them. Brennan found the ride exhilarating, but he fervently hoped that no one was hurt by their exuberant passage.

As they reached the foot of the mountain, spilling out into the valley, Arabella headed away from the town, galloping instead into the grassy fields to the west, the rest of the herd following. Then she began to slow her pace to a canter as she crossed the valley toward the river. At its bank, she came to a stop.

As the others milled around her, she called, "You are on your own now. Have a good day. Just remember not to let yourselves be caught too quickly!"

The horses whinnied their good-byes and began to move down the bank to drink from the cold water. Emma's black gelding and Brennan's roan followed Arabella into the water, drinking thirstily before following her across to the other side.

"We'll be safer traveling across country rather than following the road," Arabella explained. "I guess you should know, Lady Emma, that you are riding Minuit, and you, Lord Brennan, are riding Rouget. Where do we go now, Lady Julia?"

"To the Meadow of the Larks," Julia answered. "And as quickly as we can, Arabella. We need to get back to Hannah and the prince and that's where they were going."

"Then, come on Minuit, Rouget," Arabella called. "Let's be off!" And the three Angeluscustos and their horses started toward Nidwald and the Meadow of the Larks.

The horses, led by Arabella, walked leisurely now, the exhilaration of freedom and the thunderous mountain descent forgotten in the placid quiet of the afternoon. The warmth of the sun and the sweet smell of the alfalfa through which they walked lulled them into a sense of well-being. The kids, on the other hand, still nearly quivered with excitement and nervousness.

Brennan's arm ached abominably and he wished the apothecary had left him some medicine to calm the throbbing. His mind kept going back over the events of the morning. Why had the Duke wanted to know where the Gwencalon was? He had asked about both the Gwencalon and the prince, but the entire charade with Lord Gabin had been designed to find out where the Gwencalon was.

The prince hadn't been rescued when they set that up. He needed the prince, obviously, so he could kill him and produce his body to the people. That Brennan understood. But what difference did the Gwencalon make? Was his influence over the people so great that he could prevent the Duke from carrying out his plans even if the Duke had the prince, or the prince's dead body?

Julia's thoughts dwelt on the loyalty that the animals --- dog, cat, horses, even the rats --- had shown to the prince's cause. Obviously the Duke and his son were not universally liked at the castle. She wondered if that loyalty might come in handy again somehow. She must keep it in mind. The ability to converse with the animals was really useful, she mused. What a great asset it would be for a veterinarian. She remembered reading the Doctor Doolittle books when she was younger. How much better it would be to be able to ask an animal where it hurt than just to guess. And Arabella. She would miss her so very much when they left to go home!

Emma sat quietly on Minuit's back, running the events of the day through her mind. She had been frightened at the thought of meeting the duke on her own, but knowing that an invisible Julia was backing her up had made it easier. She had been proud that her voice had not quavered when she had announced to the guard, "I demand to see the duke immediately! He is unlawfully holding an Angeluscustos in the dungeon and I have come to get him." When an astonished and mildly amused guard had ushered her into the duke's presence a few minutes later, she had felt emboldened enough to repeat her demand. Even the duke's laughter had not moved her then. She had remained outwardly calm even though her insides were like Jell-O!

And then, the events in the throne room had been really fun. She wished Brennan's phone hadn't run out of battery power because it would have been so funny to have video taped it and watched it later! Of course, she had to escape with Brennan, so she knew they had missed much of the action, but she was sure it had been as funny as the first few moments had been! Being an Angeluscustos could be frightening at times, but at other times it could be really entertaining, she thought.

They had continued moving to the north, keeping west of the river and therefore away from the main road where they might encounter curious travelers. Now Julia remembered that when Lord Bernald had brought them from the Meadow of the Larks to Charlesville, the river at been always at their right.

Now, going back toward the Meadow of the Larks, it should have been on their left, not the right! They were on the wrong side of the river to traverse the narrow ravine between Mittewald and Nidwald! She also realized that the water seemed to be running faster now as they gradually descended toward the Great Sea.

"Arabella," she asked, apprehensively. " Shouldn't we ford the river before it gets any deeper and stronger?"

"Oh, don't worry," Arabella answered, "We'll come to another road soon that joins the main road, and we can cross on the bridge."

"Good thing. The water looks a lot rougher here than back when we crossed it before."

"It runs north toward the sea here. See that mountain peak that looks like a man's face?" Arabella motioned with her nose.

"Yeah, I see it."

"Just beyond that the mountain range breaks and the valley carries the river down through Meerwald and to the sea. Behind us to the south are the Vautrais Mountains and to the north and east ahead of us is the Annecy range. The valley slopes downward and the river runs faster as it goes down," Arabella explained. "One of the roads to Meerwald follows the river but on the east bank, and a lot of wagons go that way with goods to be shipped off. That's why the bridge. We'll be to the bridge shortly. It's just past this grove of trees."

"How much longer to the Meadow of the Larks?"

"Another couple of hours or so at this pace. But we're pretty well rested. We can move faster once we've crossed through the ravine."

They were soon through the copse, the kids dodging low hanging branches with ease at the walking pace of the horses, but as they broke into the open again Julia pulled Arabella to a stop, halting everyone.

"What's wrong, Julia?" asked Brennan.

"Look! There's the bridge we need to cross and that looks like men guarding it."

"Brennan?" Emma asked. "Are those the duke's men?"

"I'm afraid they are," Julia answered.

Brennan was dubious. "I don't see how they could have beaten us here. They couldn't have caught the horses this quickly."

"I don't know either," Julia argued, "but look. They're searching that wagon."

And indeed, the men had stopped a wagon and seemed to be looking it over carefully. As they waved the wagon on across the bridge, Julia turned Arabella back into the trees. "Let's get out of sight before they notice we are here," she urged.

Brennan and Emma quickly followed suit, the three of them dismounting and creeping closer to the edge of the grove on foot to watch. As they watched, a solitary rider approached at a canter on the main road and two of the half dozen men quickly mounted horses to intercept him, even though he was obviously not coming towards the river bridge. The kids observed as the rider was stopped, apparently questioned, and then allowed to proceed unmolested. Brennan pulled his sisters back, deeper into the trees.

"Arabella?" he asked. "Is there another way across the river?"

"There's a ford a ways back," Arabella answered, "but the ravine is narrow into Nidwald, scarcely wider than the river and the road. If the duke's men are guarding the bridge, they will have the road through the ravine closed off completely."

"Is there another way through?" Brennan pressed?

"Maybe a goat trail over the mountain, but nothing that I would know about!" Arabella sniffed.

Emma looked at her brother and sister. "Then what do we do now?"

Brennan and Julia looked at each other and then Brennan sighed. "We find a safe place to rest and think. We have to figure out how to get word to the Gwencalon. Maybe we can cross over the mountain somehow."

"But how?" Julia asked. "We don't know these mountains; we don't know where trails might be!"

"I don't know, Julia. I just don't know."

15 A TEMPORARY CHANGE IN PLANS

The three led their horses through the trees away from the guarded bridge, remounting as they reached the open meadow once more. Brennan pulled himself into the saddle with great effort, hoping that the girls hadn't noticed. In addition to hurting badly, his arm had started to bleed again. They needed to get somewhere more secure so he could have the girls bandage his arm again to stop the seeping. Not only was it making him weak, he feared leaving a blood trail that a tracker might find and follow. He turned Rouget away from the trees and back the way they had come. Some scattered farmhouses on the far side of the river, smoke curling from their chimneys, suggested warmth and possible help.

Julia had noticed how slowly and laboriously Brennan had dragged himself up into the saddle and how he slumped, swaying a bit as he rode. She, too, had noticed the farmhouses and although they could house supporters of the Duke, she felt they had no choice but to stop at one. Brennan needed rest and food. She imagined that his arm was very painful and the hard ride they had coming down the mountain could not have been easy on him. She made sure she rode close by his side in case he should need support. Emma, following Julia's lead, moved Minuit up on Brennan's other side. And so they rode for a while.

The ford, when they reached it, was shallow, but the water rushed across the rocky river bed and each of the horses lost its footing at least once as they picked their way across. But by some miracle, none of the three Wests fell off, although Brennan seemed to sag even lower on

Rouget's neck. They headed toward a scattering of farmhouses just a little ways beyond the river, and Brennan roused himself enough to ask, "Do any of you horses know the people who live here? Are they loyal to the royal family, do you suppose?"

Arabella answered first, her position as the late queen's horse still giving her status in the stables.

"I know no one this far from the castle. Rouget? Minuit?"

"No," Rouget answered. "I've been through here before, but I don't know anyone."

"Neither do I," Minuit responded. "Still, I'd think chances are that they remain loyal. Most everyone except those who live in the Duke's own lands in Meerwald would be die for members of the royal family."

"Then let's stop here," Julia concluded, looking at Brennan from the corner of her eye. "I for one am tired of riding and getting really hungry. Maybe they will feed us."

"I'm hungry too," Emma piped in.

As they turned toward the farmhouse, Julia noted that it was different from the village houses. Several stories high, it had wide doors on the ground level that stood open, giving her a good view of piled straw just inside the doors. A man stood in the doorway watching their approach, a lanky brown dog at his feet, his hackles raised. The farmer's wrinkled face was clean-shaven below a narrow brimmed green hat with a jaunty feather in its hatband. Dressed in brown trousers, well-worn boots and a green jacket much like the one the kids were wearing, he had a pitchfork in his right hand and his left rested on the head of the softly growling dog. As they came to a stop before him and he saw who they were, he leaned the pitchfork against the door, and moved forward to great them, quieting the dog with a soft word.

"Afternoon, youngsters. What can I do for you?"

Julia spoke quickly, forestalling Brennan who was beginning to sway in the saddle. "We are Angeluscustos, called by the Gwencalon to protect the prince. My brother was injured and needs food and rest. Can you help us?"

The farmer stared at them for a moment and then repeated "Angeluscustos? Here?" in a wondering voice. Then, as if shaking himself from a dream he assured her, "Yes, yes," and hurried to Brennan's side to help him dismount.

"Pietre," he called. "Come take care of these horses." A young boy of perhaps ten ran from the depths of the barn to gather up the reins of the three horses as the girls also dismounted. "Come inside, young Angeluscustos, and we'll take care of this young man. Come, come!"

He led them up a stairway, supporting Brennan who was clearly unsteady on his feet. As they crossed a balcony, the dog hard on their heels, he pushed open the door and called out to his wife that they had company. She came into the room, wiping her hands on her apron to gasp in dismay at the sight of Brennan, drooping at her husband's side.

"Bring him to Pietre's bed, Hans. What is the matter, young man?"

"I, someone cut my arm yesterday. I think it has started bleeding again," Brennan answered. "Please, I don't want to bleed on the bed," he objected as Hans led him to the bed.

"No fear," the woman assured him, taking off her apron. "I will lay this on the bed under your arm while I look at that wound. Help him off with his jacket, Hans."

Emma and Julia stood with Hans on one side of the bed while an embarrassed Brennan submitted to the assistance of Hans and his wife as they removed his jacket. His torn shirt, like his jacket, was caked with blood, some of it obviously fresh and some of it dried and black. The farmwife scurried back to the kitchen for hot water and clean linens and then she gently soaked the shirtsleeve away from the wound so Hans could help Brennan out of it.

"Is it infected, Greta?" Hans asked his wife as she carefully inspected the long, jagged cut.

"No, it doesn't seem to be. Someone has put honey and sugar on it and stitched it up, but the horseback ride has opened it back up a bit. I'll put more honey on it and bind it up again and it should be fine until tomorrow. Then the wraps will need to be changed again and new honey applied." She left again to bustle into the kitchen for a jar of honey and two smaller jars.

"I've put more honey in this jar for you to take with you for tomorrow," she explained. "In here," she lifted the second stoppered jar, "is some laudanum for the pain. Give him two drops in water when the pain gets bad, but no more." She handed Brennan a pewter mug to drink from. "I've put a couple of drops in some cider for you now, because it must be hurting now."

Brennan grimaced. "It is rather. Thank you." He chugged down the cider as she cleaned, doctored and rewrapped his arm. Emma and Julia had watched with various expressions on their faces. Julia's was first filled with regret and guilt that she could not have prevented the injury, though of course there was nothing she could have done, and then with relief that it was not infected. Emma was concerned that Brennan was suffering from the arm, but also curious at the use of honey as an antiseptic.

"Ma'am," she began, as Greta finished binding the arm and tied the fabric ends together, "why use honey?"

"Call me Greta, Lady. It's an old remedy for wounds and burns and it seems to work very well. Somehow it prevents dirt from getting into the injury and those who use it recover more swiftly and with fewer complications."

"Hmm." Emma mused. "The bees must create something that kills germs and bacteria."

"What are germs and bacteria?" asked Hans.

"Tiny invisible things in dirt and even in the air that cause infections," Julia put in. "We use all kinds of creams in our world to kill them in wounds, but no one I know has ever used honey. That is so cool!"

Greta frowned. "Oh, it doesn't need to be cool. Just use it right out of the jar."

Brennan interrupted the conversation by swinging his legs off of the bed.

"Here, what do you think you are doing?" Greta asked him. "Lie back down and rest!"

"I'll be fine now," Brennan insisted. "We need to tell you what is going on and ask for some advice."

"Then come into the kitchen," Hans suggested. "At this time of day, it is the warmest as Greta is preparing our evening meal."

"Yes, and you must join us," Greta urged. "No one leaves this house hungry!"

They had soon gathered around the roughhewn table in the cozy kitchen, each with a mug of warm cider in their hands. The three introduced themselves, and then Hans began the discussion with a question that had nagged at him since Julia had announced they were Angeluscustos.

"If you are Angeluscustos, called by the Gwencalon, then the Gwencalon, the real Gwencalon, isn't dead after all?" he asked.

"No," Brennan replied. "He was saved from drowning and is in hiding."

"And he feels that the Duke will try something on the Prince's birthday to prevent the Landsgemeinde from declaring him king?"

"Yes, Sir," affirmed Brennan. "He sent for us, four of us, to rescue the prince from the castle and take him to safety. Someone at the castle betrayed us to the Duke and Lord Gabin pretended to be the prince. We had to split up, two of us with the real prince and two of us pretending to believe that Lord Gabin was the prince. But the Duke's men came after us and Lord Gabin knifed me as Julia escaped. Then she and Emma returned to the castle to rescue me while Hannah, our other sister, took the prince to safety."

Hans and Greta listened in silence. Then Greta asked, "But how did you come to be here? We are far from any main road and far from the castle."

"Running from the castle, we crossed the ford at the village near the castle to get as far off the main road as possible. We need to get to the Meadow of the Larks in NIdwald," Julia explained, "but the Duke has men guarding the bridge over the river and we don't know how else to get there. Then Brennan was getting weak again, so we knew we needed to find a safe place to hide for a while. We found your farm," she ended simply.

"But we don't want to endanger you," Brennan hastened to say. "So if you can tell us where to head, we'll leave you in peace."

At that moment, PIetre came into the kitchen, taking off his coat, and introductions were made around the room. Pietre was obviously excited to be with the Angeluscustos and he could not take his eyes off of Brennan, eyeing his bandaged arm with admiration.

Hans quickly related to Pietre what the Angeluscustos had told him. Then he paused a moment in thought. Then he continued, "I hate to send you out again, PIetre. But the Duke's men may come by looking for these three. I want you to ride Bessie and take their horses down to the ravine. Tether them there and walk back. It shouldn't take you longer that half an hour, and if anyone comes looking for the Angeluscustos, the horses won't be here to betray their presence. You can take them over the mountain into Nidwald, can you not?"

"Of course," PIetre responded, pleased with the task his father was entrusting him with. He hastily put his coat on again. Greta kissed her son and assured him she would keep his meal warm until his return. With a final look at the Angeluscustos, Pietre left to hide the horses, anxious now to get them quickly out of sight. Hans took the kids to a storage room behind the kitchen, pulled back a rug, lifted a trapdoor, and guided them down a wooden ladder that descended into the barn below.

"We use this in the winter," he explained, "so we can care for the animals when the snow is too deep to walk through. I intend to send

158

Pietre as your guide, but should anyone come before he returns, you must grab your things and go down this ladder. You will need to do it in the dark because we won't be able to chance them seeing a light." He showed them a surprisingly light trunk that, when slid to the side, revealed the opening to a tunnel.

"The trunk must be pulled back in place from inside the tunnel," he cautioned. "Then if you follow the tunnel to its end, it will open into the ravine where your horses await you. Ride to the end of the ravine and then continue to head north. Keep out of sight of the road, but make sure you are traveling parallel to it. As you near the ravine between Mittewald and Nidwald, the mountain on your right will come ever closer to you. When you can go no farther without returning to the road, stop and wait for Pietre. He will come to guide you into Nidwald."

Brennan and the girls nodded their understanding and they climbed back up to the storage room and into the kitchen where Greta was just setting out the evening meal, a meaty stew served with thick bread and butter. By the time they had finished and the girls had helped Greta clear away the dishes, Pietre was back and ready to hungrily attack his own food.

During the meal, Greta and Hans had asked more questions about the rescue of the prince and about the world they came from. With Pietre's return, however, Hans returned to the subject of the Landsgemeinde and the trouble that the Gwencalon must expect. The kids could supply no more information to Hans, but from him they discovered that Lord Bernald had sent soldiers around the country warning the men to come armed to the assembly.

"Not obviously, you understand," he explained, "but we must be prepared to defend ourselves and our prince if the Duke tries to keep control through force. Rumor has it that he has even called in some Kummerians to help his own men 'encourage' us to vote as he wishes." He slapped the table with his palm. "We will not stand for that! The prince is royal blood. The duke is not, though he will argue to the contrary.

His great, great grandfather was a, shall we say, a love child of the king's great, great grandfather and a young farm girl from Meerwald. The king's great, great grandfather could not marry the commoner, of course, and legitimize the boy, but he did make him a Duke and gave him lands in Meerwald. So he is descended four generations back from an ancestor who was only half royal blood and he himself is not well-liked, even though his sister was wife to the late king and mother to our prince."

"So the late king married a cousin?" Julia asked, aghast.

"'Tis a common thing for nobles to marry first cousins," Hans answered. "But the queen would have been related only through her great, great grandfather. That is pretty distant. The only problem is that her brother would be himself king."

At that moment, the dog, who had been lying in front of the fire, sleepily watching his master as he talked with the Angeluscustos, began to growl. The whinny of a horse sounded from the yard and they heard the sound of voices in the courtyard.

"Go!" Hans ordered in a loud whisper as rough pounding sounded at the door. A loud voice called, "Open up to the Duke's men and be swift about it!"

Emma, Julia and Brennan quickly arose and grabbing their Schulmappes and cloaks, they hurriedly followed PIetre to the storage room. As they carefully climbed down the ladder, Pietre followed them, pulling the trapdoor carefully shut above him. Then they could hear the soft thud as Greta replace the rug and quietly shut the storage room door.

Hans' voice called, "Patience, patience! I am coming! I cannot move as quickly as I once could."

They had all reached the bottom of the ladder before they heard the scuffle of booted feet on the ceiling above their heads. Pietre quickly moved aside the trunk and guided them into the low opening, first Emma, then Julia, Brennan and finally he, himself. Voices came faintly as he quietly pulled the trunk back into position.

"What is this?"

"Only a storage room, my lord."

"You, search it! And where do these stairs go, man?"

"To the attic, my lord, but there is nothing up there but old trunks and broken furniture."

"Up here men! Quickly now!"

Hans' voice came again, "You are wasting your time, sir. No one is up there."

"We will judge for ourselves!" The authoritative voice said harshly and Pietre pushed Brennan. "We must go now!"

Brennan fumbled for Emma and Julia's hands in the dark as Pietre eased past them to take the lead. Emma grabbed his arm as he passed her and clung to him as he hurried them deeper into the dank tunnel. Soon they heard nothing but the quiet shuffling of their feet on the dirt floor, the sound of their nervous breathing, and the occasional scuttle of tiny feet scurrying away from them.

"Are those rats?" Julia whispered in a horrified voice.

"No, we are only field mice," came the plaintive answer. "Please don't hurt us!"

"We aren't going to hurt anyone," Brennan assured the voice.

Pietre, who didn't understand mouse speech, hissed, "What are you talking about? Please continue to be still!"

"Nothing, Pietre, sorry."

"Here," Pietre finally said, stopping. "I'm going to look outside to make sure no one is about. Wait for me to return."

The three waited in silence while Pietre crawled out beneath some bushes and disappeared into the night. Soon, however, he returned and ushered them out.

"No one is around. I saw the duke's men ride away from the farm heading toward the Bruner's farm. We should be well on the way to the bridge before they have finished there."

The moon was rising into the clear night sky, lighting their way through the ravine. Brennan appreciated the light as they dodged stones and rocks along their way, but he feared that their passage through the night once they left the shelter of the ravine would be visible for miles around them. Still, it could not be helped. They couldn't simply wait to be found. Their only hope now was to reach the mountains before their passage was detected.

Several hundred yards into the long ravine they came upon the horses, who seemed glad to see them. Even Pietre's Bessie looked at them with interested curiosity, suggesting to Julia that Arabella and the other two had spent the time relating their exciting exit from the castle to the other horse. They mounted in silence, but Julia, who had begun to think of the horses as part of their team, quietly explained to the horses where they were heading, much to the astonishment of Pietre.

"Why are you explaining our plans to the horses?" he asked.

"Because they are our friends," Julia explained. "And because they can understand us."

"Can they understand me, too?" he queried?

Arabella answered that one herself. "Sometimes we can, but not always. Your speech is difficult for us."

"She says sometimes they can and sometimes they can't," Emma translated. "We Angeluscustos can converse with all animals, just as the Gwencalon can," she explained. "It is quite helpful at times!"

"I should imagine so," Pietre returned. "Well," he turned Bessie to the north and started her moving. "We'd best get going. We need to reach the mountains as soon as possible. We'll be easy to see in this moonlight, but then, we'll be able to see the Duke's men, too. Come on."

And with that, they began picking their way to the end of the ravine where the ground rose gradually to the level of the meadow. There they turned away from the river and the road to begin picking their way through fields and woods.

ELIZABETH ANDERSON

16 HAPPY REUNIONS

Hannah found her second ride on the Dragon de Neige less intimidating than her first, mostly because the sun was out and she could see where they were going. Still, she looked out and down rather than straight down. The view was incredible and the feel of the wind in her face, ruffling her short hair, was exhilarating.

The sun sparkled off the snow-tipped mountains like diamonds sprinkled on a wedding dress, a stark contrast to the still green fields below. Like a patchwork quilt the mowed and uncut fields spread out between the mountains, connected here and there by silver ribbons of river and streams. Along the mountains, tumbling waterfalls fell in torrents from the rocky massive and she wondered which one was the wonderful waterfall that connected this world to her own. Luckily the Gwencalon and Mr. Higgley would know, because she could never pick out the correct one from among so many.

In only a few minutes the ride was over and the Dragons de Neige were landing neatly on the high meadow from which they had left a few days ago. With a new appreciation for the feelings of animals, Hannah thanked her mount for a safe and comfortable ride to which the dragon replied with a courtly bow of his head and a friendly smile that displayed an impossible number of sharp teeth.

Lord Bernald and Prince David were walking ahead with Sachi and Hannah hurried to catch up with them. She was pleased to see Lord Bernald's arm across the prince's shoulders as they talked animatedly. He had seemed so lonely in her dream and had sounded so bitter when he spoke of the jealousy within a royal family. Lord Bernald was only his godfather, she knew, but he seemed to genuinely care for the prince and that cheered her considerably.

They returned again to the home of Ugo and Amea, this time passing through a village that was very much alive with chattering Barbegazi who all bowed as the prince walked past. The men were polishing bows, or sharpening their short swords on stone wheels that they turned by pushing wooden peddles thrust through the stone. They were obviously preparing for war and Hannah felt chilled at the implications.

The women had paused from their chores to hold their awed children back out of the way as Lord Bernald, the prince, and Hannah passed, and she realized from the whispers of "Angeluscustos" that her presence awed them nearly as much as that of the prince. She felt humbled and inadequate. Her apparent skill of putting individuals to sleep seemed impossibly meager and she feared that they would expect far more from her than she could ever give. Then immediately she felt guilty for feeling unequal to whatever might come. God had sent her. He would provide her with whatever tools she needed when the need arose.

When they entered the house, Amea met her with a hug and helped her off with her coat before handing her a mug of warmed cider. The small room was so crowded with people that the new arrivals could scarcely walk. The Gwencalon was seated before the fire with Ugo and several men dressed in rich fabrics and wearing wide metal necklaces such as Lord Bernald wore, each adorned with semi precious stones. She realized she must be looking at the noblemen of Serenia.

As Amea faded into the background, the Gwencalon announced, "Gentlemen, Lord Bernald has brought us one of the Angeluscustos and our prince, Prince David."

The others rose as one and bowed low to their prince and nodding their heads to her before showing him to the preferred seat by the fire, and ushering her into the one next to it. Then with many smiling faces and congratulations to Lord Bernald for bringing the prince safely here, they settled down again, noblemen and Barbegazi elders, to discuss how to proceed.

The Gwencalon began. "Lady Hannah, my dear, I know that you are worried about the others so I am happy to tell you that word has come that they have fled the castle and should arrive here tonight." Hannah smiled in relief. "Now, Lord Bernald. If you will give us your news."

Lord Bernald leaned forward and began. "As you already know, I waited for the Angeluscustos and the prince outside the castle, and I witnessed the arrival of about 50 men from Kummer."

"From Kummer?" came a shocked query from one of the lords.

"Yes, from Kummer. A loyal castle servant was able to overhear their leader's conversation with the Duke and so we now know most of the Duke's plans for Wednesday. He had intended to starve Prince David to death and present the Landegemeinde with the prince's body," he said to gasps of horror from those around him.

"Unfortunately for him, he waited too long to put his plan into action and the Angeluscustos rescued the prince before it was too late. The prince was weak, but as you see," he paused to smile at his godson, "my filleul is very much alive!"

The prince nodded and smiled. "Thanks to you, Parrain, and to Hannah here and the other Angeluscustos! I shall be forever grateful to them."

Hannah blushed, but said nothing.

Lord Bernald continued. "But the Duke had a secondary plan. He has made a pact with King Reichter of Kummer. He will allow them free passage through his lands in exchange for their support of him as our next king."

"What!" one nobleman exclaimed. "How can the Kummerians support his candidacy?"

"With their soldiers," Lord Bernald answered grimly. "They have already sent the squad of 50 men to the castle for the Duke's use and a larger group awaits in the south near Engle's Pass to march on the Landsgemeinde to subdue our people if they will not voluntarily elect the Duke as king."

Angry and dismayed cries arose from both the men and the Barbegazi.

"This means war!" cried one of the noblemen.

"What must we do?" asked another nobleman. "The Landsgemeinde is scheduled for Wednesday morning and it is already Sunday evening. That gives us little enough time to raise the army."

"I don't suggest we try to raise the army," Lord Bernald objected. "You are correct that we have little time. But even worse, the men attending the Landsgemeinde will be trapped in the town square. A dozen archers on the rooftops or upper balconies could kill many of our people. I want to avoid that at all costs."

"So then, what?" queried another. "What do you suggest?"

"I have already taken the step of sending word to as many villages as possible, warning the men to come armed to the Landsgemeinde. As you know, Ugo is the headman of this Barbegazi village. He has promised us his assistance and that of some other Barbegazi groups. I suggest that with their support, we take a party of as many horsemen as we can quickly assemble to meet the Kummerian forces in the south. With the Barbegazi supporting us from the air, we can drive their forces back."

One of the noblemen, a bearded man of middle age, leaned forward. "So, Bernald. Without the Kummerian forces, the Duke will have only his own men to control the assembly."

"His own men and the fifty or so men that King Reichter has already sent to the castle. But because we can guess what he intends, we can prepare with our own men and the Barbegazi to forestall them."

Now Ugo entered the conversation. "We Barbegazi are as anxious to see Prince David on the throne as you are. You can count on our full assistance."

There were murmurs from the noblemen as they debated the merits of the plan. Then the Gwencalon interrupted them, saying, "And of course will we have the Angeluscustos healer with us to deal with any injuries our men may receive."

Hannah straightened up, looking startled. Realizing suddenly that they Gwencalon was referring to her. "But, no, that is not my gift," she objected.

The Gwencalon smiled at her. "But Lord Bernald saw the two men you put to sleep, my dear. And what is sleep but the relaxing, healing process of the body? Yes, when he saw that, he knew that you were the one."

"But" Hannah began.

"My dear Lady Hannah. The very first Angeluscustos had the gift of healing and so have the Angeluscustos ever since."

"But my dad never mentioned that when he told us about the first Angeluscustos."

"An Angeluscustos does not brag about his, or her, gifts, my dear. But you are most certainly a healer. You will go with Lord Bernald and the others to insure that none of our men die in the battle if battle there must be."

"You don't think there will be a battle, then?"

"Oh, not much of one anyway if the others get here in time. Your brother has a very useful gift that will turn any battle to our favor. Let us wait and see."

Lord Bernald interrupted. "Pardon, Gwencalon, but we can not wait too long. It is a long ride to where the Kummerian forces wait and we only have two days to get to them, turn them back, and return for the Landsgemeinde."

169

"Patience, patience, Lord Bernald. All in due time," the Gwencalon soothed. "For now, let us all have some food and rest while we await the others."

Hannah could never say later exactly how the hours passed. Obviously the prince was still physically weak, but emotionally he seemed recharged. Everyone wanted to talk with him, clap him on the back, shake his hand. Amea kept a plate of food in front of him and he ate hungrily in between answering the questions that his lords kept eagerly thrusting at him. He described the changes he had observed in the personnel of the castle, including who was still loyal to him and who was not, making sure they understood that Bruno had betrayed the Angeluscustos to his uncle.

He ably enumerated the number of guards that the Duke had called to the castle and where they had been stationed until the time that the Duke had ordered him locked in his rooms. The men, already angry at the Duke's perfidy and his traitorous agreement with Kummer, grew steadily more furious as the prince related his treatment for the last few weeks, especially in the dungeon.

Hannah, witnessing their fierce loyalty and their unwavering resolve to secure the kingdom for their prince, thought she would not want to be aligned with the Duke in the coming struggle.

No one, in the course of the afternoon, paid any more attention to her except Amea, who came to sit with her from time to time "letting the men talk about what men talk about when they get together." Hannah hoped she would be included in the discussion of their battle plans, but for now she was content to listen to Amea, who asked her questions endlessly about home life and food in her own world.

She was intrigued at the thought of a machine that washed clothes for you and wondered if perhaps Ugo could rig something up like that, perhaps with peddles like the knife sharpeners. She could not believe, however, that a machine could adequately clean dishes. That, she concluded, was something better done by hand. "Some food must simply be scraped off," she argued. "Surely a machine would scrape too hard and break the dish!"

Hannah learned, in turn, that Amea had only recently married the young chief of the village, and that in addition to being madly in love with Ugo, she was also proud of her new status as his wife. Hannah especially wanted to know why the Barbegzai lived in the mountains and not in the valleys with the other Serenians, and Amea cheerfully explained.

"It has been thus for generations," she began. "We do not look like them, for one thing. They are so much taller and have small feet and naked skin! For a long time they despised us because we were different, but for the last several hundred years we have gotten along much better.

We live high on the mountains because it is more peaceful here and because we are well suited to the cold and snow. Our long hair keeps us warm, and our large feet allow us to move easily over snow. The men farm on the lower slopes of the mountains during the summer, raise some cattle, some chickens, and some pigs. During the winter they make weapons and leather goods and we women weave rugs and tapestries that we sell in the villages in the valleys. We keep watchmen who hold vigil over the valleys and warn the villagers of impending avalanches and other dangers with a series of loud whistles. In return, the people in the valley provide us with fruits that will not grow up here and pottery that their women make from the river mud."

"And you have the Dragons de Neige," Hannah contributed.

"Yes, the Dragons de neige also fare better in the snowy regions of the high alps. We take care of them and they provide us with quick transportation to the valley when we must go there. Oh, but excuse me. I must see about the evening meal for everyone."

"May I help?" Hannah asked.

"Oh, no, Lady Hannah, you are an honored guest!" Amea answered, shocked.

"Please, Amea. I feel useless, and besides, having something to do will help me stop worrying about my brother and sisters. The Gwencalon said they won't be here for several hours. Keeping busy will help the time pass more quickly for me. Please."

Amea looked at her for a moment, and then smiled. "Yes, of course, you may help" and the two moved into the kitchen area where Amea put Hannah to work peeling and slicing vegetables.

The afternoon wore on. Amea and Hannah finished preparing an elaborate meal and handed out plates to everyone before sitting down with their own. Hannah had quickly grasped that women were usually excluded from men's discussions and that the men felt more comfortable when she was not sitting in their midst. It rankled for a 21st century young women, but this was their world, not hers. She would do what she could when the Gwencalon called for her help. In the meantime, she courted acceptance and approval by staying in the background and helping Amea.

As if he could read her thoughts, the Gwencalon looked over at her as she sat beside Amea and said, "Lady Hannah, we do not mean to ignore you. You have done wonderful things so far and your help later will be invaluable. However, now we discuss what changes Prince David will need to make once he assumes the throne. You, my dear, would be terribly bored." He smiled. "When the others arrive, we will discuss our plans for dealing with the Kummerians and for the day of the Landsgemeinde. Then you and the others will be included for we will need your skills badly."

Hannah nodded. "I'm fine," she assured him. "I just wish the others would get here!"

The Gwencalon frowned. "Yes, I thought they would have been here by now, also." He turned to Ugo. "Ugo, can you send someone out to look for the other Angeluscustos? We should have had word of their arrival in the Meadow of the Larks by now."

"I will see to it at once, Gwencalon," Ugo responded with a quick look at Hannah. "Don't worry, Lady. We would know if they had been caught again." He grinned. "We have spies at the castle, remember!" He threw on a jacket and hastened out the door, sending a blast of cold night air to set the flames dancing in the fireplace.

Hannah and Amea had finished washing the dishes and clearing away the bits of food that remained by the time Ugo returned. He caught

Hannah's eye before announcing to the Gwencalon that the Angeluscustos had been found.

"They are coming across the mountains rather than down the valley. The duke has posted men at the ravine and they went north to miss them. I have sent men with mounts to meet them and bring them on. They will be here in a matter of minutes!"

Hannah sank thankfully into her chair, reluctant to admit that she had been worried, but elated nonetheless that they would soon be here. The others talked excitedly among themselves and Hannah realized that with the arrival of her siblings, the actual business of this group would finally get under way.

Ugo explained that he had ordered fires lit in the council hall that had a long table big enough to seat all of them including all four Angeluscustos. As soon as the others arrived, they would move to that building to begin their serious discussions. Although it probably took only a few minutes, it felt like an hour to Hannah before the door burst open and Emma, Julia, and Brennan burst through, followed by a shy young boy who was clearly intimidated by the crowd in which he found himself.

"Hannah!" Emma squealed and the three all tried to hug her at once. "We have had such an adventure! Julia made herself invisible and I let myself be captured and then the rats and the cat and dog helped and all the horses and we rescued Brennan!"

"Yeah, Hannah! It was pretty cool!" Brennan chimed in.

"Yeah, you should have seen Lord Gabin when the rat was on his shoulder and the cat was climbing his leg!" Julia added.

"Oh, it sounds exciting!" the Gwencalon interrupted. "But now we must get you something to drink. And who is this young man?"

"Oh," Brennan said. "This is Pietre. We stopped at his father's farmhouse because my arm was bleeding again and so he brought us here."

"Oh, I forgot Julia said you had been injured!" Hannah gasped. "Let me see it. Maybe Amea can do something for it."

The Gwencalon looked at her meaningfully. "Maybe you should do something about it, Lady Hannah! Take him into the bedroom. Amea will set out some cider and the others and I will go on to the Council Hall. After we have made plans, we will escort Pietre back to his father's farm."

"Only to the valley at the end of the trail where they met us," Pietre corrected him. "That's where we left our horses. I was going back to take them all to my father's farm again."

"Very well. We will take you back to the horses," the Gwencalon agreed.

At that moment, Prince David stepped forward to clap Pietre on the shoulder. "You and your family have served your country well this day," he assured him. "You certainly know that the three you brought here are Angeluscustos. They saved my life and now you have surely saved theirs. I, Prince David, thank you and I will see that you and your family are amply rewarded."

"You, you are Prince David?" the boy gasped, hurriedly bowing to him. "I am most honored to be of service to you, your Highness!"

"Indeed you have already been of service. What is the name of your father, Pietre?"

"Hans of Longmeadow," Pietre replied proudly. "He served your father the king in his last battle against Kummer."

"Then I owe him much," David smiled. "Now drink and then go take care of my horses which you left in the valley. Tomorrow we will come for them at your father's farm."

"Yes, your highness," Pietre responded, bowing again before hurrying into the kitchen in the wake of Julia and Emma who were already sipping hot spiced cider.

As the Gwencalon, the prince, Ugo and the lords departed for the Council Hall, Hannah reluctantly took Brennan into the bedroom and had him sit on the bed.

Then she had him remove his coat and took his arm in her hands.

174

She did not want to do this. What if the Gwencalon had been wrong? What if she did not have the gift of healing? What if she did this and nothing happened? What if she just did it wrong?

"What's going on, Hannah?" Brennan asked, puzzled.

Hannah was silent for a moment before answering. "The Gwencalon says that I have the gift of healing. I can put men to sleep, you see, and he says that is a by-product of the healing gift. But, I'm afraid. He sent me in here to heal your arm and tomorrow we march against the Kummerians and he expects me to heal anyone who is injured in the fighting. What if I can't, Brennan?" Her voice was anguished and her eyes sparkled with unshed tears.

Brennan, however, approached the problem logically and matter of factly. "Well, who would have thought Julia could make herself invisible or that I could call down a wall of fire? We're not the ones doing these things, Hannah. God is doing them through us. If He wants you to heal, then you must heal. If the Gwencalon is wrong," he shrugged, "well, no one is here to see but you and me!"

Hannah reluctantly agreed. "Okay. I'll give it a try." Laying one hand on the side of his arm where slight seepage from the wound could again been seen, she quietly whispered, "God, if this is Your Will, heal Brennan now." She felt a current of something run from her head down her arms and exit her body through her hand where it lay on Brennan's arm.

Brennan's arm jerked as he felt first an electric tingle run along the line of the wound followed immediately by a feeling of warmth that began in his arm and quickly filled his entire being with a wonderful feeling of well-being. After the first shock of feeling the current run through her, Hannah began to slowly unwind the bandages, and when they were removed, lifted the padded fabric that protected the wound to find, nothing. The skin was as unblemished as it had ever been. God had healed the arm.

"See, Hannah." Brennan said. "Now you know that the Gwencalon is correct and that you do have the gift of healing!" And they both were silent a moment as they individually thanked God.

Finally, Hannah said, "Let's go join the others. You need a drink after your long journey and I am sure they are waiting for us in the Council Hall." Brennan agreed, gave her another hug, with a whispered, "I have missed you, Hannah!" and then they went to the kitchen to join the others.

17 PLANS ARE MADE AND CARRIED OUT

The war council, because that, Brennan decided, was really what it was, lasted a remarkably short time. The Gwencalon opened the meeting with a short prayer to the Holy One, and then turned the meeting over to Lord Bernald. Brennan realized that he must be the most important and powerful of the noblemen in Serenia, because everyone deferred to him. Hannah had already told him that Lord Bernald was the prince's godfather, and although Brennan wasn't entirely sure he understood that relationship, he did understand that Lord Bernald cared deeply for the prince, feelings which the prince obviously returned.

Lord Bernald began by asking Ugo to pass on the information that the Barbegzai had gathered on the number and location of the Kummerians. Ugo, obviously honored by this deferment, stood on his chair so that all could see him and clearly and concisely gave his report.

The Kummerians, about a hundred in number, had camped in a small clearing near Engle's Pass which led from the border between Mittewald and Oberwald into neighboring Kummer. The pass lay only a two hour ride from the capital, Charlesville. They had managed to come undetected, except by the Barbegazi, over the mountains from Kummer, through the same pass where the prince's father and his men had been ambushed many years before. Their camp was hidden from the roads by the thick forest that grew along the foot of the mountains there. The Barbegazi normally kept to themselves and did not interfere in the disputes of the valley dwellers, but Ugo's father had been saved from a bear by the former king, and a close friendship had grown between the men. In honor of that relationship, Ugo and his people had allied themselves with the prince's cause. So the Barbegazi in the southern mountains had also sent word to Ugo about the Kummerian arrival in Mittewald. He in turn had told the Gwencalon and Lord Bernald, verifying what Duffy had overheard in the castle about the Duke's compact with Kummer.

Lord Bernald's plan was simple. Each of the Serenian noblemen had brought only a small number of men with him, so the Serenian force would be about the same size as that of the Kummerians. Thus the element of surprise would be very important. Lord Schuman, Lord Rhiener and Lord Perrault would take their men along the east edge of Mittewald to attack the Kummerians from the south. Lord Einstadler, Lord Altvater, and Lord Killian would ride into Oberwald and attack from the west. Lord Bernald, Lord Witmer and Lord Speilburg would ride the main road after bypassing Charlesville, to attack from the north.

The Barbegazi, mounted on their Dragons de Neige, would fly down from the mountains in a first wave to attack the Kummerian soldiers from the air. They were excellent archers, and Lord Bernald hoped that the sudden flurry of arrows falling on the Kummerians would cause them to attempt to flee. That would be when Brennan would come in.

A small group of Lord Bernald's men would escort Brennan to the foot of the pass to Kummer where he would create a wall of fire to drive the Kummerians back into the arms of the Serenian soldiers who would be waiting for them in the woods on all sides. Once the Kummerians had surrendered, Hannah would be brought in to heal wounds on both sides.

"We want to prevent Kummer from interfering in the Landsgemeinde," Lord Bernald explained, "but we don't want to cause a war if we can avoid it. Rather than kill, we need to capture."

"Humph!" grumbled Lord Schuman. "If they dare to come into our country to interfere in our business, they deserve anything we do to them!"

"Agreed, Schuman," Lord Witmer responded, "But we don't want our prince to have to begin his reign with a war. Lord Bernald has the right of it. Let's show some restraint here."

"All right. I suppose you are right." Lord Schuman turned to Ugo. "Do all the Barbegzai know to shoot to wound rather than to kill?"

"They know," Ugo assured him.

"What do we do with them once we have captured them?" queried Lord Killian.

"We take their leader to the Landsgemeinde to testify against the Duke. Then we send them all home, without their weapons!" responded Lord Bernald.

That comment elicited chuckles from the men around the table. Then the Gwencalon spoke. "Prince David, you and I will go with Lady Emma, and Lady Julia to the farmhouse of young Pietre's father. We will wait there for the return of our forces and go from there to the Landsgemeinde on Wednesday."

"I thought I should go with my parrain," the prince objected.

"No, Filleul," his godfather responded. "The whole point of this is to present you safe and healthy to the people on your birthday. We cannot put you in danger before that day. Half of my men will go with you, although since the farm has already been searched, I don't think you will be in danger there."

"All right, Parrain," the prince conceded. "I will do as you suggest."

His godfather laughed. "Until your birthday, Filleul, it is an order, not a suggestion!"

The prince grinned. "As you say, Parrain, until Wednesday."

Hannah and Brennan found themselves bundled back into their coats as the men intended to travel by darkness. Brennan, who had had little real rest since coming to Serenia, still found himself energized and ready to go. Hannah was unhappy at once more being separated from her younger sisters, but at least this time, she reasoned, they were with the Gwencalon, the prince, and some armed men.

The lords dispersed to collect their men who had been sheltering with various Barbegazi families. The Barbegazi would transport them to the places where they had left their horses in the valleys and then go on to the southern mountains to be ready for their part in the upcoming campaign. Lord Bernald called Hannah and Brennan to his side, and, bidding the others good-bye, they walked out into the night.

The ride on the Dragons de Neige was as bad as the first time, Hannah concluded. Everyone rode double since there were more men than dragons and in fact, the Barbegazi had to take the dragons back for the rest of the men. Brennan sat in front with Hannah's arms wrapped tightly around his waist. Again the darkness prevented them from seeing where they were going. They simply lifted off the ground and then quickly dropped through the starry night to blackness below them.

Hannah gripped Brennan more tightly until he called above the whistling wind, "Loosen up, Hannah, I can't breathe!"

Lights were on in farmhouses here and there in the valley and on the lower slopes of the mountains, and it was impossible for Hannah to distinguish between the starry night sky and the light-dotted mountains. Thankfully the ride was short and soon they had landed and were dismounting as Barbegazi claimed their dragons and took off again into the night.

Once more Lord Bernald sorted them out of the scores of armed men and pointed them to horses that were being held by one of his men. They mounted the horses, again the mountain horses, the *Einsiedler* like they had ridden that first morning, and waited for Lord Bernald's signal. After the last group of men had arrived and Lord Bernald had conferred briefly with the other lords, the men split into two groups, and moved off towards the ravine leading to Mittewald, one group on the road, the others cross country.

The ride must have lasted four or five hours and the sky was turning light gray, streaked in the east with pink, as Lord Bernald at last stopped in the lea of an arm of rock that jutted out from the mountains to nearly close the valley as it wound into Oberwald. The mountain here had sheered off in the remote past, scattering the narrowed valley with large boulders and scree. Just around the cliff, the mountains again settled into the gentler, tree studded slopes that existed in Mittewald.

It was among those trees, which extended down into the valley itself that the Kummerians had camped. Just behind them and a little to the west was the road that led up into the mountains and eventually through them to Kummer. To this road, Lord Bernald sent his lieutenant Cerles and two others with Brennan to secure the road and thus cut off retreat into Kummer.

Everyone else dismounted, securing their horses to a long rope that two of the men had hastily set up. They would proceed from here on foot, silently creeping through the trees to set up a ring around the Kummerian forces. Lord Bernald left a couple of men to stay with Hannah there in the protection of the cliff until the confrontation was over. The injured would be brought back there for her care when the fighting had ended. Hannah found a comfortable looking rock, and sat down to wait.

As Lord Bernald and the others departed on foot, the two men left with her took up positions from which they could see anyone who came their way. Hannah supposed they were unhappy at being left to babysit her rather than engage in the fight, but they showed no disappointment, simply doing what Lord Bernald had told them to do. Sighing, she settled in herself, pushing worries about Brennan and about her own upcoming duties aside. Instead, she began to pray silently that everything would go well and that no one would be killed.

Brennan was excited as he and his escort moved quietly into Oberwald. To avoid the sound of galloping horses, they walked their mounts along the road through the narrow mouth of the valley and then immediately off the road to avoid the clomp of hooves on the hard surface of the road. After a couple of miles, the group crossed the road to the mountains where they dismounted, secured their horses, and moved up onto the mountain above the road to the pass.

"Now we wait," lieutenant Cerles said to Brennan.

"When will we know it's time?" Brennan asked.

"When everyone is in place," he answered, "the Barbegazi will whistle and then begin their attack from the air. When we see them fly over, you will create the fire."

"Okay," Brennan said, taking a shaky breath. Excitement and fear of failure coursed through his body. "I can do this," he whispered to himself. "I can do all things through Christ who gives me strength," he quoted.

Suddenly a shrill, long whistle sounded through the dawn air, followed by the heavy flapping of dragon wings as dozens of Barbegazi appeared in the sky, bows at the ready. Thick pine trees shielded the clearing where the Kummerians camped from Brennan's view, but he could guess when the Dragons de Neige were over it from the flurry of arrows that the Barbegazi suddenly released in a relentless shower.

Cries of surprise and pain were quickly augmented by the clash of swords as the men in the clearing sought the shelter of the surrounding trees only to meet the armed Serenians who waited there.

"Now!" ordered the lieutenant, as a few men broke from the trees and scurried toward the road to the pass. Brennan swept his arm in an arc that crossed the base of the road, thinking of fire and saying, "Stop them!" in an authoritative voice. He was immensely relieved to see fire spring up in a head high wall before the men, driving them back into the trees. By now, the Barbegazi had ceased their flights and soon the sounds of shouts and clashing swords had also faded away. A Serenian appeared at the base of the road to wave them down, and Brennan lowered his arm, allowing the fire to die away to ash. He and the others mounted their horses, and, skirting the remnants of the fire, picked their way carefully back down to the valley.

Hannah and the men with her had faintly heard the sharp whistle of the Barbegazi and watched them dive on their Dragons de Neige to rain arrows down on the still sleeping Kummerians. The men with her became alert, but no soldiers fled their way. The Dragons de Neige gradually disappeared from the sky and soon a half a dozen Serenian soldiers appeared with orders to bring Hannah and the horses to the Kummerian camp.

"Lord Bernald says we may as well make use of it until we need to move off again," one soldier reported.

As they mounted and rode the mile or so to the camp, driving the horses with them, one of the soldiers told about the short-lived battle.

"It was a great victory," he bragged. "We had managed to capture their sentries without raising a warning, so the Kummer soldiers were all asleep until the Barbegazi whistle woke them up. Before they knew what was going on, the Barbegazi were sending arrows flying down into the middle of them. They scattered towards the woods, most of them without even their weapons, but we were waiting there, on three sides of them.

When they found us, a few of them fought, but most fled toward the pass, but were driven back when a huge wall of fire sprang up there. The ones with weapons laid them down pretty quickly then, and they all surrendered." He smiled at Hannah. "Your brother did well, Lady! Now you will take care of the few who are wounded."

"Are there many?" Hannah asked.

"No, only a handful," he answered, "and most of them not badly. All in all it was a very successful campaign!"

Hannah quickly saw that he was correct as they dismounted to lead their horses into the wooded area that protected the Kummer encampment. The clearing had no doubt seemed large enough for the company of Kummerian soldiers who were camping there, but now it was crowded with double that number of men and several Barbegazi including Ugo. The wounded had been taken to one side, Kummer and Serenian soldiers alike. The other prisoners were being roped together, their hands tied in front of them, their weapons piled onto a farm wagon that one of the Serenians had borrowed from a nearby farmer.

The soldier who had related the course of the battle to Hannah and the others took her to the group of wounded, where Lord Bernald stood talking to a tall, redheaded man with a bleeding gash in his left shoulder. As Hannah walked up, Lord Bernald noticed her and said, "Ah, Prince

Lethin. Here is our healer who will see to your wound. Then, we shall leave shortly for Charlesville."

"And my men?"

"They will be escorted to an abandoned manor house just inside Mittewald. They will be kept there until our business in Charlesville is concluded. Then, the new king will decide the fate of those who dare to interfere in the internal politics of Serenia! Now, Lady Hannah, if you please, tend to Prince Lethin first, as befits his rank."

And with that, Lord Bernald walked a little ways away to speak to one of his men who then moved closer to stand guard on the prince. Hannah realized that she could not comfortably reach Prince Lethin's wound, so she instructed him to sit down beside the other wounded.

"I do not need your aid," he told her curtly. "See to my men."

Hannah looked him directly in the eyes and responded, "The sooner you cooperate with me, I sooner I will be able to tend to your men. Again, please sit down!"

The guard took a half a menacing step forward and Prince Lethin reluctantly sat. She crouched next to him and moved aside the fabric of his shirt to see that he was bleeding from a single stab wound that had penetrated deeply into his muscle. She laid a hand on the wound and said quietly, "Be healed!" Again that mysterious current ran through her body. Prince Lethin did not move, but his eyes widened in surprise as the current entered his body. Hannah removed her hand, checked the wound site that was now unblemished skin, and stood.

"You will be fine now," she told him.

"I," he stammered, "I thought you were an apothecary!"

"I am an Angeluscustos," she corrected him. "Thank the Holy One for your healing," she admonished him as she moved on to the next wounded man, leaving him staring after her open-mouthed.

Few had actually been wounded during the skirmish, and none seriously, so Hannah completed her task in only a few minutes. Then, locating Lord Bernald, she told him that she had finished, and he thanked her with a smile.

"Find your horse, then, my dear," he told her. "I wish to retrieve the prince before mid-afternoon and we need to see the prisoners settled before then."

Hannah moved to where she had tied her horse, noticing that most of the other men had already retrieved theirs and moved out of the woods. As she untied her mount, she watched the controlled activity around her. The prisoners, roped together into a long line that now included those whom she had treated, were being herded out of the woods and into the valley proper. A few men remained behind to clear all vestiges of the camp so that it would look as if the men had left of their own accord. The wagon with the weapons had already moved out toward the road, its load covered from curious eyes by a leather tarp.

Hannah led her horse out of the woods where she met an excited Brennan, who eagerly told of his part in the rout. Mounted at last, Lord Bernald moved to the head of the column, waving for Hannah and Brennan to follow him. They in turn were followed by two of Lord Bernald's men carefully guarding Prince Lethin who alone of the prisoners had been permitted to ride.

The other lords followed closely behind, chatting and laughing among themselves, now that the campaign had been successfully ended. Two long, double columns of men aligned themselves on either side of the walking prisoners, carrying banners that designated the particular lord whom they served. In the rear of the columns came the captured horses.

It was impossible to move such an immense group secretly, especially under the clear sky of the fall morning. But it was the northern reaches of Oberwald that they moved through and the southern region of Mittewald to which they traveled, and both of those lords rode with them, their banners fluttering proudly in the breeze. No one who observed their passage would tell the Duke's men what they had witnessed.

Once through the narrow neck that served as the passage between Oberwald and Mittewald, the caravan followed the main road for perhaps and hour before turning onto a smaller road that led to an obviously abandoned manor house. The outer defensive walls, constructed of thick timber, still stood intact, but the roof had collapsed on part of the main building. Enough remained, however to provide shelter for the prisoners, though perhaps not the greatest of comfort. It developed that the lords Schuman, Rheiner, Altvater and Einstadler, who were from Oberwald, and Unterwald, would continue on to Charlesville in preparation for the Landsgemeinde.

The lords Perrault, from western Meerwald, and Killian and Witmer from Nidwald, would wait until dark to head for the capital so that the direction from which they arrived would not be remarked upon. Lord Spielburg, whose old manor house this was, would also proceed to the town openly, but not until the next morning. Lord Bernald sent half of his men to Pietre's home to get the Gwencalon, the prince, and the other Angeluscustos and take them to his manor house where he would meet them with Prince Lethin, Hannah, and Brennan.

They would move to the meadow at the edge of Charlesville on Tuesday morning to take part in the festivities that would precede the Landsgemeinde on Wednesday. Cloaked and hooded, the Angeluscustos, Prince David, and Prince Lethin would be hidden in plain sight among Lord Bernald's entourage. Several of the best archers among the Barbegazi would be with them. In the meantime, Lord Spielburg would leave a group of his men to assist the rest of the Barbegazi in guarding the prisoners.

With plans thus decided upon, the group settled in for a simple meal before the first group left for the capital. Brennan and Hannah found a sunny spot to sit, suddenly wondering after the excitement of the morning, what they would do to while away the hours until their evening departure.

"I wonder how things went with Julia and Emma?" Brennan asked.

"They had the Gwencalon with them as well as the prince and some soldiers," Hannah pointed out. "They will have had an uneventful journey and be quietly waiting for someone to come and get them."

Unfortunately, she couldn't have been more wrong.

18 A NOT SO UNEVENTFUL JOURNEY

By the time the others had left, Pietre had finished his drink and was ready to take the prince, the Gwencalon, Emma, Julia and their two guards back to his home. Some of the Barbegazi youths took them on the Dragons de Neige to a high meadow in the spur of mountains between Nidwald and Mittewald.

From there, one of them, a young bearded lad named Fiscus, would guide them the rest of the way down the mountain on foot to where they had abandoned the horses early that evening. Despite his white hair and beard, the Gwencalon scrambled over the rocks as easily as the others and despite the limited light cast by the lanterns the Barbegazi had provided them with, the descent went relatively smoothly.

Julia lost her footing once, but as she was following the prince, she only slid into him. A more experienced mountain walker, he managed to retain his footing as well as stopping her slide. He helped her up, solicitously asking after her welfare and brushing aside her apologies. The rest of the descent was uneventful. When they were near the foot of the mountain, the Gwencalon sent Fiscus home and the other six climbed the rest of the way down to the valley.

And that was when they encountered the first problem. The foot trail emptied into a small canyon formed by a rocky outcropping that swung out into the valley and curved to run horizontal to the mountain for about a hundred yards. One of the many waterfalls that peppered the mountains, anchored the canyon, emptying its water into a small pool from which a stream meandered to the river. The canyon was secluded, but had provided both plentiful grass and water for the horses. This was where Pietre, Brennan and the girls had left the horses hobbled; yet, they were no longer there.

Pietre, painfully aware that the prince had charged him with taking care of the castle horses, and equally aware that his father could not afford to lose his own horse, was nearly frantic with panic. Julia called for Arabella, but no answering whinny came back to her. The Gwencalon simply shrugged and told Pietre they would just have to walk to his father's house.

As Pietre began to lead them out of the canyon, one of the guards, a man named André, sidled up to the Gwencalon and said to him quietly, "I don't like it, sir. If someone found the horses, they may be lying in wait for us. These valleys have lots of trees, ravines, and rocks that could hide any number of men."

"Agreed, André," the Gwencalon answered. "But we have little choice. We must get to the farmhouse to meet up with Lord Bernald's men. Just be vigilant."

And they were all vigilant, creeping silently along the road, wary of every shadow and every rock, their four lanterns shaded so that they only cast light on the road before them for a foot or two. But no one appeared to challenge them. The moon was peeking from behind clouds when a mysterious pale shape appeared in the distance, starkly outlined against the dark sky. André waved them all to shelter behind some nearby rocks, but as the shape drew closer, it became apparent that it was a riderless horse.

"Arabella!" cried Julia, dashing from cover to meet the horse on the road.

"Thank heaven I have found you!" Arabella exclaimed. "Some of the duke's men found us and recognized that we were from the castle stables. When they unhobbled us, that stupid farm horse took off for home! I tried to stop him, but he wouldn't listen to me!"

Emma and the others watched while Julia carried on a short but intense conversation with the horse before returning to where they had gathered on the road when they realized the horse was alone.

"Arabella says some of the duke's men found the horses and recognized the royal brand. Pietre's horse took off for home and they took the others and followed him, leaving one man to follow us when we came back for the horses. They have set a trap at the farmhouse for us, and with the man following us, they will have us surrounded."

André and Olivier, Lord Bernald's men, spoke earnestly to the Gwencalon.

"Now that we know we are being followed, you and the others should go on with the lanterns and we will wait here in the dark until he comes," said André.

"Exactly," concurred Olivier. "He won't be expecting us if he sees the same number of lanterns moving off. We can't afford to have him behind us when we reach the farmhouse." He turned to Pietre. "How close are we to your home, Pietre?"

"About four kilometers, I'd say," Pietre answered. "There's a ravine just about halfway there where we can shelter and wait for you. If they are at the farm, they may be using my parents as hostages! We'll have to rescue them!"

Prince David agreed. "Absolutely, Pietre. We will not let your parents suffer for being loyal subjects!"

"I like your idea about catching our spy!" the Gwencalon agreed. "Lady Emma, hop onto the horse. Lady Julia, I'm afraid you'll have to walk and carry Olivier's lantern. I'll take yours, André. Good luck, gentlemen. We'll wait for you just inside the ravine so be watching for it."

"It starts just to the east of the road by a big Walnut tree that overspreads the way. The descent to the ravine is gradual at first, so just go to the east of the tree and follow the descent until you find us," Pietre instructed them hurriedly.

The prince tossed Emma up onto Arabella's back and the others started down the road again as André and Olivier melted into the darkness on either side of the road.

Emma and Arabella followed the road with the others walking in a scattered pattern behind them, trying to maintain by the placement of the lanterns the fiction that André and Olivier were still with them. They did not talk, simply moving as they had moved before, deliberately but carefully.

When at last Pietre ran up to guide Arabella past the Walnut tree and into opening of the ravine, Julia was surprised that they had reached it so quickly. She had been thinking of how to use their powers to rescue Hans and Greta, Pietre's parents, and she was anxious to convince the Gwencalon and the prince to allow Emma and her to go in alone.

Pietre led them into the ravine until the walls of the deepening canyon hid them from the road. Then he stopped, and turned to the Gwencalon. "I will go back to watch for the others," he offered. "The rest of you should wait here."

Emma slid off Arabella's back, thanking her for the ride, and then sank gratefully to the ground next to Julia. The prince and the Gwencalon sat also, glad to rest after the long walk they had finished. Julia leaned toward them and began to talk earnestly.

"Your highness, Gwencalon," she began. "Emma and I should go in to the farmhouse to find Pietre's parents and get them out. I can make us invisible and Emma can walk through walls. Anyone we are touching can do the same. André and Olivier can come with us to subdue any guards and tie them up. Then, after Pietre's parents are safe, we can go after the others, still invisible. It worked really well when we rescued Brennan!"

"Invisibility? That would certainly make things easier. I would like to help," the prince offered. "These are my subjects and they are in danger because of me!"

The Gwencalon considered for a long moment, studying the young prince. Then he nodded. "You are correct, Prince David. Lady Julia's invisibility will give you some protection, however, so you must agree to hold onto her until everyone is dealt with."

The prince grinned. "You have my word, Gwencalon!"

The Gwencalon then turned to Julia and Emma. "Be wary, my ladies. Being invisible allows you to move freely without detection, but if someone shoots or strikes with a sword, you could still be injured or killed."

"We know," Julia assured him, "and we will be careful."

At that moment, they heard the scuffle of boots on the loose rocks of the ravine and Pietre came into view with André and Olivier. Pietre was leading a horse and the others were pulling a slightly battered man between them. André shoved him to the ground, where he sat, glaring up at them through eyes that were starting to swell shut. Having no rope, they had not yet bound him, so the Gwencalon produced the sash from his robe and Pietre his neckerchief and they tied his hands securely behind him and gagged him before moving some distance away to discuss their plans.

The Gwencalon quickly explained the plan to send Julia, Emma and Prince David in first to secure Pietre's parents and to determine the location of the Duke's men. Olivier and André were shocked at the thought of sending children, even Angeluscustos children, to do a man's job. André warned that their prisoner had volunteered the information that five men waited at the farmhouse.

He and Olivier suggested that the safest way was to steal the horses back and go on to meet Lord Bernald, but Prince David pointed out that Pietre and his family wouldn't be able to go home if they didn't remove the Duke's men. Julia, never considering that Lord Bernald's men knew nothing of her unusual gift, broke into the discussion.

"Once we've gotten Pietre's parents to safety, I'll just take you two around to the Duke's men invisibly and you'll be able to capture them easily."

"Invisibly?" André questioned, shocked. "What do you mean by that?"

"Oh," the Gwencalon laughed. "We forgot that you do not know! Angeluscustos have special gifts, you know."

"Yes, yes, we know," Olivier answered impatiently. "Are you suggesting that this one can make us invisible?"

"Quite!"

The two men looked at each other and then at the tall and slender young girl who gazed back at them with clear, brown eyes. At that moment, a woman's voice called "Pietre! Oh, it is you!" And Greta and Hans appeared from the darkness of the ravine to embrace the boy as he and the others leapt to their feet.

"Mère, Père!" Pietre cried. "We were coming to rescue you!"

"No fear, my son," Hans grinned. "We rescued ourselves!"

"We are thankful that you are all right, but how did you manage to escape?" asked Prince David.

"Oh," Pietre said, abashed. "My prince, these are my parents, Hans and Greta."

"Prince David?" Greta asked in awe, sinking into a curtsy.

"Your Highness!" Hans said with a bow. "Please forgive us for not recognizing you!"

"There is nothing to forgive," the prince assured him. "My uncle has long kept me away from the people and I no longer look like the eight year old boy you must remember. No doubt you do recognize the Gwencalon, however, and these two Angeluscustos?"

"Yes, yes, of course," Hans concurred as he and Greta bobbed their heads in recognition of the others.

"How did you escape?" asked the Gwencalon, motioning for everyone to be seated again. "And can you tell us where the Duke's men are waiting?"

Hans chuckled. "These men are from Meerwald and are not so familiar with how we live here in the upper valleys!" He looked at the Angeluscustos to explain, "In Meerwald, the houses and their barns are side by side with connecting doors, but here, as you know, our barns are below our houses. Bessie came back with five men following her, a couple of hours after you had left.

They had the Angeluscustos' other horses with them. They came into the house and demanded to know where the Angeluscustos had gone, and when we said we didn't know, they locked us in the storage room. So, we opened the trap door, climbed down the ladder, and crept out through the tunnel in the barn into the ravine, and here we are!"

"And do you know where the men are now?" demanded Olivier.

"Not for sure," Hans answered. "One took the horses around behind the farmhouse to the fenced pasture, two hid somewhere in front of the house and the other two were inside with us. By now, of course, they could be anywhere."

André wrinkled his brow. "Okay. I suggest the young Angeluscustos makes us invisible and we take out the men outside the farmhouse. Then we can deal with the ones inside."

"If I might speak, sir," interrupted Julia. "I can only make you invisible if I am touching you when I am invisible. But Emma's gift is to walk through walls as if they are not there. Anyone she is touching goes through with her."

André and Olivier gawked in astonishment as Julia continued. "I suggest that Olivier goes into the house with Emma, through the stable wall in back, up the ladder, and through the storage room. That brings you out in the back of the kitchen. If the men are waiting in the front of the house, you can sneak up on them. I can take André invisibly to find and take care of the ones who are outside."

The Gwencalon nodded. "That sounds like a good plan, Lady Julia. The rest of us will bring the prisoner but stay in the rear until all is safe."

"Père," Pietre piped up. "What of the dog? Won't Chasseur bark when he hears someone?"

Hans considered. "I had forgotten about Chasseur! We had him in the storage room with us so that the men would not hurt him. We left him there, so if you go into the house through that room he will be there. Without one of us to stop him, he may attack you and he will most assuredly bark at you."

"Then I will go with them," Pietre offered. "I can climb the ladder and quiet Chasseur before he makes enough noise to let them know we are in the house with them."

"Oh, no!" Greta objected, touching Pietre's arm protectively.

Prince David tousled the boy's hair. "I think we must let him go. Once he has quieted the dog, he can keep him out of the way until my uncle's men have been subdued."

Nodding again, the Gwencalon agreed. "Indeed, Hans. We must send him."

At Greta's sound of distress, Olivier spoke. "He will be safe, Lady. Once in the house, he and the dog will guard Lady Emma in the storage room. They can escape down the ladder if things go wrong."

"They will not go wrong," André insisted. "Olivier and I served in the King's Royal Guard until the Duke brought in his own men and dismissed us. Lord Bernald took us on until the prince becomes King and has need of us again." He finished proudly, "The Royal Guard are always the best soldiers in the five cantons. We will not fail to overcome the Duke's men, especially with the help of the Angeluscustos!"

The Gwencalon turned back to the prince. "Since we have no one to rescue, Prince David, I suggest that you stay here with us. No," he said as the prince began to argue, "no arguments! You owe it to your people to remain with us."

Reluctantly, the prince nodded.

André turned to the Gwencalon. "I would suggest, Gwencalon, that we get started. Even with a moon the darkness will help us, but the darkness will soon be gone."

In the next few minutes, the group hastily arranged itself. The prince insisted that Julia and Emma should ride Arabella and Greta the other horse while the men walked with their prisoner. Led by Hans, they moved back out of the ravine and onto the road to continue their journey to the farmhouse. Quietly and with the lanterns dark, they followed the road. The moon had totally emerged at last, lighting their way from a now nearly cloudless night sky. As the road entered a small woods, Hans stopped.

"Once we leave the trees, we will be in sight of the farmhouse," he explained.

"Then the boy, the Angeluscustos, Olivier and I must go on alone," André concluded. "When it is safe for you to join us, I will signal with a lantern or send the boy to get you."

While the others settled in to wait, André, Olivier, Pietre and the Angeluscustos started out of the woods, headed for the back of the farm. To minimize the chance of being detected, André and Olivier reminded their little band of warriors to try to walk quietly and without talking. Because the moonlight cast shadows on the ground, André suggested Julia use her gift of invisibility. As they crouched together behind some rocks, Julia instructed them to hold hands and then she whispered, "Make us invisible." Olivier's eyes widened in shock, Pietre gasped, and even Emma was startled as suddenly no one appeared to be where only seconds before they had been.

And so they proceeded across the field in a horizontal line, linked hand to hand, but unable to see either their own arms or the arms connected to the hands they clasped so tightly.

19 THE ASSAULT

The sky was beginning to lighten to the gray that is still night, but hints at the coming dawn as the four attackers halted to confer within a few yards of the house. Huddled on the ground behind a stand of bushes, they were able to drop hands, and Julia became visible again. Ahead, they could barely make out the rough wooden fence of the paddock and the shapes of horses slowly moving about within it.

As they watched, a shadow detached itself from the darker shadow of the house and moved along the fence towards the back of the paddock. In quiet whispers, André directed Emma, Pietre, and Olivier to slip through the paddock and into the back of the barn as soon as he and Julia had dealt with the guard by the fence. He had gotten assurance from Emma that slipping through the wall was soundless and therefore safer than going in by the wooden door which might creak, alerting the guards to their presence.

At his signal, Julia grasped his arm and silently whispered, "Make us invisible, please!" André and Julia immediately disappeared from view, and André's voice seemed to come out of the air as it whispered, "So, then. Watch the guard. When he goes down, you three get to the barn."

"D'accord," Olivier whispered back. Then, as the grass rustled, he reached out toward where his friend and the Angeluscustos had been. Nothing remained but the cool air of the dying night. He settled back to watch the guard who had now reached the end of the paddock and was leaning against the fence as he gazed into the darkness.

Julia kept a firm hold on André's arm, hurrying to keep up with him as he moved swiftly and silently toward the guard. She could not see her outstretched arm, nor the firm, muscled arm that her invisible hand clasped tightly, and she wondered if she would ever get used to this bizarre invisibility. André slowed his steps as they neared the guard and then stopped only a few feet from him. Stooping, he felt around for a stick, a stone, something to throw, but nothing was there.

Then he felt Julia wiggling beside him and he felt her press her Schulmappe into his hand. Grasping it, he tucked it against his side with his arm, feeling for the strap with his right hand. Then, letting his hand slide to the center of the strap so that the bag was balanced evenly from his hand, he swung his arm back and slung the bag forward to arc behind the guard, bouncing off the top rail of the fence with a thwack and landing on the ground behind him with a satisfying thump.

The horses shied nervously at the sound and the guard swung around to look, swinging his flintlock rifle up to his shoulder. The scuffle of feet was almost lost in the noise of the horses, but the sentry heard André and Julia and swung back to be met by André's knee to his abdomen followed by a bruising blow to his chin as he doubled over in pain. The sentry sank to the ground, unconscious, as André pulled the rifle out of his nerveless hands. Julia caught sight of Emma and Olivier climbing between the rails of the fence and moving hurriedly through the restless horses, but then André was pulling her toward the front corner of the farmhouse in search of the other guards.

Emma, Pietre, and Olivier had crept quietly behind where they presumed André and Julia to be, watching the guard at the paddock. When a Schulmappe suddenly appeared out of nowhere to whack against the fence rail and fall to the ground, Olivier grabbed Emma's hand and broke into a run. They reached the paddock as the guard dropped to the ground.

Olivier lifted Emma over the bottom rail as Pietre scrambled over, climbing hurriedly after her. Worried at the commotion caused by André and Julia, the horses were milling around, and Emma whispered soothing words to them as she and the others moved swiftly through their midst. She thought she recognized Rouget in the throng, but she couldn't be sure in the fading night, so she just patted his nose and hurried on.

At the wall to the barn, Emma grasped Olivier's hand and whispered, "Grab Pietre's hand and don't let go of either of us! Then just keeping coming after me and don't stop!" As Olivier did as she had instructed, Emma put out her other hand, pushing it through the wall and following after it.

Olivier hesitated only a fraction of a second before following Emma closely, but Pietre was not so sanguine, resisting the pull of Olivier's hand. Olivier, however, gripping him tightly, even when he tried to pull back, yanked him through the wall behind him. Once in the barn, Pietre looked about him with wonder, surreptitiously touching his legs, his head, making sure that he was all there.

"Where's this ladder?" Olivier asked in a whisper. "We need to get into the house quickly."

"Uh, this way," Pietre answered, as he moved past the others to head for the far end of the barn. He reached for the ladder and began to climb. As he reached the top, he pushed gently on the trap door, easing it up a crack to whisper, "Chasseur! Here, boy!"

As he pushed the door open fully, Emma and Olivier could hear the scrabble of nails on the wooden floor above them and the soft whine of the dog as he greeted Pietre. Emma and Olivier joined Pietre in the storeroom, Olivier quietly easing the trapdoor back into place. Pietre quieted the dog and then turned to face Olivier for further instructions.

Olivier carefully tried the door, but it would not budge. "Lady Emma, I had wanted you to stay safely in here, but it seems I need you to get me out of here. But," he admonished her sternly, "I want you to stay back out of the way. Understand?"

Emma nodded.

He turned to Pietre. "Will that dog attack on order?"

Pietre nodded. "At my signal, he will attack anyone or anything."

"Then hold onto the dog and bring him out with us. Bien, Lady Emma. Let us get on with it!"

Emma took Olivier's hand and he grabbed hold of Pietre who had already hoisted Chasseur into his arms. She slipped her head through the door, looking to see if anyone was in view. Seeing no one, she continued out the door, followed by Olivier, Pietre, and a struggling Chasseur. Once in the kitchen, Olivier motioned for Emma to stay back and for Pietre to follow him. As they approached the front of the room, they could hear the murmur of voices from the beyond the kitchen door which was standing open. Olivier peered cautiously around the door to see two of the Duke's men crouched by windows overlooking the front of the house.

"I tell you," one of them repeated, "I definitely heard something from the corner of the house. One of us should check on the others to be sure they are okay."

The other man was reluctant to leave the security of the house, arguing, "There are three of them out there. If someone else is out there, they can deal with it. We should stay here."

"Well, then. Go get the farmer and his wife. We can use them as shields if need be."

The second man rose and started toward the hallway, prompting Olivier to hastily pull his head back.

He hurriedly pointed to the dog and then back toward the window. Pietre nodded and Olivier tucked himself behind the door. The man halted just inside the kitchen as he caught sight of Pietre holding tightly to the now growling dog, but before he could react, Olivier had caught him across the back of the neck with a chopping motion and he fell unconscious to the floor. A flash of brown fur sailed over the collapsing man and into the other room, followed by Pietre and Olivier, who paused only long enough to be sure the man by really unconscious.

The man at the window had turned and stood at the sound of his falling comrade, but the racing dog had caught him full in the chest before he could raise either gun or sword. The momentum of the dog's body had knocked him off his feet and back into the window shutter, which his head had hit with a resounding crack. Pietre stood a few feet away, watching, as Chasseur stood on the now unconscious man's chest, teeth bared within inches of the man's unprotected throat.

"Call him off, Pietre!" Olivier ordered. "Then find me some rope so we can tie them up."

"Chasseur, here!" Pietre called as he turned back to the storage room. The dog responded with a last growl at the downed man and then raced to his young master.

"Olivier needs a rope," he told Emma excitedly, hurrying into the kitchen. "Père has some in the barn. Do you think it is safe to go down there again?"

"Wait," Emma said. "See if he can use this." She had been busy while the others were dealing with the guards. As the first guard fell, she had grabbed a dishtowel that hung neatly from a peg by the sink and a knife that lay next to a partially cut loaf of bread. Even now, she was cutting and tearing the towel into strips that could be used for binding arms and legs together. Pietre grabbed some of the long strips and rushed back to Olivier.

"Emma cut these," he explained. "The only rope is down in the barn somewhere and I didn't know if I should go down there yet."

"These will work for now," Olivier agreed, and began binding the arms and legs of the second man. He had moved to the first man and was wrapping rag strips around his hands as the door burst open. Julia came through, followed by André and two of the other guards who were dragging their semi-conscious friend. In short time all five men were securely bound and Pietre, with a cheerful dog at his side, had been dispatched to alert the others who waited in the woods. Before long, the others had arrived and the now six prisoners had been settled in an underground root cellar with a heavy lock keeping the door securely latched. Greta herded everyone else into the kitchen for a quick meal of bread and cheese before they each found someplace to curl up for a few hours of much needed sleep.

20 THE CALM THAT WAS NOT CALM

The rest of the day passed uneventfully for all of the Angeluscustos and their friends. Around noon Greta stirred, preparing a light lunch of sandwiches and cider for everyone except the prisoners. The Gwencalon suggested, only half jokingly, that a little time of fasting might be good for their souls. Emma reasoned that since the Holy One had sent the Angeluscustos to save Prince David and the Duke and his men were fighting against the prince that made them enemies of the Holy One.

She strongly considered going to the door of the root cellar and quoting scripture to them to drive home the message, but then she remembered her store of memorized verses wasn't exactly huge, so maybe that wasn't such a good idea. And besides, this was a different world. Had God had to send Jesus to them also? She just didn't know, and she hated to ask the Gwencalon who was deep in conversation with André and Olivier.

Hans and Pietre had gone out earlier to feed the cattle and the horses, and had returned to eat lunch with everyone. After hearing the story during lunch of the assault on the house, Greta insisted on giving Chasseur some leftover meat as a reward for his assistance in subduing the guards. Emma and Julia both yawned frequently, and the others, too, were obviously tired after the long day and night of travel, but all were cheerful and excited as only one more day remained before Prince David was to be declared king.

In the early afternoon, Chasseur began barking from the courtyard where he had been sent to take up his normal post. A quick glance out the window told André that Lord Bernald's men had arrived to escort the prince to meet up with his parrain. Julia and Emma gathered their Schulmappes and Olivier went after the horses while André and Hans went down to talk with the escort.

In short order the girls had hugged Greta, Hans, and an embarrassed Pietre and the cavalcade had mounted up and headed southeast toward the manor of Lord Bernald. Julia and Emma rode side by side behind the prince and the Gwencalon. André and Olivier rode just in front of them with the rest of the soldiers arranged two by two behind them.

The ride was uneventful, if long. They passed several individuals, and when they turned east onto the main road through Mittewald, some groups obviously headed toward Charlesville for the Landsgemeinde. The Gwencalon, the prince, Julia and Emma wore their hoods up, as did some of the soldiers and except for respectful nods from those they passed, no one seemed to pay them any attention.

And none of them had any reason to spare more than a passing glance for the young farm lad sitting beneath a tree near the road that led to Lord Bernald's manor, eating the supper his mother had no doubt carefully packed for him that morning. Nor did they notice that after their passing, he had scurried to some trees where he had tethered a horse, nor that having mounted the horse, he had set off for Charlesville at a gallop.

Lord Bernald's manor, Ravenswood, was much like the royal castle except that where the castle was made of stone, this structure and its encircling walls were made primarily of the same dark wood as most of the houses in Mittewald. A tributary of the main river flowing through Mittewald meandered past the manor had been diverted to flow around the wall, creating a shallow moat. The main gate stood open and the group clattered across the wooden drawbridge into a cobblestone courtyard, surrounded on three sides by high wooden walls and on the fourth by the manor house itself.

Low buildings, which housed the stables, a blacksmith shop, and a fletcher's workshop where arrows were made, crouched against the walls. The manor itself was massive, soaring to three stories and surmounted at the rear by a watchtower that rose another story beyond the slate roof.

Their arrival created an uproar for Lord Bernald and his party had arrived shortly before them and he hurried out to meet them, followed by Hannah and Brennan. The greetings were heartfelt and joyous and after hugs all around and claps on the back, the party went inside where Lady Bernald's kitchen servants had just finished setting out a wonderful spread of meats, breads, cheeses, fruit, and cider.

Soon they all settled at the long trestle table in the dining hall to eat and to tell in turn the stories of their adventures since last they had been together with the Barbegazi. Unlike the prisoners at the farmhouse, Prince Lethin was treated more as a guest, and had a seat at the table with the others although two sturdy guards were stationed behind his chair and André and Olivier were seated on either side of him.

The feasting and storytelling carried on for some time, but well before midnight the guests were shown to rooms and everyone settled down for the night. The following morning, Tuesday, they would leave after breakfast for Charlesville to take part in the festivities preceding the Landsgemeinde on the following day. The men wanted to be fresh and alert, as did the Angeluscustos, for whatever the Duke might try next.

Lord Bernald had solemnly told them all that Prince David's uncle could not be underestimated. He had shown himself capable of anything. And, of course, Lord Bernald was more correct than he could have imagined.

By the time Lord Bernald and his guests were in the middle of their meal, the young farm lad was being shown into the presence of the Duke at the castle.

"Well?" the Duke asked him. "They are all there?"

"Yes," Bruno answered. "They were wearing hooded cloaks, but I'm sure I saw them all! Lord Bernald arrived first with two of the Angeluscustos. Then later came the other two with the prince and I think the Gwencalon."

"Good, good!" the Duke murmured. "That will be all for now. You have done well!"

"Thank you, your Grace," Bruno said, bowing himself out of the room.

The Duke turned to the captain of his guard. "Is our agent in place, Berkel?"

"Yes, your Grace," Berkel answered. "He went in today to sell rabbits to the cook. Then he hid. He'll unlock the small door after dark."

"Good work. Then burn the place down and everyone in it!"

"Consider it done, your Grace."

"Wait," the Duke said, as his captain started to leave. "Save the animals if you can. Those pesky children stole some of the royal horses when they escaped. I want them back!"

"As you will, your Grace!" And with that Berkel bowed and departed.

Shortly after midnight, Brennan awoke to a commotion outside of his window. Looking out he saw flames rising from the roof of one of the long, low buildings along the manor wall. Pulling on his clothes, he went next door to rouse his sisters and together they scurried down the stairs to see what was going on. The courtyard was filled with a line of men, shadowy silhouettes in the night, stretching from the fire out the now open gate and to the moat.

Men at the water's edge filled buckets with water and then passed them up the line to the fire. There, men tossed the water onto the blacksmith shop that was entirely consumed in flames before handing the empty buckets to the female servants who ran back to the moat with them. Those closest to the burning building were lit with a garish red light that faded and danced as they moved with the buckets. It was a nightmarish scene that the waning moon did nothing to ameliorate.

The Angeluscustos huddled together in a group in the courtyard, out of the way of the hurrying firefighters, but watching in horror the scene before them. Suddenly Julia realized that the fire was near the stables.

"Arabella!" she cried. "Has someone gotten the horses away?"

"Yes, yes. The horses are safe," a soot streaked Gwencalon assured her, ushering the Angeluscustos farther back from the activity. "As soon as the fire was detected, the horses were taken out of the stable and moved to a pasture outside the manor. They are fine."

"What started the fire?" Hannah asked.

The Gwencalon shrugged. "Fire remains a danger with a blacksmith shop. The fire must be banked every night and even then a spark might escape to ignite any straw or rags that might be nearby."

"Is that what they believe happened?" Brennan asked.

"It is the most logical cause."

Lord Bernald appeared at that moment, followed by the prince. "The fire is under control and will soon be out," Lord Bernald announced. "We were lucky to catch it so swiftly. The Smithy is destroyed, but the other buildings and the outer wall were not greatly damaged. I'll leave a couple of men to watch over the smoldering ruins, but the rest of us can go back to bed."

He shooed the Angeluscustos ahead of him toward the manor door, following the exhausted soldiers and servants who were trailing slowly toward the manor house. Soon the house had settled into an uneasy slumber.

After what seemed like ages of tossing and turning, Brennan found that he could not sleep. He pulled his clothes back on and slipped out into the hall. Ahead of him, another figure moved quietly along the corridor. As the figure passed a casement window, the moonlight illuminated his face, and Brennan realized that it was Prince David.

Hurrying after him, Brennan called in a loud whisper, "Your Highness. Prince David, wait."

The prince heard him and turned, smiling as he saw that it was Brennan who had called to him.

"Could you not sleep either, Lord Brennan?" he asked as Brennan reached him.

"No," Brennan admitted. "I just keep thinking that fire was awfully suspicious."

"I agree," the prince said as the two leaned against the window casing. "But why start a fire in the Smithy? It makes no sense."

"Unless it was a diversion and they have something else planned."

"Hmn. You could be right. Perhaps we should talk to my parrain."

"Yeah."

The two moved down the hallway, past the central stairs, and into the west wing where the nobleman's apartments were located. Suddenly a voice hailed them from the stairs.

"Filleuil, Angeluscustos, were you looking for me?"

The young men turned back to meet Lord Bernald as he reached the top of the stairs.

"Yes, Parrain," answered the prince.

"I was just checking to be sure that our guest, Prince Lethin, had not somehow disappeared during the commotion over the fire," he explained. "Did you two need something?"

"We were thinking, Parrain, that it is quite a coincidence that we would have a fire here tonight of all nights."

"And you think it was deliberately set for some reason? So do I. That is why I checked on Prince Lethin." He rubbed his face wearily. "But everything seems to be normal now except for that lingering smell of smoke. Funny, it seems stronger up here than below!"

At that moment, shouts, screams, and ferocious pounding began above them in the servants' quarters and as Lord Bernald and the two young men started toward the servants stairs, men and women clad in their night clothes started streaming down.

"The ceiling is on fire!" shrieked the cook, pushing a group of maids before her. "Bits of it fell onto Marigold's bed and lit her bedclothes on fire!"

The maid in question bobbed a curtsy, saying "Mary and I tried to put it out your Lordship, but it spread too quickly!"

"It's okay," Lord Bernald assured her, patting her shoulder. "Get to safety now. Filleuil, Angeluscustos," Lord Bernald ordered quickly, "Get everyone out of the rooms on this floor." As they split up, racing for opposite ends of the hallway, he turned to one of the footmen. "You, wake up the men in the barracks and get a fire line started again. Send two of them to get the prisoner and his guards and bring them to me."

The footman bowed hastily and hurried off toward the area where Lord Bernald's men were housed.

"I've counted the servants, your Lordship," a harried chamberlain assured Lord Bernald. "Everyone is accounted for."

"Good. Then get everyone downstairs and out the door," Lord Bernald ordered.

His wife, his children with their nurse, the Gwencalon and the prince came rushing from the west wing as Emma, Julia, Hannah and Brennan came from the east wing. He swept them onto the stairs and turned to follow them as a sudden shout and more screams arose from the hall below.

"Now what?" he demanded, quickly reaching the bottom of the stairs and pushing his way through the crowd of frightened and confused people, now augmented by the addition of the soldiers from the barracks. André pushed toward him, meeting him in the middle of the swirling throng.

"We can't go out the doors. There are archers out there, shooting anyone who tries to leave."

"A deliberate attack!" He grimaced in anger. "Then we'll go out through the tunnel. Do we have wounded?"

"Just three, my Lord. The others were missed. They are there by the door, waiting for the Angeluscustos."

"Good! Lady Hannah! We need you here."

Hannah, hearing her name, pushed her way through the crowd who were now starting to cough as smoke began drifting down the stairwell.

"I'll take care of them, my Lord," she assured him, sinking to her knees beside the first of the wounded men.

Lord Bernald favored her with a thin smile before pushing his way back to the stairs and moving up a few steps to shout above the noise. "Quiet everyone. We can't go out the doors, so we will go out the tunnel. Our enemy is outside the manor so we must be as quiet as possible. Once outside, don't talk, and try not to cough," he added with a small smile. "Let's permit them to believe we are as dead as they intended." He turned to Olivier. "Take the prince, the Gwencalon and Lord Brennan and lead everyone out through the tunnel. Take them to Fleinem's woods and wait there. The rest of us will catch up to you." To his anxious wife, who was closely holding his two children, he said, "Go with Olivier and help him keep everyone calm and quiet."

She nodded and reached up to lay a tender hand against his cheek. "I will do as you say. May the Holy One keep you safe!"

"May the Holy One keep us all safe this night," he answered her, giving her a quick kiss and one to each of his children. "Now go!"

As she turned and swept her children down the hall, Lord Bernald saw that Olivier had already marshaled some of the soldiers to begin herding people down the hallway that led to the rear of the manor house.

Olivier took the prince's arm and said "Let's lead them to safety, your

Highness, out the tunnel and into Fleinem's woods." With a nod, the prince grabbed Brennan, saying, "Help me be sure the Gwencalon is safe. I see that Lady Bernald and the children are already going."

"What about my sisters?" Brennan asked, holding back.

"My parrain has need of them, Angeluscustos. They will be fine. The Holy One will see to that!"

Unhappily, Brennan once more left his sisters to their tasks and helped the prince gather Lord Bernald's family, the Gwencalon, and the group of frightened maids that he was trying to calm, and together they shepherded them hastily along the corridor, down some more stairs, and into a tunnel. By now the smoke was thickening on the main floor and the crack of falling timbers could be heard from the floors above.

At that moment, a small group of soldiers came up to him escorting a hastily dressed but alert Prince Lethin.

"What do we do with him, your Lordship?" one of them asked.

Before Lord Bernald could respond, Prince Lethin said, "I thank you for remembering me. I perceive you have a fire. How can I help?"

"By going with these men and giving me your word that you will not try to escape," his lordship answered.

"You have my word," the prince assured him solemnly.

"I hold you to it," Lord Bernald responded, clasping him on the shoulder. To the others he ordered, "Keep Prince Lethin safe. Take him out through the tunnel with the rest of them."

"But my Lord," one soldier objected. "The tunnel is supposed to be secret."

"It cannot be helped," Lord Bernald retorted. "Now, go on!"

André had stayed behind with Lord Bernald, making sure that all of the others were headed toward the tunnel and safety. Hannah had ministered to the three men who had been wounded trying to escape by the doors and sent them on their way. Now she, Julia, and Emma, trying to breathe through their pulled up shirt tails, waited for Lord Bernald's instructions. Instead of sending them after the others, however, he led them to the library. Because the door had been closed, not much smoke had seeped into the room yet. There he stopped and turned to Julia.

"Lady Julia, my dear," he asked. "Just how many people does this invisibility of yours extend to?"

"I don't know, my Lord. Several at least."

"Well, we are about to find out. I want you to make us invisible and then Lady Emma, I want you to take us out through the library wall. It's far from any door so the attackers shouldn't be watching it closely. If the attackers are still out there, I want to find out who they are. And I want to check on the guards and the men who were watching the ruins of the first fire. I fear they have been killed. Let's go!"

The group formed into a line with Emma in the lead followed by Lord Bernald, Hannah, Julia, Brennan, and André. Julia whispered a prayer, and as they faded from view, Emma said, "Now, don't let go!" and pulled them all through a gap in the wall where no bookcases stood.

Outside most of the smoke was rising and the air seemed wonderfully clear to the small group of spies. A wing of the manor blocked them from anyone hiding near the front door and some tall shrubs gave them protection from the back. The moonlight filtered eerily through the smoke that hung in the air, giving some illumination to the clearer air near the ground. Lord Bernald stopped Emma once they were all clear of the building to rearrange their group.

"Lady Julia, I'll go first, you next, then Lady Emma, Lady Hannah and André. We will check on every fallen soldier and if one of them is alive, we will carry him to safety. That will not be easy without losing our contact to Lady Julia, but it must be done so that Lady Hannah can try to save their lives."

In silence and unseen, the five moved through the courtyard looking carefully from side to side. Movement behind a wagon in sight of the front gate warned them that men were hiding there, and they crept by them cautiously. Near the partially open front gate they found two men, one lying slumped against the gate and the other near the rope that would have sounded a bell to warn the manor of danger. Both men were dead.

By the ruined stable, however, they had better luck. Both men there were wounded and unconscious, but alive. The girls had long since moved their hands to André and Lord Bernald's arms to maintain contact while leaving the men's hands free. Now the men awkwardly lifted the first wounded man and carried him, with the girls carefully holding on to them, to shelter.

A small gap between the now empty stables and the ruined Smithy formed another nook into which they could lay the wounded man and leave Hannah to tend him. As they laid him on the ground, Lord Bernald motioned for Emma to stay with Hannah and the wounded soldier while he, André, and Julia went back for the other man.

Hannah laid her hand on the man's wounded abdomen and watched as his eyes suddenly flew open. "What. . . what happened?" he asked.

"Hush. Whisper if you must talk." Hannah warned.

"You were shot by some bad men and we rescued you," Emma explained.

Hannah explained, "They are still out there. We will get you to safety soon, but there is another wounded man we have to save."

The man sat up, feeling his stomach gingerly. "It doesn't hurt."

"No," Hannah answered. "It's healed up now."

"Oh, you are the Angeluscustos healer!" he responded in awe.

"No, the Holy One healed you," Hannah corrected him, irritated. "Now, hush! Here they are with your comrade."

And truly they were there with another body in their arms, settling him carefully on the ground.

"We need to check the guards on the wall quickly," Lord Bernald told them. "The fire has caught the wall in the back. We can't stay here much longer," he admitted, as he stamped out a spark that flew onto the ground beside him. We will return as soon as possible and then get out."

"We're okay, Lord Bernald," Emma assured him. "If the fire gets too close, we'll just go out the wall and wait for you outside."

"Of course, my dear, I had forgotten."

"Let me go with you," the young soldier said. "I'm fine now. Three of us can carry more wounded than two."

"And four even more," put in the other wounded man who had just been treated by Hannah.

"In that case, we will all go together. The stairs are at the corner. Everyone take hands and hold on," he instructed the two soldiers. "Julia will keep us invisible as long as we are connected to her, so don't let go!" The now longer chain of searchers made quick work of their journey. Two of the guards on the wall were also dead, but two others were quickly brought back from grievous wounds with Hannah's help.

As they reached the top of the stairs leading down to the courtyard, Lord Bernald pulled Julia to a stop. Below them, a group of men were gathering in consultation.

André gasped and whispered to Lord Bernald, "That's Berkel, the Captain of the Duke's guard!"

"Yes, I see," answered Lord Bernald. "This removes all doubt, does it not?"

The whistles and cracks of the fire and the occasional boom of beams falling in the manor house prevented them from hearing what the men were saying, but as they watched, the men moved out the gate, leaving the burning manor behind them.

Lord Bernald nudged Julia as soon as they had disappeared and the group hurried down the rest of the stairs. And none too soon, as flames suddenly ran along the walkway that they had just been on.

"Do we go after them?" asked André.

"No. We continue as we are, invisible, until we reach the cover of the trees. Then we go to Fleinem's woods to meet up with the others. I want them to think that we all died in their assault. Lead on, Lady Julia, across the drawbridge before it also catches on fire, then go to the left and up the hill."

The disheveled parade, bloodied and covered in soot, moved wearily across the drawbridge, up the hill, and into the trees. Then they dropped hands, became visible again, and followed Lord Bernald as he led them towards the safety of Fleinem's woods.

As the scraggly bunch neared Fleinem's woods, they encountered a group of villagers carrying blankets and quilts and lighting their path up the hill with lanterns. One of them, a short, rather chubby man brightened when he saw them. Hurrying up to Lord Bernald, he cried out with joy: "Lord Bernald! I knew you must be all right. I told my Sarah, he'll get his people out all right, just you wait and see, didn't I Sarah? And we organized everyone to bring blankets up here since you won't have had time to grab your cloaks."

"Yes, Master Pastor. I take it you saw the fire?"

"Who could miss it, my Lord, the flames were so bright and the smoke. . . we went to help, all of us. But the Duke's men sent us away again, said it was too late to save anyone. We knew they were lying and we would have tried to fight them, but what men weren't already at your manor had left for Charlesville leaving us sadly outnumbered by the Duke's men.

So we pretended to believe them and went home to gather these things and started up here as soon as we saw them leave. We knew you would use the emergency tunnel." He looked keenly at Lord Bernald. "They took all of your horses, my Lord, herded them right down the road."

Lord Bernald grimaced. "I am not surprised, though I am disappointed. Well, I must thank you, all of you," Lord Bernald said to the excited townspeople. "Those blankets will be very welcome indeed! The others should be here already so perhaps we should join them, yes?"

And so, Lord Bernald, Julia, Emma, Hannah, André, four guards, and a dozen older townspeople continued to the woods where they were soon met by one of Lord Bernald's men.

"Olivier posted sentries, my Lord," the young man explained. "The others are trying to fashion some kind of shelter for the women and children with some kind of folding knife that the Angeluscustos had. Go straight on. They camp in the center of the woods."

"Thank you, Jérome."

By now the sky was beginning to lighten with grey of approaching dawn, but here in the woods what little light penetrated the trees grew less and less as they moved deeper and deeper into the evergreen forest. The lanterns of the townspeople were very welcome as they dodged around trees and stepped over branches. They heard the soft murmur of voices and the crack of breaking branches before they could pick out the people, darker shadows moving among the trees. Olivier hurried over as soon as someone noticed him and called out, "Lord Bernald! Lord Bernald is here!"

Brennan reached the girls quickly, greeting them with enthusiasm, hugging them each in turn.

"Are you okay? I was so worried about you!" Brennan said. "What did you do? You were gone so long?"

"We're fine," Emma said matter-of-factly. "We went out through the manor wall invisibly to look for wounded guards."

"Yeah," Julia added. "We found four that were still alive and Hannah treated them."

"Then as we were leaving," Hannah continued, "we saw a bunch of the Duke's men leaving the courtyard. They were the ones who attacked us!"

"Yeah," Emma contributed, "so we followed them out and came here, meeting those people on the way."

"What about you?" Hannah asked. "Any trouble getting everyone out?"

"No. I'm kinda getting used to tunnels now," Brennan grinned. "We got everyone up here and used my Swiss army knife to cut branches and put them together to help shelter the women and children from the wind." He shivered. "It's kinda cold up here."

"Yeah," Julia agreed. "I didn't feel it so much while we were doing stuff, but it is kinda cold."

Prince David moved up to them at that moment. "We're going down to the village," he said, handing each of the girls a blanket. "The pastor is going down to light the stove in the church and we'll all shelter there for a while. Some of the men will go back to the manor in the morning to see if anything survived the fire."

"Oh your poor godfather and his family," Hannah murmured sympathetically. "They have lost everything!"

"Oh, I doubt everything," the prince responded. "Certainly most of their belongings are gone, but my parrain kept Lady Bernald's jewels and his gold in a secret room connected to the tunnel. Those will no doubt have survived the fire. Still," he shook his head, "it is a terrible loss for them and all because of my wicked uncle! I must find a way to repay him."

Brennan had a suggestion. "When you become king, can't you punish your uncle by making him pay to restore your godfather's home?"

"Yes, of course! His is a wealthy area of Meerwald with revenue from fishing and farming as well as tariffs from the merchants. He can rebuild what he has torn down!" The prince clapped Brennan on the shoulder and then turned to the girls. "Let's get going. The sooner you girls are in a warm building, the happier we all shall be."

And with that, they joined the parade of men in pants pulled over their nightshirts and women in nightgowns, shawls and blankets that was winding its way through the trees and down toward the village.

They straggling group had reached the village and begun turning down the main street toward the church when suddenly a shout went up from the front and the word "horses!" spread through the throng like fire. Fearing the return of the Duke's men with reinforcements to make sure they were dead, the survivors from the fire scurried into alleys between buildings to get out of sight. The prince and Brennan pushed the girls toward cover, but Julia resisted.

"Wait!" she cried. "It might be Arabella again. She escaped before; she could escape again!"

"Okay," the prince agreed, "watch for her, but from safety!" and he pulled her into the shadows of an Apothecary's shop. As they all watched from cover in silence, the horses swung away from the village, circling its buildings to the north and heading for the destroyed manor house. In the lead ran a beautiful cream mare, her black mane and tail flying gloriously behind her in the wind.

"Look!" Julia shouted. "It is Arabella! She's brought the horses back!" And with that, Julia turned and began running back toward the manor in the wake of the horses, followed by Brennan, Emma, Hannah, and the Prince. Lord Bernald waited only long enough to send the villagers and a handful of men to the church with the manor's servants. The rest he called to follow him as he raced after the herd of horses.

When Julia and the others finally reached them, the horses were milling around in the paddock, congratulating one another on a fine run. Arabella had noticed the people streaming up towards the fenced pasture and went to meet them, laughing as she greeted Julia.

"Oh, Julia, what fun we've had!" she chortled. "We let those men herd us docilely enough until their leader left with most of his men. Then, you should have seen it!" She laughed again and tossed her mane. "We had already talked to the soldiers' horses. They don't much care who is king, but they did like the idea of a little fun followed by a run through the night and maybe the chance of a day or two of vacation.

So, as soon as most of the men were out of sight, I pretended to be startled by something and reared. That was the signal. All the other horses started jumping around and in just a moment or two, the soldiers had been bucked off. Then we all swung around and headed north for a good run to put them off our track. So, here we are!" she concluded. "I figured you'd need us if you didn't want to walk all the way back to Charlesville!"

Julia hugged her neck and rubbed her nose. "Oh, Arabella! You are such a great horse! Thank you so much. You have saved us again!"

Arabella lowered her head modestly. Julia turned to the others. The Angeluscustos had understood what Arabella said, of course, but Julia repeated it for the prince and Lord Bernald. His men had quickly moved to the fence and replaced the bars that secured the entrance so that none of the horses would wander off. Now, since they were virtually at the wall of the manor, Lord Bernald took his men in to scavenge for anything that had survived the fire. The prince and André he sent back to the village with the Angeluscustos to report to the Gwencalon what had happened.

In the church, people were stretched out on the wooden pews and on the floor, blankets and coats covering them as they tried to get some sleep. The prince found the Gwencalon comforting some of the women and pulled him aside to explain how the horses had come to return. Brennan and his sisters found extra blankets and curled up on the floor as close to the stove as they could get. It wasn't terribly warm, but after the early morning chill outside and the shock of the fire, any warmth at all was welcome. Brennan found himself drifting off to sleep with Julia leaning against his shoulder.

21 CORONATION DAY

Wednesday dawned bright and cool, and by 9 o'clock it hadn't warmed much despite the sun, but the crowds that thronged the streets of Charlesville and wandered about the meadow at the edge of town paid little heed to the chill in the air. The grass of the meadow had been mowed and the hay gathered in preparation for this day, and now it was festooned with tents of all sizes and colors.

Flags bearing the colors of the various lords of Serenia flew valiantly from the tops some tents, while other tents were draped with the red and gold of the national flag or adorned with dangling ribbons of rainbow colors that danced merrily in the morning breeze.

Covered wagons had created a double row of merchants selling everything from honey to cooking pots, and women wandered from seller to seller, examining their wares and perhaps buying something here or there. Children raced between them, playing tag, or sat enthralled at the Punch and Judy puppet show.

Another wagon had lowered a side to produce a stage on which a small black and white dog jumped through hoops, and danced, and bowed to the crowd of enthralled children. Groups of Barbegazi were selling rides on some Dragon de Neige, which swooped around over the meadow to the delight of their passengers.

Still another enterprising gentleman had fastened four long poles together to form two large triangles, which he then connected with a long pole. From the connecting pole he had suspended two boards on long ropes. For a centime, a child or an adult could sit on the board and swing back and forth, up into the air. The smiles and cries of excitement kept the line of would be riders long and his purse fat.

Yes, the women and children of Serenia were enjoying their morning, but in the meadow few men were to be found. In Charlesville proper, they all awaited eleven o'clock, when they would move to the center square for the Landsgemeinde.

In the town, men stood on corners, smoking their intricately carved pipes and discussing what changes they might want to propose to the new king. Others crowded the coffee house, the café and the inn, all of which overflowed with men in feathered felt hats, short wool jackets and leather pants, while harried waitresses in apron covered dresses hurried from table to table with trays over laden with mugs of mulled cider, hot chocolate, and a variety of tarts.

The conversation here too centered on the politics of the day: the coronation, finally, of the young king. In a corner of each building, near the door, rested an assortment of muskets, each neatly inscribed on the stock with the initials or crest of its owner, each politely placed there as its owner entered, each ready to be snatched up should the need arise.

On the streets, too, the men carried muskets slung on leather straps across their bodies or over their shoulders, an unusual sight for a Landsgemeinde, where it was understood that weapons were not welcome. The Duke's guard, patrolling the streets in the black and silver livery of Southern Meerwald, advised many a gentleman to put away his musket, but without fail this admonition was greeted with a cheerful smile and a pat on the soldier's back . . . and the musket stayed where it was.

Scattered among this crowd of men were those serving as the guards of the various Lords of Serenia, each clad in the colorful uniform of his lord; grey and sky blue for Lord Schumer and dark blue and white for Lord Rheiner, both of Oberwald. From Unterwald were those wearing the green of Lord Altvater and the green and white of Lord Einstadler.

Lord Perrauld of Meerwald's men were in fine black and yellow. Lord

222

Killian's and Lord Witmer's men from Nidwald wore black and white and black and gold respectively. And the men who served Lord Spielburg of Mittewald were dressed in their red and white uniforms. Conspicuously absent were the red and black uniforms of Lord Bernald's men, though none commented on it.

News of the destruction of Lord Bernald's manor and all of its occupants in a terrible fire had spread quickly that morning, fueled by the whispers of castle footmen and the Duke's men. Those who heard had expressed horror at the loss, and then gone nonchalantly about their business of having fun, leaving those who spread the news wondering at the lack of feeling in the general populace.

What those who went about the Duke's business did not know, however, was that Lord Bernald's own men, dressed as farmers, had crept from tent to tent, from campfire to campfire, and from inn to café the night before, quietly assuring the citizenry that despite the best efforts of the Duke's men, all from the manor, including the prince, still lived.

Now those same men moved unacknowledged among the crowds, dressed inconspicuously in everyday clothing, carrying the same muskets that adorned the backs of every farmer and tradesman in town. There would be no shortage of weapons raised in support of their prince should the need arise.

In the castle, Duke Ferigard relaxed with a glass of wine as he contemplated the day before him. Despite the interference of those pesky Angeluscustos, things were working out just fine. His men had returned early Tuesday morning to report the total destruction of Lord Bernald's manor at Ravenswood.

No survivors had been seen escaping from the building and the guards along the walls had all been shot. The fools had let the horses get away, spooked by something, dumb beasts! But a couple of men had gone back out yesterday to round them up with orders to rope them together this time when they found them, so that would be okay.

It was a pity about the seal, the ring of state, and the scepter. Who would have thought that conniving nephew of his would have stolen them and hidden them! If he had escaped with them, they were probably buried under the rubble of Bernald's manor house. He wondered if it would be worth sending men back in a day or two to sort through the ruins. Even if they didn't find the seal and scepter, they might locate some of Lord Bernald's riches. Yes, he mused, that might indeed be a lucrative move.

Soon his chamberlain arrived to tell him that it was time to go to the Council House, and he rose slowly, majestically, already thinking himself to be king. After all, with the prince dead, and his borrowed soldiers on the roofs of buildings, whom else could they choose? He frowned at the perfidy of Prince Lethin who had apparently taken his troops home. Well, he wouldn't need them now, anyway, and just let those Kummerians try to tunnel through the mountains now! You don't back out of a deal with Duke Ferigard and not live to regret it! No, he reminded himself, as he allowed his valet to drape his shoulders with a silver trimmed black silk cloak, not Duke Ferigard, King Ferigard of Serenia!

As eleven o'clock neared, activity in the Council House became frenetic. Servants rushed here and there with messages, and the ceremonial guard, made up of retired soldiers from across Serenia, donned their black uniforms, trimmed in gold fringed sashes that crossed their chests next to the many medals that cluttered their uniform jackets.

In the council chamber itself, the Council of Elders formed slowly, gathering in groups on the left of the chamber to chat worriedly about the turn of events. Selected by the Duke from among the venerable men of Meerwald, they had lived long lives of service both to the Duke and to the late King, and many of them were anxious and unsure of the steps the Duke expected them to take this morning. Even with the death of the prince, the somewhat suspicious death, some admitted to themselves, naming the Duke as King of Serenia without considering other candidates was a risky business.

On the right side of the council hall, eight lords of Serenia also huddled in constantly changing groups of two and three. Normally there were 10 Elders and 10 Lords of Serenia to vote on the kingship and other vital state matters, but with Duke Ferigard as acting ruler and Lord Bernald rumored to be dead, they were clearly outnumbered by the Duke's handpicked Elders. What if the word they had gotten was wrong? What if the prince and Lord Bernald had perished in the fire after all? What then?

But no, it was Bernald's own men who had brought word and were even now hidden in plain clothes among the crowd of the Landsgemeinde, ready with the Barbegazi to disarm the Duke's men. And every man of the Landsgemeinde was armed as were their own soldiers, scattered among them. No, if it came to a show of force, regrettable as that would be, they would prevail! Serenia would be saved!

And then the clock struck eleven, his slow bongs echoing through the hall. The Elders and the Lords alike hastened to their seats on either side of the hall, as with a short trumpet fanfare, Duke Ferigard entered, followed by his son, Lord Gabin. Both were dressed in ceremonial jackets and pants bearing the colors of Eastern Meerwald, but the duke also wore a short, silk cloak, trimmed in silver braid and fastened at his neck with an intricately carved silver medallion with a ruby at its center.

He strode to the dais at the end of the room and then turned to face the men in the council chamber. The Elders had automatically risen at his entrance, but the Lords, of which he was one, naturally, did not give him that respect, but instead remained stubbornly seated. He cleared his throat, motioned for the Elders to be seated, and then began.

"My brothers, it should be a joyous occasion which brings us here, but instead it is an immensely sad one. As I'm sure all of you have heard by now, on Monday night, a fire started in the blacksmith shop at Lord Bernald's manor and while they thought they had put it out, a spark had apparently ignited the roof of the manor house and while they all slept, the building burned to the ground. By the time villagers and one of the patrols reached the manor, the flames were too hot for anyone to enter. There were no survivors."

He paused for reaction, for murmurs of dismay or horror, but only silence met his words, so he cleared his throat again to cover the pause, and then continued. "Unfortunately for all of Serenia, Prince David had gone to spend the last day before his coronation with his godfather. He also perished in the blaze."

He looked around the council chamber. No one stirred; no one so much as coughed. Everyone waited to hear what he would say next. Emboldened, he continued. "In such a situation, where all members of the ruling family have perished, it is your job to put forth able candidates for the kingship, to debate their merits, and to finally choose one to present to the Landsgemeinde. Do you have such candidates?"

The Lords were silent, but their comments would have gone unheeded anyway as three of the Elders stood to their feet.

"I propose the duke as king," the first shouted, while some of his fellow Elders squirmed uncomfortably in their seats. "He has led our country through ten years of peace since the death of our late and beloved king. He has the experience to lead us into the future!"

"I second that proposition," cried the second.

"As do I," added a third. "Who else is so imminently qualified for the position?"

"I am," called a clear voice from the back of the room as Prince David, dressed in neat, but borrowed clothes, strode into the hall, followed by the Gwencalon and Lord Bernald with Prince Lethin of Kummer between them, then by the four Angeluscustos, and finally by a double row of Lord Bernald's men who moved around the edges of the room to block off escape routes for the Duke and his son.

"Prince David!" shrieked a shocked voice from among the Elders. "But we were told you were dead!"

"No," the prince answered. "I am not dead, though not because my uncle has not tried very hard to see that I was!"

The room erupted into agitated conversation until Lord Altvater called out above the other voices. "That is a serious accusation, Prince David. Are you sure you are ready to accuse your uncle of attempting to murder you?"

"I am, my lord."

Slowly the Elders sank into their chairs, horror written on most of their faces. The Lords, also took their seats, except for Lord Altvater who stepped forward. "Lord Bernald, do you support your filleul in this claim?"

"I do, Lord Altvater."

Lord Altvater slowly shook his head. "But do you have any proof? I know we have proof in the person of Prince Lethin here, that Duke Ferigard conspired with Kummer for support in his bid for the crown. And I know that he mistreated you, my prince, and that he intended to oppose you for the kingship, but murder? Can he really have gone that far? You are his own nephew!"

Prince David answered calmly, "I have eyewitness testimony, my Lord. The fire was deliberately set and attackers outside the manor shot the guards on the walls and shot anyone who tried to escape the fire. Had we not had an emergency tunnel escape, we would in fact have perished. In addition, Lord Bernald, three of the Angeluscustos, and several of my uncle's men later observed Berkel, the Captain of the Duke's guard, and several of his men leaving the courtyard of the burning manor. There can be no doubt!"

Lord Altvater turned to the Duke who had remained frozen in silence since he heard the voice of his nephew ring through the hall. The shock he had felt at the resurrection of those he had been assured were dead had begun to wear off, now, however, and he tried to pull himself together to try to salvage his life something from this catastrophe.

"Duke Ferigard?"

"I have already explained," the Duke blustered. "I should not have to say this again, but I will. Berkel led the patrol that discovered the fire, but it was too late to rescue anyone. The building was an inferno. He, we assumed everyone had perished!"

"And does the captain of your guard always lead patrols through the countryside?" asked Lord Bernald somewhat sarcastically.

"Of course not," the Duke responded, turning an angry face toward Lord Bernald. "But of course, we knew that the prince was with you and we worried for his safety, and not without cause, apparently!"

Lord Bernald and the prince spoke at once, Lord Bernald in a calm but cold voice and the prince in a voice thickened with anger.

"But the prince was quite safe with me, wasn't he?" said Lord Bernald.

"But you were what I needed protection from, you!" cried Prince David.

The duke opened his mouth to answer them, but subsided at a loud command from Lord Altvater.

"Enough, my Lord Duke!   The evidence of eyewitnesses is compelling, especially when it includes the Angeluscustos." He turned to the Wests who were standing quiet and wide-eyed to one side of the dais. "Which of you saw the men at the fire?"

"We girls did," answered Hannah. "Brennan was with the prince, getting people out of the manor and away to safety."

"Would you recognize any of the men if you saw them again?" Lord Altvater asked?

"Maybe," Julia said, hesitantly. "It was dark and the flames made everything look sorta red."

"I would," Emma answered confidently. "He had dark hair and a long scar. . ."

"That ran from his right ear to his mouth," Hannah finished. "I saw it too."

Murmurs filled the room as the noblemen and the elders recognized the description of Captain Berkel.

Lord Altvater turned to the other lord and the Elders. "Do we need to find Berkel and bring him here to be identified, or is the description enough.

"I'm satisfied," Lord Killian asserted.

"That's enough for me as well," answered Lord Schumer.

The other lords assented as well, although the Elders remained largely silent.

Lord Altvater turned to Lord Bernald. "Perhaps your men would like to take the Duke into custody to be held for trial."

"Gladly," Lord Bernald smiled, motioning to his men.

"I wouldn't do that if I were you," the Duke hastily said. "Look out the window, and you will see that I have archers on every roof top, ready to slaughter the men at the Landsgemeinde if you try to harm me!"

"On the contrary, Duke Ferigard," Lord Bernald assured him. "If you look out the window, you will see that your men on the rooftops have been replaced by Barbegzai and all of your men, including the Kummerian mercenaries, have already been locked away in the dungeon where you are about to join them!"

The Duke rushed to the window, followed closely by Lord Gabin, his son, whose face was ashen with shock and fear. When the Duke drew back, having seen the unmistakable Barbegazi on every rooftop, waving Serenian flags and shouting with the crowds, he had no more to say. He stood silently while the guards grabbed his arms and escorted him out of the room. But when they would have taken hold of Lord Gabin, Prince David stopped them.

"No, not him." He turned to the Lords and Elders. "My Lords, I would ask that Lord Gabin be allowed to collect his mother and siblings and retire to their lands in Meerwald. Perhaps we can send an overseer to ascertain that the land is safely and properly tended, for my Lord Gabin now owes Lord Bernald a new manor house and many lost possessions, and I would see that Lord Bernald is fully paid back."

"Aye, Aye" agreed the Lords while Lord Gabin turned if possible, even paler.

"Lord Gabin," Lord Altvater said to him, "you are dismissed to gather you family and depart for home.

"Some of your men will eventually be sent back to till your lands," Lord Bernald cautioned him, "but someone will arrive to see that you do not take up your father's desire to sit on the throne of Serenia. It has a king!"

The Lords cheered as Lord Gabin turned to hurry out of the room, but Prince David stopped him.

"Frederick."

"Yes, Dav. . . Your Majesty?" Gabin answered turning.

"Don't leave Meerwald until you are given permission to do so," the prince warned quietly. Lord Gabin bowed his head in acknowledgement of the order and continued out of the room.

Then Lord Altvater turned to the Elders and the Lords. "We must vote to make it official," he said. "And given that all of you Elders are from Meerwald, I think for this once we can dispense with your votes!"

"Dispense with nothing," one of the Elders cried, getting to his feet. "Many of us have not agreed with what the Duke hoped to do today, but with news of the prince's death, we had no other choice. We are glad that you are safe, my prince, and we welcome you as our rightful king!"

And so the Council of Elders and Lords cast their votes and no one dared vote against Prince David. He was immediately cloaked in a royal purple robe, edged with the distinctive black spotted white fur of the ermine, and led from the council chamber in a solemn parade of Lords and Elders, preceded by the group of trumpeters who had watched the proceedings from the doorway in openmouthed astonishment.

The Gwencalon motioned to the Angeluscustos to join him, and they brought up the rear of the procession. Out through the doorway they went and into a hallway that led to a set of double doors. Footmen at the doors threw them open and the procession went through and onto a wide balcony to the sound of the trumpet fanfare and the rapturous cheers of the crowds.

Lord Altvater pushed Lord Bernald forward, and though he was dressed not in his ceremonial clothing but rather in the rough clothes of a farmer, he stepped to the edge of the balcony with Prince David at his side and raised his arms to quiet the crowd. When at long last they fell silent, he spoke.

"Men of Serenia, as many of you know, Duke Ferigard has attempted to kill Prince David and to seize the throne for himself, but with the help of the Angeluscustos, we have kept him safe!" Another roar of excited approval rose from the crowd. As it subsided, Lord Bernald continued. "The Council of Lords and the Council of Elders have voted unanimously to present him to you as the next king of Serenia. If you agree to this choice, raise your hand."

A veritable ocean of hands rose in the town square. "Anyone opposing this choice will now raise his hand," Lord Bernald continued. No one in the crowd moved a muscle. Lord Bernald grinned. "Then I present to you, men of Serenia, King David of Serenia!"

The trumpets played, the crowd roared and clapped their hands, the Lords shook one another's hands and clapped each other on the back, the Elders stood silently, and the Chamberlain handed the crown to Lord Bernald who placed it firmly upon King David's head. The Gwencalon turned to the Angeluscustos, smiling.

"You should be proud of yourselves! You have completed your very first mission as Angeluscustos very satisfactorily! Now we will all go to the meadow for the banquet and their will be speeches, oh my the speeches! And no doubt King David will have something to say about you as well! Come along, now. Let's try to beat the crowd to the meadow!"

But somehow King David had heard him above the clamor of the crowd and bid them step up to the railing with him. And so, Hannah, Brennan, Julia, and Emma found themselves standing on either side of King David, waving at the crowds below. At last Lord Bernald stepped forward to draw the king back into the building so the procession could start for the meadow. But as the double doors were closed behind them, they could still hear the muffled shouts of the crowd "David! David! David!"

King David halted in the corridor, however, and turned to his godfather. "Parrain, I would like Prince Lethin to attend the banquet as my guest. Would you bring him to me, please."

"Of course, your Majesty," Lord Bernald answered formally, and waved an imperious hand at one of his men. Prince Lethin had been held in an adjoining chamber in case it was necessary to present him to the Council of Elders or at the Landsgemeinde, and so it was only moments before he was brought before the group that waited curiously in the hallway with the king.

The prince bowed to King David and inquired, "What did you need of me, your Majesty?"

"It seems you have come to Serenia at an oportune moment," the king answered. "Therefore, I would like you to be my guest at the Coronation Banquet which we are about to attend. After that, Lord Bernald will see that you are escorted back to your men. Your horses will be returned to you, and you and your men will be seen safely to the borders of Kummer."

"I thank you, King David," Prince Lethin responded, bowing his head in recognition of the generosity of the king. "But what of our weapons? It would cost my men dearly to have to replace them."

"Not so much as it could have cost your men," the king retorted, "but, nonetheless, they will be returned. The next time a Kummerian merchant travels our roads, lawfully paying the tariffs, to deliver goods to a ship on the sea, instruct him to stop by the castle on his way home. We will load the weapons into his empty wagon and send them back to you!"

The prince had reddened at the mention of merchants and tariffs since his very presence in front of King David was the result of his own father's attempt to find a different route for merchants, one that did not include paying Serenian tariffs! But he simply bowed his head again and answered, "It shall be as you desire."

King David turned to the Angeluscustos. "Now we must walk in the procession to the meadow. It will be slow and very loud, I'm afraid, but it is tradition."

"If I may suggest, your Majesty," the Gwencalon interjected.

"Perhaps the young Angeluscustos would prefer to watch the procession rather than walk in it. If you would excuse me as well, I could take them to the meadow to await the arrival of the procession."

King David smiled. "I would like them by my side, and you also, Gwencalon, but you are right. Take them to the meadow but seat them and yourself at my right hand at the table."

"As you will, Sire," the Gwencalon answered, and with a bow, he ushered the bemused Angeluscustos back into the Council Hall, down a stairway, and along a back alley toward the meadow.

To Emma, it had seemed as if the cheering crowd would never be silent and the situation in the meadow was not much different. Small boys had hovered at the edges of the Landsgemeinde to rush back with the news as soon as a king was chosen and now while the meadow did not exactly roar, it certainly buzzed with excitement. Women were hurriedly spreading blankets on the ground to mark their eating spots and summoning their children to sit on the blankets and wait for their men to return from the town square.

Servants were loading long trestle tables with fruit and breads and meats of all kinds; fish, venison, roasted pig, mutton, and sides of beef. Other tables had been covered with white linen and set with plates and goblets for the King and the Councils of Lords and Elders. It was to this table that the Gwencalon guided Hannah, Brennan, Julia and Emma, seating them in that order next to the center chair, which was the King's seat. He then took the chair next to Emma.

"We can sit here until the King begins to come," he assured them. "But then, of course, we must stand until he is seated. Now, some protocol lessons." He looked at them carefully. "Everyone, including me, will bow low as the King passes. You, however, are Angeluscustos and have special privileges. You need only bow your head in acknowledgement that he is king, as he no doubt will do to you. As special envoys of the Holy One, you hold a special rank that permits you to sit in any king's presence without his permission and forces you to bow to no one but the Holy One Himself."

"So we don't have to get up when King David appears?" Emma asked.

"Don't have to, no," responded the Gwencalon. "But on this day, this one time, to rise would gain you the love of the Serenian people."

"We helped save him," Brennan answered. "Of course we will honor him on his coronation day!"

"And his birthday!" added Julia.

The increased level of cheers and the sound of trumpets soon announced the arrival of the men with their new king, and the Angeluscustos, the Gwencalon, and all the women and children scattered in colorful tableau about the meadow rose as one. The happy men soon joined them at their chosen spots about the meadow, and as King David moved into the meadow, everyone sank into a bow or a curtsy as he passed by.

When at last he reached their table, King David threw protocol to the wind and greeted the Angeluscustos with hugs and for the girls, kisses, before pulling out their chairs and seating them himself to the loving approval of his people. And then the Council of Lords and the Council of Elders found their chairs and followed the king as the Chamberlain seated him and cried, "Let the feasting begin!"

And begin it did. Servants carried platters of food along the King's table, beginning with King David and then moving to each end, while those in the meadow moved along the food laden tables, filling their own plates. Children ate and ran about chasing one another, musicians played, and finally, after everyone's appetite was satisfied, the speeches did, in fact, begin.

The Lords swore fealty to their king, the Gwencalon promised the blessings of the Holy One upon his reign, and Lord Bernald praised the Angeluscustos for their timely help. Then King David rose to address his people for the first time, promising a more equal representation by allowing the Council of Elders to be chosen by each canton rather than by the king.

Prince Lethin of Kummer, who had been settled between Lord Bernal and Lord Altvater at the king's left, rose to his feet as well to congratulate King David, and to promise to do all he could to promote peace between their countries.

As the speeches wore on, Emma and Julia amused themselves by playing tick tack toe on a sheet of paper that Emma had found in her Schulmappe. Brennan had begun thinking that perhaps he might not miss the entire basketball season when they returned home, and Hannah wondered, though not very seriously, what it would be like to marry this handsome young King and live out her life in Serenia.

At last, however, the speeches were over and King David rose to signal that the feasting had ended. People began picking up their blankets and gathering up their children, as those who lived in Charlesville began slowly drifting homeward. Hannah, realizing that she and her brother and sisters really must go home, found herself saying good-bye to King David.

"Your Majesty," she said. "Brennan and the girls and I must really head for home now."

"Oh, no," the King objected. "I hoped you would stay for a while so I could show you around Serenia! I know you saw some parts of it, but it was hardly an enjoyable view, fleeing from pursuers, fighting battles, and escaping burning buildings! Can't you stay, please?"

"I really wish we could," Hannah murmured, touching his arm gently. "But our parents will be worrying about us. We really must go."

King David gazed at her for a long moment. "If you must, then I suppose I can not keep you here, as much as I would like to."

"No, your Majesty." Hannah said with a sweet smile. "But we will need someone to show us where the waterfall is, so we can go back through the portal into our world."

"The waterfall?" The King frowned. "Oh that won't work. A portal is only open for a few days. But don't worry! There is always another portal. The Gwencalon will know where it is." He turned to look about him and then took Lord Bernald's arm.

235

"Parrain, where is the Gwencalon?"

"The Gwencalon? He has left on one of his pilgrimages," Lord Bernald answered.

"Left?" Hannah gasped. "How can he leave without telling us how to get home?"

Lord Bernald smiled gently at her. "He said to tell you that he will give you directions to the portal when you catch up to him on your next mission."

"Our next mission? What next mission?" Hannah asked.

"I don't know," Lord Bernald assured her. "You'll have to ask the Gwencalon!"

"But first," King David said, smiling, "you'll have to find him!"

ABOUT THE AUTHOR

Elizabeth Anderson is the pen name of Jane Elizabeth Anderson Witmer who lives in central Illinois with her husband, one of their daughters and numerous cats and dogs. Mrs. Witmer grew up in Indiana and is a graduate of Indiana State University where she was the chapter editor of the Alpha Sigma Alpha Sorority. Holding an M.S. in Secondary Education and an M.A. in English, she has taught French and English in high schools in both Indiana and Illinois as well as both literature and writing for Lake Land College in Illinois. In their spare time, she and her husband enjoy traveling, especially to Europe, although they have also been to Canada, Mexico, and Israel.
You can reach Ms. Witmer at http://jewitmer.wix.com/elizabethanderson.

Made in the USA
Lexington, KY
10 March 2015